Emma Quinn Mystery

THE RETURN

Book 1

Mariah Martin

Chrysalis Publications

Rhode Island

Fourth printing

Copyright © 2013 Mariah Martin

ISBN: 1482588013

ISBN-**13: 978-1482588019**

All rights reserved.

DEDICATION

In memory of my beloved son, Kwon

CONTENTS

This is a work of fiction.
Names, characters, places, and
precedents of law are products of the
author's imagination. Any resemblances
to actual events or people, living or
dead, are entirely coincidental.

ACKNOWLEDGMENTS

Thank you to my family, friends and
Writer's Group for your support.

Beautiful Rhode Island deserves a special
acknowledgement for its culture, vibrancy
and creative atmosphere.

WEDNESDAY: EAST COAST

The lot of the Waterman Office Complex wasn't plowed, leaving a thin layer of icy slush. Emma could barely steer the car into her small parking slot.

The weather matched her dark mood. She didn't get much sleep and woke up tense and nervous, but wasn't sure of the cause. She pushed the upset feelings aside, gathered her strength to face the cold wind and opened her car door. A rush of energy slammed her back against the seat.

"Oh, no, what now!" she screamed into the air.

Emma closed her eyes and tried to calm down, but when she opened her eyes, all she could see was a vision of a woman floating in a light beam hovering above her.

Who was this woman? And why was she appearing to her?

Having visions was not unusual for Emma; it was part-and-parcel of being an intuitive. No matter how much she wanted to sit in her warm car and figure out the vision, she had get into the office. Focusing on the vision would just have to wait until later in the day. The only time available was during the evening meditation session at the Wellness Center.

"Damn," she moaned.

Even though her sight fully cleared up, Emma still felt a little dazed by the vision. She carefully got out of the car so as not to slip on patches of ice.

The sound of a car pulling into the lot jolted her out of the altered state of mind. A chauffeur parked a black Lincoln Town Car into the space right by the door. Jack Fitzsimmons, the founder of the firm, stepped out. Emma hurried to enter the building and opened the heavy metal door. She smiled to greet him.

"Good morning, Emma," he pronounced.

Jack lost his balance a little as he stepped into the building.

"This door isn't the only hinge that gets stuck these days. My old bones are getting harder and harder to move in the morning. I'll be happy when this cold weather is over," he said.

"Me, too!" Emma commiserated with Jack.

Entering the warm building seemed to help switch his mood. "By the way, Emma, did your crocuses survive that snow we had last night?"

"I'll know later when I go home. This morning I barely had enough time to gather myself together in order to beat you to the office. And here you are! What brought you in so early? You foiled my plan."

"My dear, I've never been known to allow a full partner to outdo me even if she is beautiful."

He teased her in a way that was not her habit to allow from any man, young or old. Jack Fitzsimmons, a power broker in Providence's political community and former state senator, often used charm to control those around him. But to Emma, his teasing was just a lighthearted form of friendship. She had learned from her father how to handle powerful men. Her father was a serious man, very much the perfectionist and controlling in most matters, but who, like Jack, used humor to approach others in social situations. Jack had met his match in Emma. She could tease him right back.

At seventy six, Jack was still a formidable figure. A tall Irishman with wavy silver hair, he commanded attention not by just his height, about six and a half feet, but also by the way he presented himself. With impeccable style, he dressed in hand-tailored, dark wool suits. Even in casual situations, his presentation was formal. In all ways, he looked the part of senior partner of a prestigious law firm.

The two attorneys stopped by the back door and removed their coats, putting them in the hall closet. Before Jack turned to go to his rather large and spacious office in the front of the building, he reminded her of his wishes.

"Don't disappoint me. I need those papers by this afternoon. I have a luncheon meeting at Brown and will be back in the office around 3:00. Do you think they'll be ready for my signature?"

"Jack, that's cutting it a little close. I'd like to have more time to review all the points of the state's fluctuating laws. Could we do this tomorrow?"

"I want it resolved today," He smiled but looked at her with the focused gaze of a bull. "I'll talk to you this afternoon."

As he turned from her, Emma knew she would need to postpone all her other work to satisfy him. Since he rarely put her in such a position, she surmised that he must really need the completed document to be ready to sign. He was also, to her displeasure, reluctant to tell her the reasons for the urgency.

The day before, Jack Fitzsimmons had approached her to draw up some personal papers for him. Since her expertise was conflict mediation and contractual law, she was puzzled. "Peter is our best specialist in estate law, why don't you have him do this for you?"

"I trust your ability, Emma, to discern the right path through conflicting opinions of the law and I believe that you, not Peter, won't leave room for any personal interpretation of my wishes. I've made my choice and that's that!"

Emma snapped back, "I don't understand your insistence about this. It's not my area of expertise. I don't see how I could do the kind of quality job you desire. You of all people should realize that!"

Jack was well aware of Emma's slow rhythm in the way she organized her work with precision. He had guided her work in the firm until she had made partner. None of that seemed to matter when he insisted on having his way, as he was doing just then.

"My dear, if your father were here, he would handle

this for me. I expect you to do as good a job as he would have. You're the ranking full partner, are you not?"

Emma knew when to surrender.

"All right, Jack, don't remind me about Dad and his loyalty to you. I get the message. I'll take care of it for you." Silently, she added, "This is the price I pay for being so competitive with my father."

The firm of Fitzsimmons, Morrison, and Quinn specialized in institutional law. It represented universities and hospitals in the Providence area. Emma's father, Andrew Morrison, Jack's first partner, was now retired. Since Jack's daughter Anne had no interest in the practice of law or in having an administrative place in the firm, Emma had worked hard to prove that she was worthy of taking over her father's position. But in this moment, she wished her father still worked at the firm so he could handle Jack's demands.

What was going on with Jack? She didn't feel comfortable managing his secret desires without knowing his motives. Were his demands the sole reason for her fretfulness?

Her office, on the second floor of the two hundred year old building, looked like so many other law offices.

The old plaster walls, softened by tones of ivory silk wallpaper, held a large display of university diplomas and licenses to practice law in Rhode Island, Massachusetts, and Connecticut.

A client would notice nothing unusual about the room except for the quality of the art and the clutter on Emma's desk. Several large watercolors, originals by Anne, Jack's daughter, and her best friend, were displayed around the room. Emma had been given them in return for handling Anne's grandmother's estate. Against the soft muted decor, these paintings stood out. They played with sharp lines, busy images, and fluid light spaces. During short moments of reprieve from the tedious details of law practice, Emma found that staring into the spaces of the paintings helped her clear her mind.

Today she didn't glance at them on her way to her desk. She picked up her appointment book, went over to the corner of her office that was set off as a private conversational area, and sat in one of the rose Queen Anne arm chairs. It was sometimes easier for her to make scheduling decisions away from the piles on her desk. Her assistant kept all her appointments in a digital appointment calendar, but Emma clung to the comfort of her paper calendar. She restructured her day to meet Jack's expectation.

Moving back to her desk, she set her appointment book down amidst the piles of files that filled every corner of the extra-large cherrywood top. Photos of her twin sons lined the outer edges of the desktop.

Emma swiveled in her chair to look out of the large paneled window behind her. A shelf under the window displayed her collection of stone Buddha statues, Native American fetishes, and an assortment of crystals. The office staff often teased her that she not only had twins but was also a twin herself: one, a compulsive lawyer fanatical to details, and the other, a woman of gypsy blood, dreaming of other worlds.

Feeling clearer, she turned around and called her secretary. "Donna, please tell Alice that I want her to join me in the conference room in an hour."

"Would you like me there to take notes?"

"No, that won't be necessary but please make some magic with my schedule and move today's appointments to next week. Hold all calls for now unless they're from Mr. Fitzsimmons or his family."

Emma wanted extra fortification for the day. She left her office and went across the hall to the lounge. The coffee was her favorite blend, Kenya roast. She enjoyed that magic moment when her senses took in the aroma of coffee and her mind jumped with excitement from the stimulation. Her yoga teacher, Patrick, had encouraged her to give up caffeine, but after trying several times, she had given up. And certainly today wasn't a day to deprive herself.

By 9:15 she was ready to get going on Jack's wills, a living one and an estate plan. She spread out the list on the conference room table to show her assistant what had to be in the final wills. Alice arrived on time and looked over the list.

"Alice, I need you to check on the latest news coming out of the state concerning living wills. Please look up Atkins vs. Rhode Island Community Hospital to see why the court prevented them from canceling the request of the patient. I don't need to tell you how important this is. It involves the will of our senior partner."

Emma had come to depend on Alice and dreaded the

imminent change when her favorite clerk would graduate from law school and take the bar. Perhaps she could persuade the other partners to invite Alice to join their team. Working to please the senior partner in such a personal situation could only help Alice in her bid for a position within the firm. And, Emma intended to make Alice look as good as she could.

After Alice left to do her research, Emma went to the outer office. She leaned on her secretary's desk and stared off for a moment. Then, in a soft but strong voice, she said, "When we finish reviewing the documents, it will need to be ready this afternoon for Mr. Fitzsimmons's signature. One other thing, Mr. Fitzsimmons has asked me to insert a clause concerning his choice of guardianship. You and I are to be the only ones to witness this aspect of the will. He insisted that the information be kept confidential."

"Mr. Fitzsimmons is choosing someone other than Anne?" Donna asked.

"Yes, his older daughter, Dr. Julie Taylor. He's very insistent about it being clear in the document that she's his choice."

It irritated Emma to be in the dark about why Jack was doing this, but she didn't push him to explain. She had learned over the years that he didn't like his motives questioned.

"In all the years I've been with the firm I've never heard him or anyone else speak of Julie." Donna looked puzzled.

"Me neither," said Emma. She shrugged. "I vaguely

remember my dad mentioning something about Jack's older daughter. It didn't seem a subject open to be questioned." Emma didn't let on to Donna how confused she felt that her friend, Anne, never mentioned her sister.

"Mr. Fitzsimmons has always been respectful to those of us working here, so it feels right to give him the same consideration," said Donna.

"I'll give you the section to type in Dr. Taylor's name after Alice gives you the sections she's finishing. Before giving it to him to sign, I'll need a few minutes to go over it. Mr. Fitzsimmons will be back around 3:00, so stay available to witness and notarize it."

"How many copies do you need?" Donna asked.

"The usual three for normal filing, and one more to be sent to Dr. Bell over at Providence General."

"No problem."

Emma retreated to her office and went over every detail, making sure the will was just as Jack wanted it. Three hours later, Jack signed it with Alice and Donna as witnesses.

After they left Jack took hold of Emma's hands in a firm grip. "Emma, I'm aware that you were put on the spot by taking care of this for me in such a rush, but now this old man can relax."

"I'm glad everything has been prepared according to your wishes," she affirmed.

"Now, have a courier run a copy of this to Providence General and tell him to give it to Dr. Bell, and to no one else. I want him to sign for it. Remember, you're not to

9

speak about the contents of this will with anyone . . . especially Anne and Tom. Don't bring up Julie's name or indicate in any way that I chose her. Believe me; I have my reasons for not choosing Anne. Do we have an agreement about that?"

"I'll respect your wishes in this matter but I have to confess, choosing your estranged daughter Julie is shocking to me. It puts me in an odd position with Anne." Emma hoped that Jack would explain the situation, but he ignored her concern.

"Just make sure that this stays between us."

The intensity of his request deepened Emma's discomfort. As he walked out of her office, he looked at the photo of her children, commenting in a strange way, "Prepare them for disillusionment. The world is full of surprises that could tear them apart."

His words left her speechless. A cloud of fear enveloped her. She couldn't help but wonder, "What, Jack Fitzsimmons, are you preparing for?"

Putting aside her concern, she called for a courier to pick up the folder.

2

WEDNESDAY: WEST COAST

It was before 6 a.m. and Julie Taylor was already up preparing for her day. An aroma of fresh brewed coffee lured her to the kitchen. She wrapped her hands around a mug of Kona roast to chase the chill of the California morning away.

There was another chill she couldn't seem to shake off, the anxiety left over from a nightmare. Julie forced herself to switch focus away from the dream to the demands of work. In charge of Stanford University's Artificial Intelligence department, put a world of pressure on her shoulders. With teams at MIT and Cal Tech biting at their heels, her team had worked day and night until they had won the bid from NASA to design part of the Mars Development Program. The project needed to be finished perfectly and without delay. Her reputation was on the line. With no time to linger on her personal confusion, she headed for the den to review messages from her office.

A whimper and whine came from the bedroom, interrupting her focus. A smile softened her face. Julie put aside concerns about her dreams and work to enjoy a moment with Dixie, a black and white fifteen-year-old Shih Tzu. The dog waited at her bedroom door. When Dixie saw Julie, she spun around in circles in front of the french door that opened to the backyard.

"It's okay, sweetie, here you go," said Julie.

The small fragile dog limped across the back patio to the yard's grassy area.

Still chilled, Julie stepped out into light. Normally this time of waiting for her dog was Julie's few minutes of relaxation before getting ready for the day, but today her body just wouldn't loosen or let go of the panic. The images of her dream returned to haunt her.

She climbed for hours to reach the clearing at the top of the canyon. Dazed, she walked beyond the trees and stood on one of the large limestone rocks jutting over the edge. The air was still except for the sound rising from the river far below. The fast moving water crashed against the rocks sending a frightening roar that echoed against the canyon's walls. She jumped away from the edge, tripped on a rock and fell toward the edge of the canyon. A tree stump stopped her fall. She crawled back to safety higher up on the rocks. Gasping for air, she called out, "What can I do? Oh God, I'm all alone!"

After a few minutes, a voice came from the other side of the canyon. Her father stood on the far ledge. Julie looked up and yelled out to him,

"What are you doing? Get help!"
Frozen, he stared at her with an empty gaze.

Julie forced the images to the background of her mind and looked around for Dixie. While her elderly dog moved around the backyard, sniffing here and there looking for just the right spot, Julie took in how her home comforted her. It had been one of her good decisions to find the courage to settle down again.

Ten years before, to celebrate getting tenure at Stanford, Julie had chosen to purchase this sandy colored stucco house rather than go on vacation. She had set out to create beauty in the abandoned yard. She transformed the space with truckloads of soil, fertilizers, and plantings from a forlorn desert landscape to a lush one with greenery and flowers, nurturing it until it became the private sanctuary she intended it to be. It bloomed abundantly with lemon, kumquat, pear fruit buds, and the spring blossoms of California poppies.

Now, taking in the beauty before her, centered her energy and dispelled the shadow cast by the nightmare.

Julie hugged the coffee mug to her heart letting its warmth seep into her skin. Her mind drifted to times with her mother and the quiet rhythm of gardening together before her childhood had fallen apart.

Early in the New England fall, they would plant the bulbs for the next year's bright spring flowers. Her mother showed her the tricks of putting garlic on top of the bulbs so the squirrels wouldn't dig them up for winter food. They giggled watching the squirrels start to dig and then jump away from the garlic.

She finished her coffee, set the mug on the table, and squatted by the flowerbed close to the door. She plunged her hands, still warm from the coffee mug, into the cool earth to feel around the base of her wild yellow rose bush. A gentle pressure guided her hands deeper into the dirt. It had been a long time since she felt such a direct sense of her mother's presence.

"Mom," her heart whispered. The sense of connection lingered and then faded into the past.

Julie rummaged through the layers of cultivated soil to grab onto the invading weeds intertwined with the rose's roots. Yanking the weeds out of her flowerbeds never failed to give her a sense of satisfaction, but today not even clearing out several invading roots calmed her nerves.

She wiped the dirt off her hands and clapped to get Dixie's attention. The dog's eyesight had deteriorated to the point that she could no longer see her mistress unless she was right in front of her. With a little skip in her step, the dog came over to the patio steps where Julie had put her food.

"Come on, old girl, it's time to eat," Julie said as she coaxed her dog onto the top step. "Take your time. I'm going to get ready for my run."

Maybe if she ran really hard, the wind would clear her mind of the darkness. She put on her sweats and warmed up for her morning run. A quick glance in the mirror confirmed that her short dark hair was tucked away from her soft blue eyes. For a woman in her late forties, she still had a trim figure and the glowing soft skin of her Irish heritage.

"Finished, Dixie? Come back inside. I'll see you after my run."

Julie left the house and headed down Middlefield, crossed over Homer, and turned up Channing on her way to the park. She pounded and pushed through Eleanor Pardee Park, forcing her breath and body to move in unison, ignoring the thoughts racing in her mind.

If only the run had worked, she'd be back to her usual composed self, but by the time she got back to the house, the scary dream images flooded her thoughts again. What was bringing her into this powerless and confused state? She called her therapist and left a message on his voice mail, "Dr. Goldberg, would you be able to me at noon? The panic is getting worse."

She had tried and then stopped taking the medication that her therapist recommended. It created a fog in her mind. She didn't have the patience to keep changing medications to find the one that worked. In her frame of thinking there wasn't enough time for that process. Research was her life. What if she lost her analytical powers? What if the anxiety took over her mind? Whether or not to take medicine was a choice, but doing without therapy didn't feel like an option. She had to find the answer. What was the cause of her troubled mind?

Julie left an envelope with weekly payment for her housekeeper, Isabella, an energetic older woman with a face that was a canvas of cultural blends—Mayan, Anglo, and Chinese. Isabella appreciated the beauty and the value of the artifacts and instruments that Julie had collected during her travels with her ex-husband. He had been too busy shooting photos and making deals to notice or care about the treasures his wife gathered. His best gift to her was his last name, Taylor. Relieved not to be identified with her family, she kept the name when they divorced. It had an anonymity about it that pleased her.

What if they hadn't met in graduate school? What if she hadn't gone to her roommate Anne's photography exhibit? What if she hadn't been so stupid as to believe the cloak of illusion he created around himself? Shaking her head as if she could toss off her disturbing thoughts, Julie petted Dixie and walked out the door.

****

The traffic through town was at a standstill. Stuck in her car, she could barely control the surges of fear gripping her stomach and sending irritating pulses of energy under her skin. Would today's session finally clear up her confusion? She doubted it, but longed for the truth to be uncovered.

Perhaps Dr. Goldberg would nudge her harder today to remember more of her past. In their past sessions, he had been able to help her admit that in addition to having an active mind and a strong body, she also had a deep, vulnerable self. His traditional appearance put her at ease. Close to her age, he held himself in a calm, grounded way.

His neutral attire of gray and beige tones and his soft-spoken manner contributed to his non-threatening persona. None of his personal likes or dislikes displayed on the surface. He was the consummate therapist, but for Julie, not having control over the process was the worst part of it all.

The cars edged along taking her through several lights and then stopped again. The traffic jam gave Julie time to review what she had recently exposed in the therapy sessions.

When he pushed her to talk about her sexual encounters, she admitted, "Look Dr. Goldberg, I'm not good at choosing the right man."

"How so?"

"Well, my first love, Dan, had all the appearances of being the perfect mate, but he abandoned me when I left for college."

She described how they spent their childhood together. Their parents socialized in the same circle and had beach cottages next to each other. In high school they dated and fell in love.

"I thought I could count on Dan. He was there for me when my mother died, he was there for me when I went to boarding school in Vermont, but he copped out on me when I went to Berkeley. He stayed in Rhode Island and went to Brown. I never saw him again."

"Relationships of youth most often end. What about after that?"

"I went from the nice guy next door to the wild type.

Right before graduate school, I married a man who almost destroyed my life. Not a good track record. Now, I don't want attachments or complications—no intrusion into my life."

Julie did not want to care again. She just wanted the nightmares to go away, but Dr. Goldberg prodded her to speak of her marriage and of meeting her husband at a college art exhibit.

She recalled the exact moment when they had met, the turning of life to the dark side. It had been the gallery show of the senior photography class. Most of the crowd didn't notice the tall, very thin man with shoulder-length, wavy black hair, dressed in black jeans, black tee shirt and a black leather jacket with a camera slung over his shoulders. He was quite a sight to Julie. He went from picture to picture, commenting as he moved along. The others either gathered around him trying to see what he saw in the photos or stepped out of his way in an annoyed reaction. She stood at the door and watched him take control of the room.

He swirled through the room and stopped in front of her on his way out.

"Are these yours?" he asked.

"My roommate's."

"Her use of shadow is dynamic. This place is stuffy. I need a drink. Why don't you join me?"

His energy was magnetic. One drink had led to another and a long conversation about the meaning of photography and life. This handsome, creative man pulled her into his world with an intensity of energy that matched he intensity of thinking. His free flowing look contrasted with her well-trimmed body and hair.

"And how did you get swept away by this man?" asked Dr. Goldberg.

Julie recounted how after graduation, they bought a VW van, fixed it up for camping, and went on a trip across the Northwest. One night, while feeling playful and wanting to enjoy the cool mountain air, they threw their sleeping bags onto the roof of the van. Julie looked up to see a full moon above them. Encapsulated in the magic of the moonlight, they laid back to watch the stars dance in the sky.

"Many young people have such times of intense feelings, slipping into the magic of life as a balance to the seriousness of their studies. Was this the first time you allowed that experience?" her therapist asked.

"I never had the luxury of magic before Jim," Julie answered.

She went on to describe how seeing Jim in the light of the moon and stars wove a spell around her. He seemed to know just the right way to touch her. His hands woke up her cells and warmed the deep reaches of her body. His kisses possessed her. The thick walls she had built around her emotions melted away. She surrendered her heart and opened her body. They made love until the stars dimmed.

"Seems like your passion for each other was strong," said Dr. Goldberg.

"It all seemed good for a while. We married in a small town along the south Oregon coast and honeymooned by camping out in the Redwood National Forest in northern California making love under the tall ancient trees."

"Such a sudden commitment doesn't seem congruent with your serious nature. Some deep need must have activated for you to behave in that way. Are you aware of what it was?" probed the doctor.

Julie reported how alone in the world she felt. Jim came along and presented himself as her shining knight.

"He knew how to charm me. Like the time he decorated our bare apartment in student housing with bouquets of flowers and scented candles in a dozen different sizes. Over a catered dinner, he suggested that I set aside my plans to start graduate school so we could travel for his work."

"And you went along with his suggestion?"

"But how could I have done that so willingly? It scares me that I was so easily talked into walking away from my research plans. I can't ever let that happen again."

"Julie, when you face what made you so vulnerable you can make more conscious decisions to lead a healthy emotional life."

She sat quietly, pensive.

"You don't believe it's possible, but exploring your inner world will give you more positive choices in your personal life. How did your ex-husband convince you to give up on your own plans?"

Julie went on to describe how Jim had appealed to that part of her that wanted a normal family life--and how she was willing to sacrifice so much to have that life.

"He sounded so assured, so confident that his plan was going to work out. He told me that we'd make big bucks on his assignments and then I could go to graduate school free and clear, without money worries."

She had longed to belong to someone. His pleas had moved her to commit herself, body and soul, to him. Without hesitation she had given into his wishes. But things didn't turn out as she expected.

"How so?" asked Dr. Goldberg.

"I put off my education for several years to travel with him. He claimed that his photography assignments were the reasons we went to South America. It all became addictive. Jim shooting his camera click after click while I carried his equipment. How could I have missed the truth that it was all a ruse for his drug dealing?"

Julie's hands shook. She gripped her hard. Her body convulsed until a deep sob rose up in her belly and with its release, she sunk into a quiet, still stance. She looked directly into Dr. Goldberg's eyes and declared, "They can't be trusted."

"Who's 'they'?" he asked.

Julie didn't answer him in that session, but in her next appointment she explained.

"One morning in the mountains of Ecuador, I woke up to an empty bed. Jim had passed out on the balcony. I didn't wait for an explanation. Something took over. I packed up, headed back to California, and applied for a doctoral program in computer science."

"You have achieved great success in science. What

about relationships?"

She admitted to him that although she experienced the fervor of sexual passion with her lovers she never had another intimate relationship; nor did she want to risk a deep connection again.

"In creating a wall around your emotional self, did you come to believe no one would care enough to ever find you?" her therapist asked.

"Never thought about it like that," she said.

"Maybe you have forgotten so much of your earlier life because of something you don't want to feel," he suggested.

What was it that she could not bear to face? This morning, the pain in her head was intense enough to make her want to remember, but it would have to wait until her noon session.

The traffic cleared. She raced to work. As she drove through the two tall columns at the campus entrance, she looked off to the side of Palm Drive at the eucalyptus trees towering over the palms. She found herself sympathizing with them. Like her, they were transplanted to California and had rooted themselves.

From the way that the mist lifted over the Santa Cruz foothills, Julie thought that it would be warm enough later to spend her afternoon break in the Rodin sculpture garden. It pleased her that Stanford displayed the sculpture castings of Rodin in prominent areas around the campus grounds and in the garden.

Julie looked through the college grounds at her favorite statue. She never tired of the power of Rodin's

Burghers of Calais since she first saw the originals in Paris during a college student trip. The bronze forms enthralled her with their beauty and intensity.

She thought of her favorite sculpted face and wished that Rodin was there to carve a heavy dose of bravery into her.

After turning right onto Campus Drive, she went into the side parking area of the Gates Computer Science Building. It was quite a different structure from the old Terman building where she had spent so much time in graduate school.

What if the present stress and headaches blocked her professional success and opportunities? She had a lot to lose. She valued the part she played in maintaining the atmosphere of cooperation between Stanford and the technology businesses flourishing in Silicon Valley. She enjoyed not only working with other scientists in business and government around the globe, but also being one of the top women innovators in her field.

Her corner of the building was almost empty. She welcomed the quiet atmosphere of her office and the predictable comfort of the academic structure. Julie reviewed what had to be completed that day in order to initiate the next stage of research, and then settled into getting as much work done as possible before the next team meeting.

The morning video conference with her team and their colleagues at MIT went well except that she had some trouble focusing. Her head ached. Her back and neck muscles were hard as a board. Lack of sleep was wearing her down and disrupting her focus. Right before noon, she slipped out of the building and headed across town to her therapist's office.

* * * *

She walked into his waiting room just as Dr. Goldberg was opening his office door to greet her.

"Julie, I'm ready for you."

The design of his office helped create a safe, healing atmosphere. There were no harsh lines in the soft gray and blue decor. With the thick curtains drawn, the room seemed isolated, separated from the world. In this cocoon-like atmosphere, Julie believed that no one would ever know the secrets exposed in the sessions.

"You seem very agitated; sit down for a moment," he said in his kind tone.

He guided her to the blue armchair in front of his desk.

In the act of sitting in the chair, Julie transformed herself from the sophisticated professional to the frightened, vulnerable woman she hid from others. She looked across the desk at Dr. Goldberg; her words stuck in her throat.

"Julie, what's upsetting you so much?"

She sank further into a very still state.

"It's all right, just tell me, what has you so tense?" His reassuring tone coaxed her into sharing her fears.

With her head bent, she muttered the answer, "They're getting worse, a lot worse--and more frightening!" Julie told him about the changes in her nightmare.

He guided her to the recliner and suggested that she lean back. She had the sensation of disrobing, leaving the ego's mask on the chair seat while she lay down on the recliner. She closed her eyes, took several deep breaths, and directed her thoughts inward. She nodded to signal that she was ready. He asked her to recall the dream she had the night before.

"I'm in my bed, unable to move. A large swirling force picks me up and whirls me around. There are things spinning in the whirlwind but I can't see what they are. I try to scream, but no sound comes out. I try to grab something to stop the spinning but everything moves too fast. Just when I feel that I'll disintegrate from the swirling force, it stops and I'm planted on a high plateau of rocks." Julie's breathing quickened.

"Go on, I'm here," Dr. Goldberg encouraged her.

"I look down into a canyon of sharp ledges and a raging wild river at the bottom. It's the same dream I've had a hundred times before, but in this one, across the gorge, standing on the ledge, is my father."

"What does he do?"

"At first, he has his hands over his eyes and then, he takes them down and reaches out to me. I can see his eyes. They're empty but there are tears on his face. All of a sudden Nana's there with him. I can't stop shaking, I can't . . . I can't catch my breath . . . I'm spinning around!"

Dr. Goldberg touched her hand, giving a familiar signal to move her focus away from the panic. He spoke in a soft, low tone, "Julie, go to a safe moment in the dream."

"The tornado stops spinning. I'm put down on solid ground—I don't know where I am!"

"Observe yourself. What do you see?"

"I'm in my teens. I'm lost and alone. There's no one to call for help. Where am I and why am I here? I'm afraid to move . . . I . . . I . . . might fall down . . . I'm going to die!" Julie let out several loud screams.

"Julie, Julie, it's all right. You're not dead. You're here, safe. Return to observing the dream." Dr. Goldberg tried to bring her back from the terror, but the emotions took over.

"I can't move! Help! Help!" Julie trembled as she cried out. "Oh, my God, no one comes! No one hears me."

She cried for a few minutes and then became very quiet.

"What's happening?" Dr. Goldberg asked.

"Dan comes and I'm not alone anymore."

As the trance subsided, Julie opened her eyes and looked around at her analyst and the office. She sighed, "Oh, thank God, I'm okay."

She sat up and stretched her neck. Her body tingled as her blood flow increased its rhythm, and her brain waves returned to normal levels. She stood and walked over to the chair, transformed back to the adult personality.

"Dr. Goldberg, what does all this mean? And, why is Dan always there?"

"Well, your nightmare images are opening your mind to the level of consciousness that holds repressed memories. Dan is someone you once trusted. For a time, you felt safe with him. He imprinted as the protector archetype in your subconscious." Dr. Goldberg looked at her in his assuring way, "Trust yourself, Julie. If you remember what is hidden, you'll be ready to face it and save yourself."

His support helped, but she still felt uneasy. She made an appointment for the next day. Julie did not want to do any further memory recall without the consistent support that Dr. Goldberg was able to give her.

All she wanted was to be free of the nightmares, but although she was committed to therapy, she was still reluctant to face the cause of her fears.

When she arrived at the laboratory for the afternoon run of the latest program, she blocked out any thoughts of her inner state, concentrating on the task at hand. For the afternoon, she assumed once again the stance of a composed woman, an expert in her field.

3

THURSDAY: EAST COAST

Emma snuggled under her down comforter to enjoy a few minutes as she passed from the dream state to consciousness. Even after an extra ten minutes of sleep, she didn't want to move. She turned toward the light to watch the sun rising over the bay and geese skimming along the water's surface.

The eastern sky lit up; Emma slid out of bed. She went over to the window to greet the dawn, "Good day, dear Sun. May God bless my day with light."

After a trip to the bathroom, she returned to her bedroom. She looked through the large windows that stretched from floor to ceiling. She did her morning yoga sun salutation and then, in a practiced act of surrender, sat cross-legged on the round meditation pillow placed on the floor at the foot of the bed. Taking several long, deep breaths, Emma closed her eyes and let her mind focus inward.

She wanted the light of a still mind and the peace that it created in her heart, but this morning Emma couldn't shake off the uneasy feelings.

Her obsessive worry about Jack kept intruding into her ritual. She struggled to stop the spin of anxious thoughts. "I let go and I let God . . . I let go and I let God." The simple yet powerful chant was repeated over and over until her mind and heart were calm, and concern about Jack dissolved.

About twenty minutes later bird sounds brought her back into outer awareness. They came from the radio that was set to turn on with this special effect when the public radio station started its day's programming. Opening her eyes, she gazed out of the window at rays of the morning sun dancing on Narragansett Bay. The sky was streaked with soft golden light, with bursts of orange and red dancing around the clouds. Swans floated with the tide, heading down the bay toward the marshes as they looked for their regular nesting place among the tall reeds. Their graceful white bodies made a startling contrast against the dark gray water. Sea gulls circled and dove into the water, scooping up the fish that the swans left in their wake.

She was tempted to find a way to stay hidden in her sanctuary all day. But instead, she sprang up to face whatever the day was going to bring.

In the hall, she listened for the familiar sound of the boys getting up and showering. Hearing the water of the shower but not much movement, she headed down from the third floor sanctum to the second floor. She banged on Matt's door.

"Come on, Matt, get going! You can't be late again or you won't be able to play in the game Friday."

"Uh, I'm up," Matt muttered.

"Go get your clothes out of the dryer while Sean's in the shower," Emma told him.

"Oh, come on Ma, can't you get them?"

"I can, but I won't. Now get going."

Sean got up on schedule but took his time in everything, while Matt just couldn't move.

Emma tapped on the bathroom door, opened it a crack and called, "Sean, finish your morning soak. I want some hot water left!"

"Just a minute, I have to rinse my hair."

Emma laughed, "What hair? You cut it all off this winter for basketball. Get out of there and get going."

Hearing the water turn off, she returned to her upstairs suite. Showering, dressing and putting on her "face" took about twenty minutes. Before joining the boys downstairs, she threw casual clothes and her riding outfit into an overnight bag.

Getting two seventeen-year-old boys out the door by 7:00 was a great feat she struggled with every school day. At times she felt overwhelmed by dealing with their very different personalities. She wondered how two boys, who were so bonded in her womb, could be such polar opposites in their personalities.

Sean's whole focus was on his social life. He loved sports because of the team experience; he hated being alone and always sought connection with others. Matt on the other hand was more of an introvert and a dreamer. As an assertive woman who was used to making things happen in her life, she found mothering Matt a lesson in patience.

When she went downstairs to turn on the coffee maker, Sean was in the hall switching back and forth between jean jacket and leather biker jacket.

"Just pick one; your brother will be down in a minute. I don't want to have to call in a late excuse again."

"No problem, Mom, Andy's older brother is picking us up today."

He kissed her, grabbed the jean jacket and went out the back door, "Tell Matt to hurry. Paul hates waiting for him. See ya, Ma."

A few minutes later Matt pounded down the stairs. Emma looked up at her son, who seemed disturbed about something. "What's wrong with you?"

"Mr. Anderson will kill me if I forget my book again!"

Emma helped Matt find his math book. "Now settle down and try to have a good day. Sean's outside. . . . He wants you to go out and stand with him so Paul doesn't have to wait."

He put on the jacket his brother had dropped, and left.

Once they were out of the house, Emma poured herself a cup of coffee, heated a raisin scone from Sweetie's Bakery in the microwave, and sat down at the kitchen table where Sean had deposited her morning reading material. She started with the Providence Journal for local news, comics and her horoscope; then she scanned the Times for national news and checked The Wall Street Journal for business news and the health of her stocks. A woman of rituals, these habits helped her transit each day moving from mothering to professional demands.

This morning, ritual didn't help. Emma folded the paper and slapped her palms with it. "Damn it, Jack! What's going on with you? What's the hurry?"

Her mother used to tease her that she was a personal barometer for others' inner storms. She tried to shake off her concern. She didn't need more chaos in her life and she didn't have time to let any more worry interfere with her life.

Emma left a note for the twins about what to cook for their dinner and where she could be reached that evening. After work she was heading out to Abbey's Run for a ride through the woods on her gelding, Knight. There would be enough time between the ride and dinner to review a contract that Anne was negotiating with Clark's, the art gallery in New York City that displays Anne's work.

Today the sun was strong and the ground dry. The earth had heard her cry yesterday for warmth. She put on a light wool coat and grabbed her briefcase and garment bag with her riding outfit. She was set to face whatever was waiting for her at the office, knowing that after work she would be in the country. Backing out of the garage she looked at the flowerbed in front of the house and noted that the crocuses were still growing uninjured by the snow. They were ready to peek through with spring's first bright colors. "I'll have to bring one to the office for Jack when they bloom."

While weaving through traffic on Allen's Avenue, she mentally reviewed cases. By the time she got to the office, she felt prepared for the day's challenges, unaware of the big one heading her way.

****

At the end of the day, she and Alice left the building together. She made a mental note to find a free evening to go dancing with Alice, but this was Thursday, a night she reserved to restore herself. The twins had meetings at school, so they wouldn't be home until late. There was no need to be overly concerned about them. This was an evening with nothing to feel guilty about, nothing to worry over, with nothing but time for herself!

Emma maneuvered through downtown to head out of Providence, but just beyond the city limits, traffic was bottlenecked. Sitting in bumper to bumper traffic gave her a chance to listen to Bonnie Raitt's blues. The music of lost love moved her. Even though she had gotten through the heartbreak of losing her husband, she often felt lonely and hoped that someday she would love again. In the meantime, she belted out the blues with Bonnie.

The late afternoon sun beckoned her to the stable. Her weekly rides on Knight, her horse, helped her accept how different life had become since she had been widowed. She went from being a full-time wife squeezing in time to study law to being a full time lawyer trying to find brief moments to study life.

Before his death from lung cancer, Bob had helped her face the transition. Even though he grew weaker and weaker over the last year, he spent time preparing and supporting her in becoming stronger. Before the disease became severe, he had taken over care of the boys so she could develop her career.

Bob had lost the opportunity to relax long before he died. The last year of his life was full of preparations, but they did manage to create one last mutual experience, learning to meditate. It helped Bob deal with the pain and gave Emma a way to ease the burden of caring for a husband with a fatal illness.

After his death, she continued to meditate, not just for the relief it brought but also for the joy and peace that grew in her heart. Although she welcomed the calmness of a trance state, Emma was somewhat uncomfortable with the gift it brought her, a deepening of her natural intuitive sense. Sometimes it felt good at work to be able to perceive the true intentions of her clients, but at times it was distressing. It was also uncomfortable to sense a change in others' lives before it happened like she felt about Jack that morning during the salutation to the rising meditation. She just couldn't shake the feeling that things to come were not going to be smooth for Jack or anyone around him.

The traffic thinned out. Emma's mood lifted as she exited into the country area of northern Rhode Island. The songs ended and in the silence, she felt a sense of gratitude for the good things that were happening in her life, like having a horse and a safe, beautiful stable to board him. Last year, she had bought Knight as part of her attempt to build a new life by returning to the things she enjoyed in her youth. Jack had suggested that she accept his daughter, Anne's, invitation to board her horse. It seemed the best choice since she already knew the land and trails around their family estate, Abbey's Run.

****

The friends, Anne and Emma, had bonded during a summer camp experience. Even though Anne was just a freshman and Emma was a junior in high school, they rode at the same skill level at Champlain Valley Riding Camp in Vermont. After that intense experience, they spent many weekends exploring the woods and racing on the trails of Abbey's Run, the Fitzsimmons' family estate.

At sixteen, Emma pulled somewhat away from Anne to date and socialize with her classmates. Anne got involved with the art community and their friendship naturally faded.

Years later, they grew close again when Emma joined the firm, and Jack invited her out once again to Abbey's Run.

At first when they reconnected, it seemed strange to Emma that Anne had always lived on the estate, but then she realized that Anne had lost her mother at such a young age so she clung to what was familiar. She lived at home during college and went to Rhode Island School of Design as a day student. Anne married very young while still in school and was pregnant with her first child, Richard, when she graduated. There was never a time when Anne lived alone.

Emma had moved to Boston while in law school and returned to Rhode Island after marrying Bob. They started their family right away with the birth of the twins, Matt and Sean. Her life had seemed so planned until her husband got sick. Becoming a widow when she was so young left Emma sympathetic toward Anne's need to have her family around her. Loss drove them both to be possessive of the ones they loved.

Anne and Emma weren't the only ones to hold on so tightly. For years, Jack and his mother, Martha, lived in the house with Anne and her family. After she died, Jack moved across the driveway to an apartment behind the garage. Anne and her father transformed the small home built in 1886 into a beautifully maintained estate with a large main house and a carriage house, which once held the horse and buggy. Now, it was transformed into a four-car garage, a studio and an apartment. The new horse barn was on its own spot of land near the north meadow.

Jack had turned over ownership of the estate to Anne and Tom when they married. On more than one occasion he told Emma how relieved he was that his daughter had married a responsible, bright man who wasn't afraid to be with a strong, exciting woman. Not many of the women Emma met in the professional world had Anne's creative gifts.

A woman of extremes, Anne could lose herself in painting large abstract pieces then turn around and take a tight rein in training horses. She nurtured her family with flare and intensity, making sure that each child had the freedom to follow his or her dreams. But with equal energy, Anne set up a structure within the home that everyone had to follow to keep peace.

No matter what the reason that Anne stayed at Abbey's Run, Emma was relieved that it was within half an hour of the city so she could get to her horse. As she entered the country hide-a-away tucked in the woods of North Smithfield, Emma considered her attachment to Anne. Her late husband, Bob, used to question her about their friendship.

"Why do you keep going to Anne's? What are you gaining by having such an unpredictable relationship?"

She had defended her choice, "Anne provides me with lots of surprises. I'm never sure whether I'll get hugged or challenged. I like to keep things predictable, but Anne likes to stir things up. Oh well, it makes for an interesting friendship."

Emma liked the attention the two friends received whenever they entered a room together. Being physical opposites in appearance, they complemented each other. As a lawyer, Emma kept her blonde hair neat in a shoulder-length cut that set off her thin face. In contrast, Anne's curly red hair flew out around her oval face, setting off her pale, freckled complexion. Emma had inherited a small frame from her mother while Anne, like her father, struggled to stay within the slightly overweight range.

In any challenging situation, Emma had the tendency to hold back until she felt clear about what outcome her response would create.

Anne, on the other hand, threw herself into life, reacting first and discovering the outcome as she went along. But aside from their physical and personality differences, their commitment to their families and friends was alike. Emma enjoyed her friendship with Anne because of their similarities, not their differences. Both women had independent natures and strong emotional ties to those they love.

In recent years, Anne had become Emma's greatest support. In return, she took over more and more of the legal matters that Anne didn't feel comfortable asking her father to do.

Emma would visit Anne when she needed an energy boost or the comfort of an extended family. But on days like today when she was tired and worried, Emma could only take being with Anne in limited doses. She wished she could avoid seeing Anne so she could just ride in the woods and put her premonitions about Jack out of her mind. She didn't like hiding anything from Anne. It made it hard to keep her promise to Jack not to mention anything about Julie. How could she face her friend and not open a conversation about the unmentioned sister?

The music ended just as Emma pulled up to the barn. The sun's brightness was lessening but there was still enough light for a short ride. She got her riding outfit out of the trunk, and went to the stables. She didn't see anyone in the yard, but to her dismay, Anne was in the barn rubbing down her filly, Lightning.

"Hi! Look at my beauty, Emma. She's going to be as spectacular as her mother. Do you want company on your ride? We have lots to catch up on."

Anne continued brushing the chestnut filly, but looked up with an intensity that Emma wanted to avoid.

"I agree, we haven't had much time lately just to chat, but today won't work for me. If you don't mind, I need some time alone to gather myself together. I've had a difficult week at the office. Hopefully, Knight will take care of the ride today so I can lose myself in the spring air. After my ride, will I find you in the studio or the house?" asked Emma.

"You work too hard, my friend. It's a great afternoon to take a ride. Hope it lifts your spirits. Stop at the studio first and pick up the contract from the desk. Wait 'til you see my last piece. It came as a surprise, even to me. Something just took over." Anne gestured with hands up over her head.

"Anne, you always claim some force other than your own is doing the work, but we all know it's that wild, crazy spirit of yours." They both laughed.

"My new work went in a totally different direction. I'm not sure if the gallery will want it."

"I'm sure it'll be fine," Emma assured her.

Anne shut the gate of the stall and walked to the bench at the front of the barn where Emma was taking off her heels and putting on her barn boots. She stood over her until Emma straightened up and gave her more attention.

"I need your gut reaction to it. Don't hold back, okay?" Anne insisted.

"Anything you do has your unique vision in it. Trust me, the gallery wants all your work! I'm sure it'll be fine." Emma gave a brief comforting hug to her friend, "Now, excuse me, I have a hot date with Knight."

Not lingering to share any more business with Anne, she darted off to the restroom in the back of the barn where she transformed herself from a lawyer to an equestrian.

When she walked back through the barn she noted that she was alone. Relieved that Anne had gone to the studio, she looked through the barn to make sure that none of the rest of the family was nearby. Not seeing anyone, she took her time walking past the stalls, patting the horses. The smell of manure, hay, and horses were all welcome to her. The rich poignancy of earth's fertility filled her senses, dissolving the static energy left over from being with paper and books all day.

Heading out to the paddock, Emma reached into her riding pants pocket for the carrot she used to summon her horse. He was against the far gate. She stood still, taking in his beauty and the energy generated by the flexing muscles of his back and legs as he stomped by the gate. Knight lifted his head, saw her, and came right to her.

She held out the carrot on her palm and massaged his neck.

"Hi ya, big guy, ready for our ride?"

Knight neighed, his head signaling his eagerness to get going.

She attached his bridle and walked to the barn to tack him. He seemed to welcome her brushing him down before

40

saddling him. With each stroke she lost touch with the world beyond the barn.

Wistful, she whispered her needs to him as if he was her best friend. "Knight, I want us to ride up behind the fields into the woods. I need to forget all the pressures of my life and soak up the fresh air."

Emma saddled Knight, mounted him, and headed into the woods away from civilization.

****

The late afternoon air was still, warm, and welcoming. Horse and rider walked through the low meadow still muddy from the melted snow of Tuesday night. Although the steady sound of clopping hoofs cutting through the mud resonated through Emma's body in a strange pleasurable way, she realized that the condition of the ground might tire the horse. Since it might be drier uphill, she chose a path that led to a pond beyond the high meadow.

Knight trotted up the hill to where the ground was dry and hard. Once on solid ground, he broke out into a full gallop. The wind hit hard against Emma and swept away the layers of tension that she had accumulated from working. When she sensed Knight had spent his energy, she changed the gallop to a trot, then to a walk. At the far end of the high meadow was her favorite path through the woods. Knight walked along as if he knew just where his rider wanted to go, and, indeed, Emma let him take her.

Her mind cleared of thoughts. She enjoyed the late

afternoon sun that danced through the trees. Each time she took this path, the scene that appeared when the pine trees cleared away touched her heart. Before her was a feast of beauty, with the woods opening to a meadow set off by a small clear pond. Knight trotted down the pine-covered path that led to the pond. The light created a reflection of trees on the water's surface. Caressing the edges of the pond were smooth, weatherworn rocks set off by budding rosehip bushes, and wild yellow roses covered with small, emerging young leaves.

Knight knew to circle around the pond until they reached a small clearing in the rocks. Emma dismounted, leaving him to graze by the banks. She walked down to her special spot on gray slate rocks that jutted out from the water's edge. Finding a smooth flat surface, she stretched out, closed her eyes, and whispered a salutation, "Thank you, Mother Earth, for the warmth and the peace I feel here by your water."

Emma drifted into a light spacious state of mind for a seeming unending moment. All thoughts of law, institutions, and living wills faded away. In their place, she was flooded with a sense of God's presence.

Twenty minutes or so later, Emma sat up and looked into the water. In that moment the veil of separation between the physical and spiritual world lifted. She felt a connection with her late husband.

Emma poured out the concerns nagging at her heart and pleaded to his spirit, "Bob, you need to come close to us now and help. We need you. Matt's avoiding going to practice; his coach thinks he's blaming himself that the team didn't win last year. He feels he's responsible for the world, like you always did."

She remembered a time when Matt was seven and his dad took him bird watching at the Audubon bird sanctuary. He came home bursting with energy. All through dinner that night he talked about setting up a safe place for the birds in their yard. He and Bob built a large birdhouse, securing it so the squirrels couldn't climb up and steal the food. Many times that summer, Matt was late for baseball practice because he was checking on the birds' safety.

"Well, Bob, I sure wish you were here to help with the boys' initiation into sexuality. Sean is active. I'm not sure how to handle it."

Emma allowed herself to feel how frightening being a single parent of teenage boys had become. She pleaded the spirit of her late husband, "Let your presence come into their hearts and help them. And help me."

Alone, away from the world, Emma felt safe letting her heart open. She threw a few stones into the water and cried out, "Oh, dear God, sometimes . . . sometimes."

Emma's chest contracted as she struggled to admit the dark, heavy feelings at the bottom of her heart, "I'm so angry at you, Bob, for dying and leaving me alone and, damn it, I miss you! I still want you so much. I just don't want to accept that you're never coming back!"

She cried until the anger and longing subsided. Emptied, she leaned back against the rock. The sadness dissolved. She reached out and plucked a small, soft pussy willow bud. Holding it as if it were a great treasure, she gazed at the cornucopia of spring's fruitfulness. The bright yellow of the forsythia bushes and the intense red buds at the tips of the tree branches set off the beauty of the dark green pine trees. Her spirit softened at the aliveness of all the new growth laid out before her.

Emma sighed in resignation and began to remember some of the loving times that she had shared with Bob. Encapsulated in the energy of love's memory, she held onto the sense of his presence and talked out loud about what had been disturbing her during the last few days.

"Dearest Bob, I wish you were here to comfort me. I'm getting those feelings again. Something around me is going to change. I'm frightened. I wish you were here to hold me, to tell me to let go, and to trust that it will all turn out for the best like always. You'd probably also admonish me to mind my own business about Julie. If Anne or Jack wanted to talk about her, they would. Sometimes I'm so damned curious it hurts."

Emma stared into the smooth surface of the pond, envisioning her husband's image in the water. She closed her eyes until the light again filled her mind. Her worries dissolved and her curiosity settled. She surrendered to a state of peacefulness. A voice broke through the silence of her mind, "Relax, I'm here and your work will be guided. Let go."

As if he knew she was finished with her reverie, Knight nudged her head. Emma took hold of his reins, patted his neck and responded, "Good boy! Let's get going while there's still some sun."

She turned from the pond, mounted her horse and headed out of the wooded area toward the high meadow. Horse and rider made it back to the barn before dusk took full hold of the sky.

****

After grooming Knight, Emma changed out of her riding outfit, packed it in the car and went over to the studio.

It was lit up but empty. On the door was a note from Anne.

Emma,

I left the lights on for you to look at my last work and went to the kitchen to start dinner. The contracts that the gallery sent me are on the desk. If there's a problem, bring them up to the house, we'll talk after we eat. The other papers you wanted are in the drawer.

Anne

Emma mused that she would never leave her own desk unlocked; Anne had an implicit trust in the world around her. When her husband died, Emma lost that feeling of trust.

As long as Emma could remember she couldn't imagine Anne doing one thing at a time or completing something before going on to another. This was typical of her, dealing with business while cooking dinner.

Letting herself into studio, Emma headed for the large collage hanging against the back wall. She stood transfixed. Anne's latest piece stirred a feeling of anticipation in her. Her mind tried to make sense out of the harsh lines created by strips of dark metals woven into the intense bright flashes of color on the canvas. The piece stood about fifteen feet high and ten feet wide. It took up the whole back of the studio.

To get a better sense of the art piece, Emma stepped up closer to it. She tried to figure out how Anne had fixed the metal onto the canvas while making the painted part of the piece look like background. Anne seemed to have welded the pieces of metal in sharp angles to each other and somehow fixed the metal collage structure to a large canvas by bolting it to a wooden support behind the work. Emma wondered what possessed the mind of her friend.

A sudden wind came into studio from door opening.

Emma turned to greet Tom and said, "Just taking in Your wife's latest work

"It's going to be a bitch to ship but it's captivating, isn't it?" he said as he stood next to Emma.

"It unnerves me, and yet I want to study it more. It does draw you into it while repelling you at the same time. I . . . I don't know what to say to Anne."

Emma stepped back for a different perspective, but no matter where she stood, the piece still created the same disturbance in her.

"Just tell her it's one of her most interesting pieces,

which indeed it is! Art, according to the resident expert, isn't meant to soothe us as much as make us more aware of the psyche," said Tom.

He moved behind Emma and leaned over her shoulder, looking back at the work, "Whaddaya feel it says about Anne's psyche?" he asked in his thick Rhode Island accent.

"I wouldn't touch that with a ten-foot pole," Emma said somewhat lightheartedly.

"I've never been bored being married to Anne."

"Nor I being her friend," mused Emma.

Tom turned around to face Emma and asked, "Now, answer another very important question. Are you joining us for dinner? It's the Thursday night special."

Emma laughed. "Would I miss a chance to eat some of Anne's famous chowder and clam cakes, a meal I don't have the slightest skill in cooking? But before we go in, I want to go over the contract." She walked to the desk to get it.

"Tell you what, come eat while it's hot and look the papers over after dinner. There's a copy in the den for you to review."

Tom put his arm around Emma and guided her out of the studio.

"That haunting painting isn't going anywhere, but the food might not survive the ravages of teenagers," he said.

"That smell always captivates me," Emma said as she went into the kitchen.

Anne was waiting for her to begin serving dinner. She hugged Emma and called to the children, who were in the den watching TV.

"Serve yourselves off the stove and then sit down. Rose, go tell Grandpa that we're eating and that Emma's here."

Rose, at fifteen, didn't look anything like her mother. Her grandfather, Jack, loved that she was the spitting image of his dark Irish mother, with crystal-clear blue eyes and pitch-black hair. Rose's straight pose and defined features gave her a regal sense and a powerful presence in any group, but especially in Anne and Tom Riley's family. Rose stood out as the only daughter. Tom, like his father-in-law, Jack, thought Rose could do no wrong. But to her mother, Rose could never do enough. Anne depended on her to fulfill the roles of daughter, friend, and sometimes surrogate mother to her. It often caused tension between the two, but tonight seemed to be one of ease for both of them. This was a rare evening when Anne and Tom's three children, Richard, John and Rose, were all present for dinner.

For Emma, being around a bright young woman like Rose was a good balance to living with her teenage boys.

Jack came in from the den with an inviting smile.

"Emma, come sit beside me," he said with a wink and sat down.

"Rose, here," he patted the seat on his other side.

Jack lifted up his arms, touched the two women's shoulders and pronounced, "I like being surrounded by beautiful women!"

"Oh, Grandpa, you just don't want to sit between two

rowdy boys."

"No, my dear, when a man is treated to the presence of three beauties, he has to make the most of it."

"Well, I for one like being seen for my beauty as long as I can still win an argument with you," Emma smiled and added, "just don't ask me to do extra work to repay you for the compliment."

They all laughed.

"Never, never, Emma," Jack matched her lighthearted jostling.

Tom, Richard and John sat together on the other side of the round table. Anne settled between the two of them and held out her hands in a gesture for them to share a long held ritual.

"Thank you, God, for the bounty of food, family, and friends."

No one could see that Anne continued in silence to wish that her father wouldn't draw Emma into any political discussions tonight. But this evening she didn't have to worry, Jack was quieter than usual and just listened while his grandchildren reported about school. Emma compared their stories to what was happening in her twins' school. All the boys were disappointed that the basketball season was over.

Jack's silent behavior disturbed Emma, but no one else seemed bothered. She picked up Anne's tension, but assumed it was just fatigue from finishing her art piece. She tried to draw Jack out of his quiet state.

"Weren't you the head of the Clippers basketball team

in high school?" Emma asked Jack with as much casualness as she could muster.

"Oh, that was a long time ago." Jack looked up to the ceiling as if he had trouble recalling the time he was so political. "I can hardly remember my earliest days but, yes, for one year. It didn't suit me, nobody on the team would do want I wanted . . . unlike my willing young law partner."

Jack smiled at Emma but instead of feeling comforted, she felt a chill run through her.

"Mr. Senior Partner, it's a pleasure to hear about the 'old days', at least some of the time," Emma tried to return a lighter tone.

"Okay, you two," Anne interrupted them, "enough about sports and the office. Emma, I'm dying to hear what you think about my new piece!"

Anne passed the plate of clam cakes around the table. "Well?"

Emma fiddled with her fork, trying to find a way to be honest, but supportive, "To tell you the truth, it took me by surprise. I'm intrigued by it."

Anne turned to her sons, "That, my dears, is a woman's way to say, 'I hate it.'" She looked back at Emma as if to tell her that she wasn't insulted.

"I didn't hate it, but I did find it a bit disturbing. But art, as you say, is meant to encourage new consciousness, so give me time to absorb its unusual form. It has to grow on me a little."

"Grow? There is one of your new age words—GROW!" Anne often ribbed Emma about her spiritual path, for it was so different from what she believed. Anything different to her Irish soul was an open target for teasing.

Jack broke his silence.

"To become wiser, to become more human, to become more alive. Your painting, my dear, shakes us into feeling more alive," he turned to Rose, "like your poetry."

"Shakes us like our football, Pop?" Richard was quick to speak to get his share of his grandfather's attention and approval.

"Shaking your body is not the same as shaking your eternal soul . . . one you can live without."

"Shake that body!" John joked and sang at his brother, "for you don't got no soul."

"At least I've got a body to shake!" Richard chided back at his younger brother.

"Jack, why don't you take the women into the den while I help the kids clean up?" Tom suggested. He was the one who kept the order in the home.

Jack stood up and opened his arms for Anne and Emma to go along with him. Rose said goodnight and went upstairs to do her homework. The boys left for a friend's house.

Jack opened the glass doors of the fireplace.

"There's a chill in the air. A nice fire will feel good."

He built the fire and then sat in his favorite recliner.

The two friends curled up on the loveseat next to the fireplace. They all surrendered to a quiet state as they stared at the fire.

After a few minutes, Jack looked up at Anne. "I've

turned over some personal work to Emma. Call her right away if something should happen to me."

"What?" Anne looked startled.

Emma was shocked that Jack had brought up the business they attended to that day. She thought he had relaxed and put it out of his mind. She wondered what was wrong with him, shuddering at the thought that she might lose him, too.

"Your father is just being his thorough self. You know that he likes everything written down," Emma assured her friend.

"What did you have her do for you, Dad?" asked Anne.

"I've added a living will to the documents so you and Tom won't be burdened with any decisions."

"I thought you already had one drawn up." Anne was confused.

"My documents need to be updated. It's nothing for your concern."

"Well," Anne hesitated for a moment, "all right, Dad."

His answer seemed to satisfy Anne about the will but she continued to push him, "I don't like the way you're behaving lately. You're too quiet. You seem distracted and not up to par. Is there anything you need to tell us?" Anne touched her father's hand in a soft way.

"Honey, I'm nearing retirement; it's overdue." He squeezed her hand back and continued, "I'm just trying to get everything in order. Don't pay too much attention to the mental wanderings of an old man. I've a lot to think about. I'm too tired tonight to talk about the will, but I'll go over it with you and Tom soon."

Emma knew that he was avoiding the truth but tried to honor his wishes and turned the discussion to concerns over Anne's contract with a gallery.

"I'd like to review the contract. Do you have the copy?" asked Emma.

Anne went over to the desk and found it right on top.

It took about five minutes for Emma to go over the fine points of the document and give it her approval. She handed it over to Anne, "The contract's fine, but it's not clear who will pay for the heavy equipment needed to move that piece."

"Tom thinks I should insist they do, but what do you think?"

"Your work is in high demand, so keep your demands high. Insist that you'll surrender the piece only if they pick it up and pay for the shipping."

"I have to remember to stop mothering the gallery. I'm served by them, right?"

In most circumstances, Anne was forceful and strong, so Emma was surprised that she sounded unsure of herself when dealing with the gallery.

"Right! Insist on shipping costs and write it into the contract before signing it," Emma agreed.

"I'll do it tomorrow." Anne seemed assured.

Jack had dozed off while the women worked out the details.

"Now that he's not listening, tell me what's going on with my father?" she whispered.

Emma got up, paced a little and said, "Really, Anne, I just don't have the answer, but I agree he's in some kind of turmoil. Has he been to see Dan Hill for a check-up recently?"

Anne laughed, "Do you think he'd let on if he had?"
"Tell you what, let's both keep an eye on him and tell the other if we notice anything that needs to be attended to right away. Deal?" Emma wondered how much longer she could Jack's secrets.

"It's a deal," Anne said. She grabbed a wrap off the sofa's back and covered her father with it. "Let's leave him napping and come have some coffee and a slice of poppy seed cake. I found a great new recipe in the February issue of Food and Wine."

"I'm supposed to get a workout by riding, but you destroy the benefits of my labor with such rich food. But, I love your cakes, so lead on to the dessert," said Emma. They headed to the kitchen.

****

Emma drove down the long dirt driveway of Abbey's Run Lane. As the farm drifted out of sight, she turned left onto Bear Hill, heading up the winding road that led back to the highway.

Each time she passed the new developments going up on the old pastureland, her heart felt heavy with a sense of loss. She regretted that even on Bear Hill Road the open land was disappearing. Emma's body tightened as she readied herself to face the aggressive nighttime drivers.

The price she had to pay for such watchful driving was the loss of dreaminess she had experienced in the woods. Matching the mood of the other drivers, she darted around slower cars. She forced herself to slow down entering the quiet residential streets of the Edgewood neighborhood.

Emma turned onto her street and gasped, "Look at that! Perfect, just perfect!" Right before her was the full moon sitting right over her house sending a streak of light across the bay.

She parked in the garage, dropped her riding outfit on the porch and went inside. After reviewing the mail piled on the kitchen counter, she headed upstairs to the second floor, the boy's level.

Hopefully, it wasn't too late to talk with Sean about some school issues. Sean was fast asleep the lights blazing, and his schoolbooks scattered all over the floor. She lingered by his door, enjoying that special moment a mother has when her older child is asleep and she thinks how much he looks like the young boy she used to tuck in every night. She didn't have the heart to wake him for a check-in talk; it could wait. She left Sean's room and peeped into the room across the hall.

Matt was sitting at his desk doing homework. Ever since his father's death, he didn't feel secure until she was home, so she knew he would be still up even if she came in late.

The wall over his desk was decorated with a cork-like material that was covered with photos of his father and him sailing, playing various kinds of ball games, camping in Vermont's Green Mountains, and fooling around during family gatherings. Lining the shelves next to the desk were trophies he had won in horse shows, an interest he shared with his mother.

The rest of his room was typical for a teenager, with clothes strewn all over, posters of popular music groups, and the smell of musk that comes from over using cologne or aftershave lotion. Matt had just started using it and hadn't yet learned how to use the lotion, slapping it on in abundance. Emma braced herself against the powerful fragrance, entered the room, and went over to stand by her son.

Sensing that Matt needed to talk, she sat down on the edge of his bed. "Hi, do you have practice before school tomorrow?"

"At 7:00, but I've got to have this book done before the game. The coach told me that I have to pass the review test with at least a B."

Emma worried about how torn Matt felt between the demands of schoolwork and competitive sports. He had joined the baseball team because his father enjoyed the game, but now that his dad was dead, he had trouble staying with it. He thought that if he stayed with it and played in top form, he might get a baseball scholarship to his father's alma mater, Boston College.

"High school is a time to discover yourself and enjoy being young. I don't want you to overextend yourself. Have you given any more thought to dropping the team and doing what you really want?"

"Mom, you don't understand! All my friends are on the team and they depend on me. I just can't drop out!" Matt got up from his desk and paced.

Not wanting to cause him more distress, Emma relented.

"Fine, but it can't continue this way. Tomorrow I'm going to hire a tutor to set up a study schedule for you and once a week, until summer, I want you ride with me. Knight misses his favorite rider, you're the only one who can push him to his limits and stay on him."

Although she wanted to draw Matt back to some of his own interests, Emma didn't dare say out loud what she was thinking, "It's important, my sweet son, that you get away by yourself. And, remember that you're not your father, your brother, or a clone of your coach. You're a sensitive, unique person, strong in your own power. Oh, how I wish you'd remember that!"

"Mom, I love Knight, but when are we going to find the time? You work, I practice." Matt softened a little after she gave up pushing him about dropping baseball.

"How about Sunday, first thing in the morning before your brother gets up? There's never any practice then. I don't work and you don't study."

"What about your med-i-ta-tion?" Matt teased her.

"I'll make it a riding meditation that morning. How about it?"

"You got it, Mom. I do miss riding that punk horse."

"Hey, don't pick on my horse. I'll ride Anne's old

gelding, Windy. So Sunday morning, we'll be out of here by 7:00. But now, you need to get some sleep."

Emma kissed Matt on the cheek before heading upstairs to her room. She called back down the stairs, "Matt, turn your brother's music off for me."

"Sure thing. Night, Mom."

Emma retreated to her suite. To restart her life as a single woman, she had had the upstairs' rooms redesigned for her comfort and style preferences. Compelled to put aside her attachment to her late husband, she sold their bedroom furniture, took down all the prints they had on the bedroom walls, and made the room reflect her new self. On the first floor, however, the rooms were still quite traditional, with a formal living room, dining room, and a more relaxed atmosphere in the "great" room. The first floor was a good place for family gatherings and entertaining business connections, but here, in the privacy of the third floor, Emma found sanctuary.

She had tinted windows put in so she could always look out at the water and not worry about anyone looking back. The whole southeast side of the room was full of windows. Her bed, a simple futon, was in front of the window with a meditation area at its foot. Except for a statue of Buddha on a low table, an Indian woven rug displayed on the wall, and a vase full of fresh flowers, the room was empty. Most times, just entering it quieted her. But not tonight.

Her exchanges with Jack during the day and then later, at dinner, had left her feeling uneasy. Emma was never one to hold back her opinions or remain silent when discussions were illogical. But for some reason that she couldn't explain to herself, she hadn't been able to have an honest talk with Jack. His comments and demands were leading to some conclusion, one she felt uncomfortable guessing.

Agitated, she went into the bathroom and turned on the hot water to fill up the tub. She dropped her clothes and rubbed her arms to ward off a cold feeling. She wrapped herself in her favorite blue bath sheet and checked the thermostat. "What's wrong with me, it's 72 degrees." Shivering, she bent over the tub and warmed herself in the steam rising from the bath water.

Jack's words plagued her, especially the ones about disillusionment. Her gut tightened with the realization that her law partner had some inner issues that could hurt him and Anne. Fear sickened her.

She opened the medicine cabinet for healing herbs and aroma essences and poured them into the bath. She slid the mirror back into place and stared at her reflection. Her skin, like her mother's, was still smooth, her eyes were clear and bright green, and her golden hair had only a few wisps of gray. "Not bad for a forty-year-old," she thanked her ancestors for her physical beauty. Her mother used to comment that all the family women aged with grace; it was expected of them. With Emma's height--five feet, eight inches--she created the impression of grace.

As she waited for the herbs to dissolve, she continued to try to make sense of Jack's announcements. She spoke to his lingering presence, "You're never one to be bitter or hidden; why, dear friend, are you so cynical now?"

She reached up to the shelf above the bathtub and chose Chopin's piano concertos playlist on the music speakers. Her bath towel slipped off. She stepped into sweet-smelling water and lay back in the comfort of the bath. She tried to envision Jack and both their families surrounded by a peaceful spiritual light. Her ringing phone interrupted her concentration.

Disturbed, Emma got out of the tub, dried off and put on a terry cloth robe, and went into the den across from her bedroom. This room was the antithesis of her bedroom, with a desk piled high with papers, photos, and assorted office supplies, a computer, a printer, and an answering machine.

Emma wrapped the robe around her, grabbed a note pad from the shelf over the desk, and settled into the high-back chair to listen to her messages. Two were from friends, one was from her cousin, Peter, and the last one was from Jack.

"Emma dear, I wanted to thank you again for all you're doing for me. Don't forget how much I respect you . . . and depend on you in the firm." The voice on the message cracked with emotion that seemed more than the tiredness of age. He continued, "And, especially, in handling my personal matters. God bless and goodnight. See you in the morning."

Puzzled, Emma thought how Jack never called her unless there was an emergency needing immediate attention. She promised herself that no matter what, she and Jack would have a talk in the morning. No one or anything would get in the way of her confronting him. She was not going to live another day with the uncertainty of wondering what was going on with him.

As she often did with people she loved, Emma spoke to Jack as if he was in the room with her. "If you're asking me to handle something sensitive for you, you're going to have to tell me right now what's up with you."

She went into the bedroom, sank into her bed, tucked one of her down pillows under her neck and slept.

4

THURSDAY: WEST COAST

Another dream-filled night and another meeting with Dr. Goldberg left Julie feeling unsettled.

"This one was the same overall as the others but had a different ending," Julie told him.

"Go on," said Dr. Goldberg.

"My father wasn't just standing at the edge as in the last dream. He was looking over the edge and then, turning away, he walked around in circles. I felt pulled to him. Before I reached the other side of the canyon, Nana pushed me into the river."

"Relax, Julie, let the dream speak to you. Why do you think your grandmother was aggressive in this dream? Is your father trying to protect you from her, or are they both threatening you?"

"I don't understand it at all. But looking at it from here feels safe. I'm not as anxious as before, but I'm disappointed not to get to the meaning of the dream."

Her therapist reflected that even though her defenses were strong, there was a part of her consciousness that held the key to understanding her dreams. He suggested that she keep a journal to record her dreams.

"Julie, every day take some time to relax, to practice allowing yourself to be present with whatever's happening to you in that moment. These reflections will help the memories emerge."

"Right. And how can I fit that in? My schedule doesn't provide enough space or time to have consciousness as a top priority."

"How much fear do you want to continue to endure?"

"When you put it that way, I don't have a choice, do I? How can I work if I don't get any sleep?"

He reminded her that the headaches, insomnia, and nightmares were symptoms of a deeper pain. Since she didn't want to take an antidepressant, perhaps writing would help her recover the childhood memories needed for healing.

She had blocked out of her mind the experiences of her youth and wasn't pleased when Dr. Goldberg emphasized that they were of core importance in solving the mystery of her dreams. She left his office feeling agitated.

For the rest of Thursday she tried to concentrate on work but allowed herself a short break from research to prepare her speech for the monthly meeting of the Space Science Researcher's Association on Saturday. She enjoyed being with others whose interest and intelligence were compatible with her own. It also gave her a chance to socialize.

Her plan didn't work. Around three in the afternoon, a severe migraine came on. Ever since she was a teenager, her life's activities were at times interrupted by the onslaught of the kind of intense physical pain that she was now experiencing as she worked on her speech. As usual, when such headaches took over, the solution was to lie down in a dark room in absolute quiet. She knew it would take about six hours to change the severe migraine to a low-grade headache even with the help of pain medication.

There was a couch in the science building lounge, but she couldn't lock herself in it for the whole day, so she stayed in her office and tried to ignore the pressure in her head and work on the speech. But the pain took control. With no choice but to surrender to it, Julie went home. Once there, she collapsed on her bed.

Isabella was still there and came in to help her. After drawing the drapes across the patio doors, she turned off the lights and placed a cold towel over Julie's eyes.

"Would you like me to stay with you tonight?" Isabella rarely witnessed her boss being so fragile. Something was wrong. She was reluctant to leave her.

"No, no, thank you," muttered Julie. "Just get me my medicine and put Dixie in the den. I'll be fine if I lie here for a while. Go on home; I'll call you if I need you."

Isabella gave her the pills with some water, covered her and left her alone in the dark room. Julie fought the waves of nausea and concentrated on emptying her mind of all thoughts. After an hour or so, the medicine started to lessen the intensity of the pain. About midnight, her head cleared and she was able to fall asleep.

FRIDAY: EAST COAST

The sound of a foghorn jarred her awake. Thinking that the fire alarm had gone off, Emma jumped out of bed and ran to the window. She calmed down when she saw a tug was pulling an oil barge through the deep channel and sounding the horn to warn the quahogers fishing down the Bay. Their lights flashing, the boats moved through the thick fog as they approached the buoy near Gaspee Point.

Her mind immersed in the fog, she couldn't recall what day it was. It could be a day in any season since the mist cloaked the water and land. She felt muscle pain in her thighs and remembered that she had gone riding the night before, so today was Friday, the last day in a busy week.

She hoped the shower would wash away her sense of vagueness. After showering she sat on her meditation pillow. A nervous feeling kept her breathing shallow and her mind racing with meaningless thoughts.

The phone rang in the middle of her meditation. Relieved, Emma consoled herself that at least she wouldn't have to waste any more time trying to do what seemed impossible this morning, to relax.

"Emma, it's Tom."

"You need to come to Providence General right away. Jack had a stroke," said Tom.

"What? Jack?" Emma moaned.

"He's not so good. You've got to get here as soon as you can."

"He's dying?"

"I don't know." Tom rambled on as if he could talk himself into being calmer by reporting the facts--the ex-cop reporting a case. "Anne found him this morning when she went to let the horses out into the corral. His lights were on and music was playing; this scared her. Jack is such a penny-pincher—he'd never waste electricity. And, he's never up that early. She went to check on him and found him out cold on the floor by his bed."

"Is Anne with him?" Emma asked.

"After the rescue squad stabilized him, Anne had them take him to Providence General. She's in the ICU with him. But Emma, when we got there, the staff acted strange with us; the computer directed them to notify the hospital administrator, Paul Bell, if Jack was admitted."

"Wasn't Dan Hill called in to treat him?"

"Yes, but there's a problem. After Anne went in with him, Bell told me that there's something about an agreement Jack signed on Wednesday. He needs to check it with you. You better get over here right now!"

"I'll be there as soon as I can."

Emma woke up the her boys to tell them that there

was an emergency and that they would have to get themselves to school. She dressed hastily and drove to the hospital. Despite her efforts to stay hopeful, she jumped to the worst conclusion. She didn't feel ready for the struggle that intuition was warning her was about to happen.

Tom was waiting in the hall of the ICU unit. Tom, the ex-cop, the young widowed father, the agent for his wild artist and young wife, was used to turning impossible situations around for the good, but he seemed overwhelmed by Jack's illness. At first glance he looked vulnerable standing alone in the hall, but as Emma approached she could see an unfamiliar rage in his eyes.

"Emma, things are a mess!" Tom pronounced.

"How's Jack?" she asked.

"Not so good, it was a massive stroke that's left him in a coma." Tom looked toward the ICU unit where Jack was hooked up to machines.

"I haven't talked to Anne about this yet. She came in the ambulance with him. When I got here, Paul Bell pulled me aside and told me that Anne can't sign for any further treatment and that you know he named his daughter, Julie, as power of attorney."

With fury in his eyes, he turned to Emma, "What's going on?" His voice rose in anger as he continued, "Anne's been looking after him since Nana died and now. . ." Outraged, he leaned closer and fumed, "And now, she can't sign for him! What the hell's that about?"

Emma had never seen Tom in such a state. Answering him with a subdued tone, she reached out with a gentle touch on his arm.

"Tom, I'm as confused as you are. When Jack insisted on that clause in his living will, it seemed strange to me. I was going to talk to him today about his choice of medical surrogate and ask him why he involved Paul Bell. He's not his doctor."

"You did the will before getting his answers?" Tom's voice tightened with rage.

"I thought he had talked it over with you and Anne. Jack loves Anne and has always acted for her good. And, he was so insistent that it be done that I put off clearing up my concerns."

Hoping to diffuse the tension, Emma stepped away from Tom and took off her coat. She walked back and spoke in a soft, consoling manner. "I thought Jack was trying to relieve Anne of some responsibility. He's been out of sorts; maybe his thinking was clouded by his illness."

Tom was still angry, but it seemed to Emma that he had a less antagonistic stance and was trying to process what she told him.

She threw up her hands in an expression of exasperation. "Believe me, Tom, I'd never set out to hurt Anne."

Tom still stood silent, looking perplexed.

Annoyed at Tom's critical tone with her but feeling the need to keep the communication open, Emma tried again to calm him. "Look, Tom, Jack never discussed with me his relationship with Julie and Anne, nor did he ever mention Julie to me before this week. I'm not privy to your family's private business just because I work with him or do a will for him. For all I knew, he and Anne decided who would be guardian."

Emma held her ground while she waited for him to settle down and hear what she was saying.

Tom turned away. Emma waited.

He swung around to face her. "How could you let him do this?"

"Believe me, as I've said, I'm as much in the dark as you!"

Tom left her standing by the door to the ICU and stormed down the hall to check on his wife and Jack. Emma hurried after him. She pleaded, "Tom, please wait a minute."

He stood outside Jack's room, softening a little as Emma continued, "It's upsetting to see Anne so hurt and powerless. Before Anne realizes that her father put her sister, not her, in charge, we need to decide how to proceed."

Tom's shoulders lowered in resignation. "Well, it seems that Jack used you, Emma, for whatever reason, we might never find out."

Emma was relieved that he had shifted into his usual cooperative, helper mode of reaction.

"Anne and her sister are estranged. I don't know Julie at all. She left and no one's ever told me why or even inquired about her. I thought Jack considered her dead. And now, this?" Tom said.

They sat on the chairs in the hall, bewildered. A nurse

asked if she could help them, reminding them of the business at hand. Tom, sounding sad, asked Emma, "Do you call Julie or do I?"

"I'm not family. You call her and arrange for her to come, and then I can go over the situation with her. The way Jack set it up, she must come to Rhode Island in order for the judge to change the power of attorney from her to Anne. She doesn't have to stay long or be involved, but she does need to come in person. It's obvious to me that by the way he organized his papers, Jack intended that Julie would have to return to Rhode Island."

"What the hell did he have in mind? Does he want something to happen between them? But what? I wouldn't be so anxious about my wife if I knew what Jack's plan was and why."

"I understand you're upset." Emma bowed her head and rubbed her forehead as if she could peel away the confusion. "I wish I had answers for you, but I have to admit, Jack set it up so Julie has the key to this mystery."

Emma reached out to touch Tom to remind him that he wasn't alone in handling this problem. "Beats me why he chose this course of action. Of course, as Anne's friend, I'm very sorry that it was put together this way."

"Okay, Emma, I believe you. But be prepared to handle any questions Anne or Julie will have for you."

"I'm as ready as I'll ever be," Emma said. She looked into Jack's room and asked, "Do you think it would be okay for me to see Jack?"

"Only members of the family can go in unless Dan Hill

lists the person. I'll ask him to put you on the list. Jack's in a deep coma and paralyzed. They want to do all kinds of tests to determine the extent of the brain damage, but without Julie's permission they can't proceed."

They went back to the nurses' station and looked in on Anne hovering over her father.

"Whatever possessed him to do this?" Tom let out a long breath and slumped down. "I better call Julie to see if I can get her here. Will you tell Anne about the situation? I just can't face her with this."

"You go and make the call," said Emma.

Anne sat stoic and silent among the tubes and monitors and IV's. She rubbed Jack's arm, as if begging him to come back to her. Emma wondered what she was in the middle of. And what was she going to say to Anne? How could she explain it to her dear friend?

Anne noticed Emma in the hall and came out to talk with her.

"Emma, did Tom call you? I was going to wait until office hours. There isn't anything you can do here. Has Andrew been called?" Anne stood motionless, none of her usual energy evident.

"I'll call my father later," Emma assured her as she gently took hold of Anne's arm. Emma guided her into the intensive care waiting area. She was thankful it was empty. "Anne, come sit in the lounge with me, we need to talk about your Dad."

"Where's Tom?"

Emma tried to be as neutral as possible. "Tom went to

make a call. I need to go over Jack's living will with you. Remember last night, he mentioned it. After the will was signed, your Dad had a copy sent to Paul Bell. He wanted to make sure the hospital acted in accordance with his wishes."

"For God's sake, Emma, not now!"

"We have to talk about it."

"Emma, Dad's fighting for his life . . . we don't need to discuss wills or anything like that . . . just stop!"

"But, Anne, this is a formality that needs attention," Emma insisted.

Anne ignored what she was being told. Rigid and empty looking, she answered as if she hadn't heard anything, "Emma, I'm glad you're here, but I've got to get back to Dad."

Before Emma could say anything more, Anne hurried down the hall back into her father's unit. Helpless, Emma found it hard to hold back her own fears of losing Jack, her friend and mentor. Her emotions surfaced and flooded through her, almost washing away all her control.

"Hold on, just hold on. Concentrate. Stay clear," Emma muttered to herself. She left the lounge to find Tom. He had to be made aware that Anne still didn't have a grasp of the legal situation and that he had to find a way to tell her about Julie.

6

FRIDAY: WEST COAST

Julie turned to the nightstand. She reached over to tap off the alarm on her cell phone. It just couldn't be time to get up but the alarm wouldn't turn off.

She picked the phone up and realized that it wasn't the alarm. The phone was ringing. To stop the irritating sound, she answered it.

There was a man's voice on the other end of the line. "Is this Julie Taylor?"

"Yes, who's calling me at this god-awful hour?"

"Tom Riley. I'm sorry to call so early, but there's an emergency here."

"Tom? Tom who? I don't know any Tom." She went to end the call but his tone kept her attention.

"Dr. Taylor, please hear me out. I'm Anne's husband, Tom Riley."

"Where are you calling from at this time of the morning?"

"I'm in Rhode Island and calling from the hospital."

"Has something happened to my sister?" asked Julie.

"No, Anne's all right. I'm sorry for waking you, I realize

that it's only five in the morning in California but I have to speak with you. Do you want me to give you a few more minutes to wake up? I can call back in five or ten minutes. Whaddaya say?"

Still groggy from the medicine she took for her migraine, Tom's Rhode Island accent jarred Julie to be more awake. "No, no need to call back. It's just that it's so early. What's wrong?"

He reported that her father had a major stroke. It didn't look like he was going to regain consciousness. Tom did his best to impress upon her how important it was for her to hear him out. He worked at having his tone be serious but non-threatening—a way of communicating he used when he was a cop talking to a resistant witness.

Julie responded somewhat coldly that her family hadn't contacted her in years and she saw no reason why she would be needed just because her father was sick. Besides how could anyone assume that after years of estrangement from her father, she would want to rush back to Rhode Island because good old Dad was ill?

Even though the exchange with this man, Tom, irritated her, she found herself suggesting that he call her later in the day.

"Please Dr. Taylor, hear me out," Tom pleaded.

There was something about Tom that softened her response. "And, by the way, you can call me Julie." What she didn't ask out loud was, "How's Anne?"

"Julie, please hang on for just a minute and listen to what I have to say. Your father set up a living will with you as guardian and medical surrogate. Anne can't make any decisions concerning his care."

"What, not Anne?"

"No, and I'm afraid that Anne doesn't know yet. I just didn't have the heart to tell her. Emma Quinn, your father's lawyer and one of his law partners, wanted me to ask you to come back East, at least for a meeting with a judge. She's confident that she can convince the judge to assign Anne or myself as Jack's guardian."

Tom didn't stop. In his best sales pitch, he continued, "Julie, you don't even have to see your father. But please, for all of our sakes, come back today and take care of this legal matter. I'll pick you up at Green Airport and make it as easy as possible for you."

Julie was taken by surprise at Tom's persistence.

Vulnerable from the drugs and the poor sleep several nights before, she vacillated.

"I just can't tell you right now if I can come." She grumbled to herself, "I haven't been feeling good and am behind in my schedule at work; it's too hard to get away."

"Give us just one day and you can return home. I'll set up a meeting tonight with Emma Quinn, the lawyer, and with anyone else who figures in the release of the guardianship of your father."

"If I come, I don't want to see my father."

"That won't be a problem. I'll protect you in any way I can."

"How's Anne reacting to this?"

"Well, it's hard for her. She's still in shock after finding him passed out. But, if this issue of guardianship turns into a problem, it could be impossible for her and the whole family, including you. Please Julie, come back East today."

Julie told herself that she didn't want any more problems for Anne, but the whole thing felt like a terrible problem for her. What should she do? Just as she was about to refuse Tom's request, the gentle presence of her mother settled in her heart. She gave in. "All right Tom. Set it up, but I want to be in and out as quickly as possible. I'll get the next flight I can."

"Forgive me for taking the liberty, but I made a reservation for you in first class on the 10:00 a.m. flight with American. I'll call and put it on my card, just pick up the ticket at the airport. I'll meet you at the airport."

Julie put the phone down and fell back against the pillow, stunned.

"What have I just agreed to do?"

She couldn't go back to sleep even though, if she got up by six, she would have plenty of time to pack, make arrangements at the university, and be on her way to the airport by seven.

In the dark of her room she tried to guess what was happening between her father and herself. Instead of finding clarity, upsetting emotions consumed her. A bitter taste filled her mouth and the heat of rage burned in her belly.

It was hard to believe that her father dared to invade her life first through her nightmares, and now with cold, legal documents--never direct, same old dad. Hurtful, unpleasant memories of her life with him had driven her far away from home. Well perhaps now he's powerless and dying, but it sure seemed to her just like old times. "He only has the balls to ask for help when he's passed out," she silently barked.

She had a slight pull to go to Rhode Island to honor her silent agreement with her mother--to make sure Anne wasn't involved in the confusion between herself and their father. Up to this time, the best way to fulfill that promise was to stay out of their lives. Julie couldn't help but worry how her coming back into the picture was going to affect Anne.

Weighed down by heaviness in her heart, Julie fell back against the pillow. She had a dreadful feeling of foreboding. Unable to sleep, she dragged herself out of bed to get ready for her trip to the past.

After packing, Julie walked with Dixie around the backyard. She touched her flowers, shaking off the dew and clipping dead blossoms with her fingertips. It seemed that Dixie sensed her imminent leaving; she stayed right by her side.

Julie fed Dixie, wrote a note for Isabella to watch the dog and the house until Monday, and left by seven. She had plenty of time to go to the office and review the schedule for the research teams.

The campus had that early morning quiet atmosphere. The Gates Building parking lot was nearly empty. How would she explain her trip "back home?" She never discussed her past or her family, and no one except her therapist knew that she even had a living parent. There were a few nonprofessional staff at work in her department, but Julie was able to get to her office without being noticed.

A switch went off inside her mind that said, "Keep organized to keep safe."

She packed her laptop and made a priority list of things that needed daily review. She didn't want to miss any essential steps in the project while she was taking care of the legal business in Rhode Island. After arranging with another professor to handle her graduate seminar, she called to cancel her therapy session. Without any other reasons to delay, she left for the airport.

The drugs she had taken for her headache made it difficult to drive but she steeled herself to drive safely. She had agreed to go, and so she would.

Driving along the San Francisco Bay on 101, she kept herself preoccupied during the forty-minute trip to the airport by reviewing the list she had left in the office for her graduate fellows. She worried that they didn't had have all the data needed for the next quarter's grant application. And above all, she avoided thinking about the events taking her away from her office.

With her mind busy with plans, Julie succeeded in separating from her feelings. By the time the ten o'clock flight lifted off, she was composed and determined to stay that way. She had almost convinced herself that she was heading for a work conference. She needed to believe that whatever was happening to her father wouldn't disrupt her life again.

****

Tom was in the hospital hall by the phone, staring into space.

Emma approached and asked, "Were you able to convince Julie to come home and if so, when will she be arriving?"

"Julie's on a morning flight from California and will get here about seven this evening. Do you think we can find a judge tonight and get this settled before Anne gets too upset? Did you tell her about Jack's decision?"

"Tom, I tried! But Anne didn't want to hear what I had to say. She isn't even ready to face the seriousness of Jack's stroke, but for her own sake, she has to find out about the will before her sister gets here. I think she might need to hear it from you. You're the one who gets through to her when she locks herself away from others."

"Damn it, Emma, I was counting on you telling her. Now what do we do?"

Ignoring his outburst, Emma tried to soothe the situation. "Julie won't be here until late. Give Anne a couple of hours and then tell her, but make sure it's before her sister arrives. Is everything okay out at Abbey's Run, or should I go out there to check on the kids or horses?"

"The boys are taking care of the horses. Richard'll drive his brother and Rose here later." Tom bent down to hug Emma and apologized, "I'm sorry for being so gruff with you. I know Jack's the one controlling everything here, even in his comatose state. Why don't you go to the office and I'll call you if anything happens. Paul Bell, Dan Hill, and the hospital's lawyer want to meet with us when everyone's ready." As a second thought he added, "What do you think we should do about the media?"

"The hospital will take care of that; they'll be discreet as Jack insisted."

Emma gathered up her briefcase and jacket. She turned and caught Tom's attention again, "Tom, I'll talk to the office staff and try to meet with my cousin, Peter. Maybe Dad can return to the office for a short time to cover Jack's cases. It doesn't look like he'll come out of this anytime soon."

She looked into the room where Jack was still under the white sheets. Her voice heavy with sadness, she continued, "If he pulls out of this at all."

Emma left the hospital, walked to her car, and collapsed.

Shaking, she gripped the steering wheel and cried out, "Damn you, Jack Fitzsimmons! You better not die on me! You just better not!"

On the way to the office, she rehearsed ways to break the news to the staff. She pulled into the driveway, disappointed not to see his car and driver, not to be able to compete with Jack about who got to the office first. Controlling the impulse to cry, Emma called out, "God, please help me not fall apart."

Emma went into Jack's office to review his schedule. She would have change or handle his appointments. To her surprise, he had cleared his schedule of important cases

For about the last month. How could she have missed what he was doing? Jack had looked busy, but he had been just covering social meetings with committee heads or administrators.

"He knew, he knew, damn it. Why didn't he let on to anyone that his health was so precarious? Why didn't he tell me? Did he even tell Dr. Dan how he was feeling? And if Dan knew, why didn't he clue his family in on the situation?"

She left his office with the uncomfortable feeling that she was being used. Jack had something in mind by bringing his estranged daughter home to handle his end-of-life issues and perhaps even his death. There was some reason she had no clue about, and he obviously didn't trust her enough to tell her. She couldn't help wanting to know what he had planned and why he had her draw up his living will knowing full well how close she was to Anne.

She muttered to herself, "Now it's too late to back out. I'm in the middle of it, whatever it is!"

Emma spent a couple of hours making calls and informing the staff. And since she was not going to get home until late, she set up rides for her sons to their sports events. By mid-morning her nerves were spent and her neck was tight as a rod with tension.

She decided that after meeting with Julie at the hospital, she would try to head back downtown to the Wellness Center for the Friday night meditation group with her teacher, Patrick. She craved support from the spiritual world to help with the trauma of the pending loss of her mentor and the awkwardness of having his daughter so disregarded. Emma felt powerless as she had when her husband had been dying, and she was never good at feeling out of control.

The afternoon's full workload helped occupy her mind and settle her nerves a little, but her psyche was in turmoil. At 6:30, she headed over to the hospital to meet the mysterious daughter, Julie. If Jack wasn't going to be conscious again, they needed to enforce his wishes defined in his living will.

Who was this person, Julie? What was she like? Emma hoped that she would be pleasant, cooperative, and not cause any more pain to her Anne than she was already experiencing. If the judge was available, it could all be taken care of by the end of the evening. Jack Fitzsimmons' family and friends could then focus all their attention on adjusting to his illness.

Weaving through rush hour traffic on North Main Street, Emma tried to avoid thinking about Anne's reactions, not because she didn't care but because of the possible problems that could come between them. Emma couldn't bear to think about losing any one else dear to her.

****

"Ma'am, we're landing!" The attendant nudged Julie because she seemed so settled in her sleep.

"Please, you must wake up. The pilot has announced we'll be landing soon. You need to put your computer away and put your seat up in the full, upright position."

Julie sat up and struggled to follow the airline attendant's directions to get ready for landing. She tried not to think too much about how far she was from home, or what she was going to have to face.

After she put everything under her seat, she looked out of the window at Narragansett Bay. An electric shock jolted her, shaking a deep part of her out of a trance. Her mind flooded with memories--sailing on the bay, dining on quahogs in her favorite clam shack outside of Point Judith, getting cartons of Rocky Point clam chowder, and water surfing through the waves of Scarborough Beach.

Disoriented by the past and present crisscrossing each other, Julie peered down at the roof of the suburban houses of Warwick. The plane flew right over them, landing just beyond one of the local roads. She recalled a lecture by her freshman high school civics teacher. "Be proud of Rhode Island, for it's a state unlike any other--small but large in its self-image. Its cities are crowded but it's spacious in the rural areas. It has a mixed ethnic population, and gracious in its provincial views. It's a place where the rich and poor live side by side."

It was all strange but familiar to Julie, and all of it was frightening to her. Lulled into the illusion of peacefulness by the staid, polite living style of her California home, Julie hated coming back to the intense, chaotic Northeast.

Just flying over Narragansett Bay and approaching T. F. Green airport put Julie into a slight panic. The pace of life sped up; the other passengers grabbed their bags from the overhead bins and rushed by her. They all seemed in a hurry to get somewhere important, but she felt reluctant to face where she had landed. She waited until the plane was empty before leaving. All the while she fought the intrusion of her memories.

In a daze, she left the gate area and walked down a modern new runway to the baggage claim area and exit. She walked down the fancy lit hall as if it were a death walk.

Everything was so different. It used to be a small, crowded building with a satellite-like domed lobby right out of the 1950's. She couldn't wait to exit the new modern building with sophisticated decor and bright atmosphere. The normal busyness of an airport exit area with taxi stands, buses and people waiting to be picked up, further unsettled her. Was she really in Rhode Island? Just as she started to think that she had flown into the wrong city, she heard her name.

"There you are." Tom was out of breath. "You must be Julie."

"Yes, and you're Tom Riley, right?"

After they confirmed identities, Tom hugged her. His large build and enthusiastic energy encased her. He didn't seem to notice that Julie was overwhelmed and his intimate way of greeting her, shocked her. Not hugged in a while, Julie stiffened in his embrace.

"Sorry I wasn't here sooner. I wondered if I'd recognize you but, there's no doubt about it, you and my daughter share the same genes, the same blue, sparkling eyes and dark hair." He stepped back and looked at her.

"You also look so much like your grandmother."

"So, I've been told before." Julie had difficulty responding to his warmth.

"Do you have any luggage?"

"None checked. All I have is this carry on."

Unaware of the extent of the trouble that her father had set up between her and her younger sister, Julie had assumed that Anne would be at the airport. Although they weren't close at all, she wasn't aware of any open hostility between them. On one level, she still thought of Anne as a child and was shocked to meet a brother-in-law who obviously was not young.

She thought that Anne knew the reason she stayed away was because of their father, not because she didn't care about her. She had stopped thinking about her Rhode Island family. She took it for granted that they had stopped thinking about her. It was for survival; it was practical, at least for Julie.

Julie expected that after a meeting with the judge, she would see Anne for a bit and then catch a night or morning flight back to the West Coast. She had put out of her mind the earlier phone conversation with Tom when he mentioned how upset Anne was over the her new involvement with their father. Even though she felt a stirring of attachment to her sister, Julie had no intention of being around their father. She had too much invested in maintaining her way of being.

Tom took her bag and guided her through the crowded airport. As they went out the automatic doors, a whiff of salty, damp, cold air blew against her skin, startling her. To Julie, even the molecules of the air seemed to move faster, with more aggression. Tom guided her to a new red Voyager van was parked nearby in the short-term lot.

Julie was taken aback by the name Abbey's Run Stables printed on the side door. She struggled to not to let Tom witness her distress of seeing such a bold reminder of her childhood home.

As nonchalant as possible she said, "I like your red van. Looks like it would be good for carting kids and equipment around, it would be hard to fit a horse in the back seat."

"Now wouldn't that be a sight!" Tom smiled and unlocked the door for her. He slapped his hand on the roof. "This bright red was a concession to my preference for the sporty look."

It felt good for Julie to laugh.

"All kidding aside, I'd be lost without the room." He spread his arm in an open gesture, "Hop on in."

She settled herself as Tom maneuvered the van out of the parking lot. They circled back around the airport, taking the access road to the interstate. Julie noticed that nothing was the same. Lining the sides of the access road were the standard signs of development: motels, restaurants, and condominiums. They closed in on her. She tried to take command of her unease by starting a conversation.

"So, is Anne at the hospital?" she asked again.

"No, she's gone back to the farm to talk with our kids. They're very upset over their grandfather's stroke. We also have horses that need attending to since they didn't have the morning grooming."

"I didn't think about how it would affect the children. Tell me what they're like," asked Julie. She was trying to find a common area of interest with this stranger whom she was entwined with in a twist of fate.

"Rose, well, at sixteen looks just like you. She's the caretaker of the clan but also very outrageous at times. She likes to read and party; she loves to argue just about everything. In that way, she's a lot like her Grandpa."

"My niece, then, takes after Nana but doesn't have her quiet temperament?"

"Rose can match her brothers any day when it comes to verbal scrapping." Tom seemed to be playing along with Julie's need to avoid talking about her father.

Grateful that he was so pleasant to be with, Julie wondered if he demonstrated such ease and protective aura to everyone, or was he just going out of his way for her because of Anne? Perhaps he didn't realize that being treated with such care was just what she needed.

The highway was crowded with the rush of people heading to the city for a night out. Julie tensed as they made their way through the evening traffic. She blurted out a criticism. "Drivers in Rhode Island haven't changed; they're still aggressive and impulsive."

"Uh, ump!" Tom agreed but didn't seem bothered by the other drivers.

Julie felt a little like she was in a war zone, but Tom didn't notice. He just continued describing the children.

"Richard's a chip off the old block--he likes to put everything in order. I just hope he shoots higher than being a cop like his dad. John has his mother's sensitivity and creativity. An explorer at heart, he loves new ideas, making things, and stirring the pot with radical opinions. He just started a drawing class, but his real love is music. They're both athletes."

"I remember Anne always drawing and being so frustrated when she ran out of paper." Julie allowed her thoughts to drift into the past. In the caring atmosphere that her brother-in-law had created, Julie almost forgot why she was in her home state.

Whenever there was a pause in the conversation, Julie looked out the window. She was shocked by all the construction in Providence, especially all the new buildings near the State House. She could still see the white marble of the State House dome lit up, beautiful against the evening sky. It was one of the few buildings that were familiar to her. It was a little comforting to feel connected to something, even if it was just a building.

When Julie was a little girl, her mother would take her to the State House building to visit her father--the senator. Inside the open lobby, she loved leaning her head as far back as it would go, looking up at the top of the dome. Her father often told her the story of how it was a unique dome, how there were just three others like it in the world. The young Julie thought her father worked in a magical place, and others also knew he was special.

"The State House is kept in good condition. I forgot

how beautiful it is." Julie didn't let Tom hear her other rambling thoughts.

"It stands out, doesn't it?" Tom agreed. He turned off of I95, crossed North Main Street and went up the hill towards Providence General Hospital.

"Julie, I hope you won't think me presumptuous, but I'm wondering, don't you want to see your father? He's unconscious. Far as we can guess, he's not aware of anyone. So if you want to visit, you won't have to deal with him. It might be your opportunity to put things in order. I'm sorry if I'm being too personal."

"For reasons I don't wish to discuss, I'm not interested in settling anything with my father," Julie answered.

"Forgive me. My wife always accuses me of acting like a cop who keeps pushing people until all the pieces of the mystery fit together--even ones that aren't any of my business. So, I'm sorry for pressuring you, but I do appreciate your coming east to clear up the legal issues. You won't hear another word about Jack from me."

"No harm done." She withdrew and was quiet for a few minutes. "Thinking it over, I might as well stop by and see him." And to herself, she thought, "Then maybe the nightmares will stop."

Soon they were at Providence General Hospital. They parked and went up to the ICU unit where Jack lay in total stillness. Julie hesitated as she stepped off the elevator and without flinching, followed Tom down the hall, through the thick safety doors and into an area of the hospital eerie with the silence of ill and dying patients.

Tom stopped at the nurse's station to introduce Julie to the nurse in charge.

"Mrs. Howe, I want to introduce you to Dr. Julie Taylor, Mr. Fitzsimmons' oldest daughter."

"Dr. Taylor, let me assure you that we're doing all we can for your father."

Julie bowed her head in response, hiding her reaction.

The nurse guided Julie into her father's room. "Don't get upset by all the machines and tubes; they're for keeping your father alive."

The plump, middle-aged woman checked one of the IV bags, then stepped back to give Julie some privacy with her father. "I'll leave you alone. I'll be right outside."

Julie just stood there for a moment, wondering if this was the man she had been afraid of for so many years. Her emotional self, awakened by coming home to Rhode Island, was emerging. She had been like her plain London Fog coat, with the bright, complicated design hidden inside, but now the force of her soul's confusion turned her inside out. Primal, raw emotions flushed through her. Tears streamed down her cheeks, washing away the remnants of restraint.

Tom leaned on the counter of the nurse's station using the time to appraise his sister-in-law. Julie sat focused on her father and didn't seem to notice that he had left the room.

"Mrs. Howe, please tell Dr. Taylor that I stepped outside for a smoke and I'll come to get her when her father's lawyer arrives for the meeting," Tom said.

7

THE MEETING

Tom stood outside the hospital entrance pacing, unaware of what was going on around him. Lost in his anxiety, he didn't notice Emma walking towards him.

"Hi, Tom."

"Oh, I'm sorry, Emma, I didn't see you."

"Any change in Jack's condition?"

"He's alive, but just barely." Tom lit up a Marlboro.

"It must be rough right now. You and Jack are very close. I haven't seen you smoke in years." Emma wished she could say something to ease his tension.

"Shit, you have no idea! When I told Anne about the information in the will, she stormed out of the hospital. Right from that, I had to meet Julie at the airport."

Tom smoked, sucking in long drags and blowing out with heavy breaths. "Emma, what's going on here? Jack faces death, Anne's raging, and Julie, to my surprise, seems like a nice woman who looks just like my daughter."

"Is Julie with her father?"

"Yes, and, sitting there crying her eyes out, is the sister that supposedly abandoned Anne. It bothers me that she's not anything like what I thought she'd be," Tom said.

"I don't know what to make of it all. I'm also bewildered. You're a cop—you know that there are always two stories or three, or more, to every situation." She wanted to redirect his energy to the issue at hand. They could deal later with the reality of the "missing sister."

"Yeah, yeah, you're right. There's a whole lot more here than we might ever understand." Tom sounded more resolved to let the mystery go for the moment.

"There'll be time to deal with Julie later, but right now we better go up. The doctors are waiting for us."

"I have to sit in for Anne. And I don't even know what's going on with her or where she is right now."

Tom tossed the cigarette onto the sidewalk, twisted the toe of his shoe over it several times and said, "I'm so irritated at not having any control over how to protect my wife!" He clenched his fist and grunted, "It makes me so God damn angry!"

"This isn't a good spot for you to be in. We'll take care of the meeting, settle whether Julie is staying or not, and then I'll help you with Anne," Emma said in an attempt to reassure him.

He wasn't acting like his usual take-charge self. Emma decided that she would have to be the person with strength, at least for the time being. She took hold of Tom's arm and walked into the hospital with him.

On the way up to the ICU unit, Tom seemed to settle into his usual reserved demeanor. They stopped by the nurse's station. Tom turned to Emma, "You wait here. I'll get Julie."

Tom went into Jack's room. He gently placed a hand on Julie's shoulder and spoke in a hushed tone, "It's time to go. Mrs. Quinn, Jack's lawyer, is here."

Julie reached for her purse and looked for her compact. She saw a tear-streaked face staring back at her. "I need a minute to get myself together."

"We'll be right outside."

Somewhat shaky, she stood and smoothed out her clothes. She took another look at her father. He looked nothing like the tormentor in her dreams. Steeling her emotions to handle the meeting, she went over to the sink, took a moist cloth, and wiped her face before going out into the hall.

Her tall, imposing brother-in-law was standing next to a professional looking woman she assumed was the lawyer. She had stepped back into her father's world and wondered what was to come from it all.

"Julie, this is Emma Quinn, your father's lawyer and partner in his firm."

Emma Quinn had a presence about her that helped to put Julie at ease. Julie sized up the character of her father's partner. She seemed to be a person of substance. A fair-skinned beautiful woman in her forties, Emma was serious yet seemed welcoming. Despite Emma Quinn's connection with her father, Julie liked her.

"I'm so sorry about your dad. I just can't get over what's happened."

Not responding to Emma's distress, Julie said, "Mrs.

Quinn, it's no secret that my father and I've been estranged for many years. I'm not sure why he set it up for me to be here. Perhaps you can enlighten me."

Although she sounded cold, Julie's eyes gave her away. Emma saw the veil of fear over her pupils and the look of sorrow shrouding her face. Emma felt she'd better be careful, for Julie looked as though she'd already been very hurt.

"I'll tell you what I can, Dr. Taylor. But right now, we should head upstairs to the conference room. Dr. Bell, chief of staff, and Dr. Hill, your father's physician, are waiting for us there." Emma moved the three toward the elevator.

"Well, Mrs. Quinn, I do hope that this can be handled without delay." Julie wanted to impress upon her sympathetic brother-in-law and her father's lawyer that she had no intention of staying in Rhode Island. She regained her bearings to present a strong facade.

They left the ICU and took the elevator up several floors to a conference room. During the ride, Emma observed Julie. To her surprise, she felt an instant liking for her. She looked just like an older Rose. Her dark hair was in a stylish short cut. She had clear blue eyes and the soft skin of the Irish. Trim and athletic, she dressed conservatively, in a dark blue silk-blend suit.

Julie took the time in the elevator to think about her trip home to California. Her feelings of turmoil for her father were already subsiding.

When they arrived at the door of the conference room, a tall man with an imposing aura reached out to Julie. "Dr.

Taylor, I'm Dr. Bell, your father's friend and an administrator here at the hospital. I hope our meeting is helpful to you during this trying time."

He guided her to a chair at the head of the conference table then introduced her to the doctors on the team. But before she sat down she was stopped short. Her father's doctor, Dan Hill, came up to her. Everyone at the meeting could see how stunned Julie was at meeting him.

"Dan, is that you? You're one of my father's doctors? It's impossible!"

He went over to Julie, hugged her and whispered in her ear, "Yes, I'm that forlorn boy of eighteen who you kissed good-bye. It's sure good to see you, even under these circumstances."

Dr. Hill turned to the others present who were shocked by the personal greeting and explained his embrace of Julie. "Dr. Taylor was my best friend growing up." He pulled the chair out for her and told her, "We'll catch up later."

The room filled with a wave of tension. Tom and Emma looked at each other as if to say, "Did you know this?" Both were surprised by Dan's announcement. Tom leaned over to Emma and commented under his breath, "What the hell's going on here!"

"Got me," Emma whispered back to him as she tried to keep her composure.

Julie sat down with Dan Hill next to her.

"Before we begin," Dr. Bell seemed to want to speed the meeting along. "I want to express my deepest concern for your father. We here at Providence General all hope that he'll have an easier time of it than he's having now. We're doing our very best for him."

"Thank you, Dr. Bell, and all of you." Julie gazed around the table and acknowledged everyone present. Without emotion she continued, "I'm here to clear up the legal situation and return to California as soon as possible. Mrs. Quinn, you said that in the meeting you would explain the unusual dictates that my father wrote in his living will. Please do so."

Emma opened her briefcase and laid out a copy of the papers while Paul Bell clarified the hospital policy of following the patient's wishes as stated in a legal document and not overriding them unless a legal guardian or judge gives the hospital authority to so.

"Dr. Taylor, please read your father's statements before discussing the options," asked Emma. She handed Julie the papers and sat back to observe her reading them. Although Julie Fitzsimmons Taylor showed no emotion, her body tensed and her eyes watered a little.

Julie projected the image of a vibrant, intelligent woman who commanded respect. Emma wasn't surprised that Jack's daughter would conjure up such energy. What was also evident, no matter how much she protested, was how much she was affected by her father's illness.

Emma wondered why this daughter hadn't been in contact with Jack. Something must have happened, but what?

A gnawing feeling familiar to Emma took hold of her, knotting up her stomach. She was determined to uncover the answer, not just to satisfy her own curiosity, but also because she had a strong sense that Julie fit into the Fitzsimmons' clan and whatever was hidden stood in the way of reconciliation. Emma also believed that everyone would be better off if whatever had separated them was brought out into the open. She hoped it all could be cleared up before Julie went back to California.

Julie had her own preoccupations. She couldn't believe it. Dan Hill, the first love of her life, her best friend growing up and the rescuer in her nightmares, was back in her life.

Why in God's name is he the doctor? Having Dan at the meeting meant that there was someone present who knew she once loved her father. It wasn't so simple to just sign a paper and leave. Her firm resolve to remain distant began to waiver.

While combing through papers that Emma Quinn had laid out for her, Julie snatched a fleeting glance at Dan. His soft blue eyes still had that tropical water reflection, but his face was tight and tense with signs of middle age instead of soft and sweet with the presentation of youth. Julie found herself interested in him. "Hmm, the voice, the looks and the charm are all still there. Wonder how I appear to him?"

Observing Dan drew her attention away from the exasperating issue before her. She tried but couldn't get into her usual, neutral stance. She told herself that this legal issue was just another problem. It would be easier to approach the aggravation of being her father's medical surrogate with the same concentration she used in setting up her scientific projects.

Julie's attempt at rationality didn't work. It was difficult to focus on what Emma Quinn was saying. She felt vulnerable and scared, but she thought she was still managing to appear cold and distant.

"I don't want the power my father has given me in this document. Can I just turn it over to Anne? After all, she should be the one deciding these things. I haven't the vaguest idea why my father set it up this way. When can I meet with a judge to transfer the authority to Anne?"

Tom Riley spoke up, "The instruction giving you control over all his medical care and property if he should die has upset Anne. She became enraged at the statement 'only Julie knows what I deserve'. Imagine how she feels after taking care of him all this time and you not being in the picture at all. And Jack turns it all over to you."

Tom leaned forward as if he were interrogating her, "I just don't get it." His glare at his sister-in-law was full of resentment. "Anne's so upset that she doesn't want to see him or you. She won't under any circumstances accept the guardianship for her father."

To everyone's surprise, Julie agreed that Anne shouldn't be forced into accepting responsibility and that the judge could decide on another suitable guardian.

She looked around at the others, "Anne's been the daughter my father has loved and shared his life with. The illness itself must be an awful shock to her and I don't want her to experience any more trauma than she has already gone through. Who then can take over the guardianship?"

"I will," Tom affirmed.

"Okay," said Julie. She turned to Dan Hill and asked, "Do you think my father will recover?"

For the next ten minutes he discussed her father's illness. Julie tried to stay firm and not give in to the expectation that she should care about all the details.

Dan gave her Jack's prognosis. Instead of listening, she tried to figure out what Dan was remembering. He sounded so official. Was he not affected by their meeting? Had he forgotten their love? Her emotions were raw enough after seeing her father, and now, this!

"It was several hours before he was found unconscious in his apartment. When he arrived at the hospital, he was placed on a respirator. There was already quite a bit of brain damage from swelling. He's had a major stroke involving brain functions of his cortex. He's on the critical list. We don't expect him to come out of the coma or regain any significant functioning. If he stays on a respirator he could stay alive for an undetermined time." Dan's voice softened as he spoke to Julie. "Jack—."

Julie cut him off. "There's no need for any further reporting. I intend to have my role of surrogate turned over to my sister or to Tom as soon as a judge is available."

Not waiting for his reaction, Julie turned to Emma, "As his lawyer, what are the chances of taking care of this tonight so both my sister and I can get on with our lives? Once I'm gone, Anne will forgive Dad, and I'm sure things will get back to normal for her."

Emma answered, not showing how stunned she was by Julie's compassion for Anne. Her reaction didn't fit what she assumed Julie to be, a cold, unemotional person. "I've contacted a number of judges, but the first time we can meet with one is Monday morning. Can you stay in the area until then? I can arrange a place for you at the Biltmore."

"Well, it's not best for me since I'm in the middle of a big research project back at Stanford, but I guess it would be possible to stay for the weekend. I'll think about it." Julie looked around the conference table wondering how she let herself get into this mess.

Emma asked her again, "We appreciate your coming all this way; it would be a shame for your efforts to be wasted. I'll do whatever's necessary to make your stay in Rhode Island comfortable. I have a guarantee from the court clerk that a judge will meet with us first thing Monday morning."

Julie surrendered to the pressure. She told Emma and Tom that she would see the situation through to the conclusion.

Tom once again stepped in to help. "I thought you might need to stay the weekend so I made some contingency plans for your comfort. I assumed that you wouldn't want to stay at Abbey's Run with us. There's the suite at the Biltmore that the firm has available; there's also the beach house."

"That sounds best," Julie answered. She had already considered using the cottage if she had to stay overnight. It would give her time to go to the beach house her grandmother left her and sort things out.

Dr. Bell spoke up, "Dr. Taylor, if you leave town for the

weekend, the hospital should have a signed and notarized form giving the doctor permission to disconnect the respirator and monitors if your father's death seems imminent. Unless you sign this form, no action easing his death can be taken, that is until the judge releases you as your father's advocate."

Emma passed the form to Julie. "Please consider it." She put all the papers away, thanked everyone for being there and turned to Julie. "Here's my card. Call me if you agree to sign the form, I'll arrange for a notary public to meet with you. I'm at your service if you want to talk about anything or need my assistance. Otherwise, call me Sunday night so I can fill you in on the meeting time with the judge."

"Thank you," said Julie.

Paul Bell also handed Julie a card with his cell phone and office numbers and said, "Jack is a good friend of mine and of the hospital. Please don't hesitate to call me if you need any further information."

Emma spoke to Dan before leaving. "Would you call down to the ICU to put my name on the list of visitors allowed to see Jack?"

"I'll be glad to do that," Dan assured her as he watched Julie from the corner of his eye.

Tom approached Julie and told her, "Just in case you wanted to stay in the beach cottage, I had the caretaker turn on the heat, stock the refrigerator and hook up the phone. Your father's driver is on standby to take you wherever you wish, or I could give you my car and the driver can take me home."

"You're so kind. The cottage in Little Compton sounds just right. Since Nana left it to me I haven't given it a thought, but I want to go through it to either give it to you and Anne, or put it up for sale. We can talk about that later. Would you mind if I borrowed your car? I'd like some time alone."

Tom finished discussing the particulars of her stay with Julie and went home to be with his wife. Emma felt the need to be alone before returning to the office. She went to the hospital chapel for a ten-minute reprise; her life was changing too fast and she had to hold on to her courage. Dan lingered to speak with Julie.

****

Before she could resist, Julie had found herself agreeing to stay through the weekend. She couldn't believe herself. What was happening to her? She didn't want to be in Rhode Island. But while she was there, she could use the time to clear up the issue of the inheritance from her grandmother and who should own the cottage. And then, there was Dan.

At last, the meeting had ended. Julie wanted to bolt out of the hospital and not look at anyone. She knew that everyone at the meeting wondered about her and Jack's relationship. She didn't care about their opinions; she had to get away, it was too dangerous for her to stay in Rhode Island.

After she said her goodbyes to Tom and Emma Quinn,

Julie turned around and faced Dan. He was waiting for her.

"After twenty-seven years apart, perhaps we could go for coffee."

"Do I have a choice here?"

"No!" Dan stepped closer to her. He put his head down as if to pretend being hurt and teased, "You owe me at least a coffee. You did, after all, drive off and leave me holding the ring I had saved my pennies to buy."

"I remember the condition that we stay in New England. But, coffee sounds good." Julie smiled for the first time that day, "but not in the hospital coffee shop."

"Gregg's just down the hill. You drive, and after we chat, I'll walk back for my evening rounds. But, first I have to phone down to the nurses' station to notify them that Emma needs to be able to see Jack."

Over coffee, they talked about their lives with an ease as if they had just seen each other. He filled her in on his marriage and divorce, and on his recovery from alcoholism. Several times he reached for her hand, but each time Julie drew back.

"It surprises me that we still can talk with ease. I've missed that. My life's not set up to connect with people in such a personal way. Don't be offended if I pull away a little, but it does feel good to be here with you." Julie was risking more that Dan might guess.

"We're friends, childhood buddies. I didn't take you out of my heart or my mind when we stopped being lovers and you moved across the country."

Julie felt tears coming. She didn't want to break down

in the restaurant. She blinked and studied her coffee cup. After a long, poignant pause, she tried to explain herself. "When I left for college in California, I tucked you away in a small corner of my heart. I had to leave the East Coast. After how they treated me, I could never come back to Rhode Island and so, when you didn't come to me, you became part of my past."

"Yes, yes. And I also believe that we didn't mean to hurt each other. So, while you're here, let's spend as much time as possible to enjoy our old and new friendship. How about it?" Dan took both of her hands in his and kissed them. "How about it?"

"Well, here I am back here in Rhodie and so . . ." Julie looked up into his kind eyes and allowed herself to feel okay being with him. "So, you're no longer only just a part of the past. I'd like to spend time with you, if your schedule permits. But I don't want to dwell anymore on old times. Okay?" Julie didn't tell him that he had stayed close to her in her dreams.

"Fine with me. I finish rounds about eight. If it's not too late for you, I could pick up some dinner at Magrino's. We can eat and visit at the beach cottage in private. I might have to crash on the couch if it gets too late. How's that sound to you?"

"I'd like the company. It's three hours earlier at home so I'll be up late. But I don't even know if there still is a couch there," she said.

Julie sat back, looked at her childhood friend, her teenage love, and liked what she saw. He remained a handsome guy with eyes that could pierce into the corner of her heart where her memories lived.

"True to form with your Nana, everything is still there. I gotta get back to the hospital to check on your father. I'll see you between nine and ten. Want me to bring anything special?"

"Tom's taken care of supplies, but I could use some pasta with lots of clam."

"Sure thing," he said and smiled.

"I'll drop you off at the hospital on my way," Julie offered.

As they left the restaurant, both of them were more relaxed.

8

FRIDAY EVENING

Before going back to the office, Emma went to Providence General to see Jack. Dan Hill had signed the receptionist's list granting her visitor status. It took all of her energy to enter the room. Each time she was in the ICU, memories of her husband's final days haunted her.

She paused at the door and uttered a prayer, "Please, God, help me face this."

Jack Fitzsimmons was motionless. His eyes were half-open and staring. His body was connected to several different monitors, IV tubes and a respirator. Emma pulled up a chair and gently rubbed his hand, which seemed like the only place on his upper body not attached to a machine. She just wasn't ready to lose another important person in her life.

"Jack, somewhere in that stubborn Irish heart of yours, you have a reason for creating so much havoc, but damn you, why did you have to get so sick? I need you. You're my friend. I'm not ready for you to go. You're good at creating miracles in others' lives. Do it for yourself. Pull yourself out of this."

She leaned over the tubes and kissed his forehead, "I love you and want you to come back to us!"

Jack continued to stare as if he was looking at a vast silent void.

After leaving the hospital, Emma went to the Wellness Center for the Friday evening meditation session. Heading down the hill to Elmore Avenue, she was overcome with emotion. She parked in front of the center and stayed in her car for a minute. She put her "lawyer self" to rest and allowed her real feelings to come to the surface. A sorrowful moan came up from her gut and she sobbed for a few minutes.

Confused, hurt, scared, and anxious, she locked the car and walked toward the center. She hoped that seeing her spiritual teacher, Patrick, would help her restore some peace in her heart. His counseling sessions and yoga classes helped her recover emotional balance and stability.

Emma felt at home at the center, embraced by its calm atmosphere. She took off her shoes and left them on the shelves provided for anyone entering the center. This little act of separating from the busy world helped her to feel that she could be sad but not overwhelmed. The meditation group had already settled themselves in the community room. Patrick was sitting cross-legged in front of the fireplace facing the group of thirty.

Soft flute music played in the background and candles lit the room, leaving a soft welcoming glow. Emma found a pillow against the back wall, relieved that she wouldn't be as exposed as those in the open space. Patrick led them in breathing exercises and a meditation. He suggested that they focus on their inner space where they experienced the presence of God.

Emma took in the love that emanated from her teacher and fellow spiritual seekers. She moved into a deep state of peace, detaching from outside concerns and busy thoughts. Time faded. Space expanded. She surrendered to a flow of restoring soothing energy.

After the meditation session the group talked and had tea together. Patrick came up to Emma.

"You looked exhausted when you came in tonight. What's wrong?"

"My boss and dear friend, Jack Fitzsimmons, had a stroke last night. It doesn't look like he'll recover."

"So, once again you're facing the loss of someone close to you."

"Do you have a moment to talk in private?"

"Come up to the office." Patrick took hold of Emma's arm and guided her to the stairs leading to the center's office. They sat on the couch for a few minutes before Emma was ready to talk.

"What I need to share must be kept in full confidentiality."

"I understand," Patrick assured her.

Emma filled him in on Jack's choice of his older, estranged daughter as his guardian and her fear about how doing the legal work for Jack could upset her relationship with Anne.

"I don't know this woman. How will our lives change now that she's come back to Rhode Island? I'm scared that Anne will be furious with me for putting her sister in the will."

"It's time for the Fitzsimmons to heal and it seems that the older sister holds the key. You might be the one to help. Anne might be grateful that you made it possible for her sister to come home. Remember that the light of God can heal all human shadows. Let the light be stronger than your fear."

Emma smiled, "How many times have I heard you say that? Thank you, Patrick. Once again you've pointed the way for me to proceed in a very difficult situation. I needed to be reminded to surrender to God."

"Why don't you go home, rest, and trust that God will tell you just what to do? Are your boys home tonight?"

"Yes. I have to take them to school in the morning. They're both on the academic decathlon team and are going out of state for a tournament this weekend. Then I'll have some time to myself. It's going to be a rough couple of days. Would you mind if I called you for some backup support?"

Patrick nodded and assured her, "I'm here to help you in any way that I can."

"Thanks, I know I can count on you."

As she retrieved her shoes from the shelf by the front door, she promised herself to hold onto the peacefulness she had experienced during the evening at the center. Tomorrow and its challenges would come soon enough.

****

Julie dropped Dan off at the hospital. Because she had left Rhode Island thirty years earlier, before she even had a driver's license, she asked Dan for directions to the beach cottage. She wandered through the East Side of Providence looking for the way back to Route 195. As if driving in a foreign country, she went down Hope Street to Thayer Street, making her way through the congested area around Brown University and the surrounding older part of the city. The colonial houses loomed close to the narrow streets, adding an eerie feeling to the evening. Her nerves and the car rattled as they made their way over the potholes and the illogical turns. As upsetting as the conditions of the streets were, the impulsiveness of the other drivers was more irritating.

It was difficult to focus on driving. She gripped the steering wheel, trying to maintain control of the barrier that she practiced putting between her thoughts and emotions. Seeing her father and Dan had confused her.

By the time she found the entrance to the highway, she was shaking from the emotions the day's events had stirred in her.

She screamed out to the universe, "I hate being here!"

But she'd be home soon and out of this God forsaken place. Julie turned on the car radio and found some soothing jazz that helped her switch her thoughts away from the present stress to the calming image of the flowers in bloom back home in Palo Alto.

Once out of Providence, she wondered which way to go to the beach village of Little Compton. What was that exit?

Everything looked so different. Unlike the vastness of California, the roads in Rhode Island were convoluted, making it necessary to go through another state, Massachusetts, to get back to the Rhode Island road she wanted. She could almost hear Dr. Goldberg reflect that the road trip was a metaphor for her life—to get to a stable place she had to take the twists and turns of her psyche. She preferred the clear path of rational thought, but to her dismay everything in her personal life seemed to be a circle. She reminded herself that she left California and came to Rhode Island, so she could find the place in her heart she once called home. Then she could return to her real home to California.

"Okay, I just went over the Braga Bridge, but I don't want to go through Fall River." She scanned the large green signs over the interstate.

If she was correct, Route 138 would become Rt. 77 and that would take her to Little Compton. As usual, Julie set up the trip in her mind as a prelude to experiencing it. Focusing on getting to the beach cottage became a calming mental exercise. Julie felt more comfortable when even after all those years of being away, the countryside looked familiar to her.

Once in Little Compton, she crept along so she wouldn't miss the unmarked turn onto the dirt road that led up to the cottage. Their property bordered the ocean on one side and farmland on the other. She turned down a lane lined on both sides with stonewalls. The cottage was just ahead. Its isolation was frightening to her as a child, but now the solitary structure was a welcome sight.

John Short had turned on driveway lights so she knew exactly where to turn into the property. Julie left her things in the car and went to see if the door was unlocked. Using the light on her phone to see, she squinted close to the piece of paper taped to the door.

Dear Miss Julie,

The key is in the place where your grandmother always left it. If you have any trouble my number is 555 0002.

John S.

She thought they couldn't still have the same hiding place. It had been over thirty years since she was at the cottage. But then again, she reminded herself, that this was New England where old habits are the root of civilization.

Julie went over to the outside wall under the bay window and bent down to find a piece of shingle loose. She moved it up, then aside and found a key. "Well, leave it to Nana, even in death she has things organized."

After opening the cottage, she unloaded the car and put her things in the master bedroom. Walking around the spacious cottage she was amazed to see many of the same vases, wall hangings, prints and knickknacks that were there when she was a child. The Hummel figurines were still displayed on a shelf over the side window. In the corner, the hand-carved oak rocking chair shone with a welcoming aura.

The cottage had been the place of comfort for over eighty years to the young children and elders. Some of the furniture was modern, but there were some other antique pieces that had been in her family for generations. When her grandmother was placed in a nursing home, her father's sister, who has since deceased, notified Julie that she had moved many of the valuables to the cottage. Julie made a mental note of the pieces to store after the cottage was sold. In many ways she was like her grandmother, always plotting, always thinking of what to do in the future. Exhausted, Julie unpacked her robe from the overnight bag.

She longed for a relaxing bath and hoped Mr. Short had turned on the hot water. She went into the bathroom, turned on the faucet, sat on the edge of the tub and waited. The old pipes cranked and moaned but within a few minutes, the tub was filling with hot, steamy water.

"Great. Are there any towels?" She opened the closet behind the bathroom door and found it full of fresh towels.

"Thank you, Mr. Short!"

Finding some of her grandmother's bath salts on the bottom shelf of the closet, Julie dumped them into the old claw-legged tub and immersed herself in the soothing bubbles.

With her eyes closed, she tried to stop her mind from racing so she could appraise what was happening to her.

She didn't belong there. Why in God's name did she agree to come back? She wanted to go back to California as soon as possible! If she could just get through the next few days, she'd never come back here!

Having made this promise to herself, she was able to give in to the comfort of the bath, relaxing at last.

To keep from falling asleep in the tub, she opened her eyes and looked around at the real pine paneling, the old-fashioned pedestal sink, and the worn ceramic tiles of the floor.

"It's all the same." Julie shivered in disbelief.

The new addition after thirty years was a skylight. Her sense of time and place became blurred. She was starting to give into the experience of being in the past.

When the water cooled, she got out, dried off, and went into the hall to turn up the heat. It was starting to get cold as the hour got late. The nightgown she had packed wasn't going to protect her from the chill in the cottage. She wrapped one of her grandmother's shawls around her and went to look for a drink. Finding an old bottle of Jack Daniels in the cupboard, she poured herself a shot.

She thought she'd just lie on the bed and read until Dan came; that is, if he came.

Putting the bottle of whiskey on the night table, Julie took her makeup case out of the bag and placed it on the dresser near the mirror. It took a few moments to notice a cardboard box on top of the dresser with a note taped to it.

Miss Julie,

Your grandmother left this box for you. She told me to give it to you when you came back. She also told me not to give it to anyone else.

John S.

Julie found a knife in the kitchen sharp enough to cut

through the thick layers of packing tape keeping the box tight. Inside was an old photo album with a letter taped the cover.

"What in God's name is this?"

She picked up the linen envelope and felt a chill run through her. It was the same kind of stationery that her grandmother had always used for official business. When she graduated from high school, her grandmother had given her a similar envelope with tickets to California and a check to cover a year's expenses. What could her Nana give her that would be of any interest to her?

A sip of whiskey warmed her. She rubbed her fingers over the fine paper trying to decide whether to open the letter or just throw it away. After a few minutes, she ripped the flap open and took out the letter.

Julie,

If you are reading this letter it means that I have died and your father has reconciled with you. I hope by now that you have forgiven me for sending you away and you are willing to take your place as the matriarch. I hand over this responsibility that I have carried, to you, the oldest cousin in your generation. Anne has been attentive and caring to your father and me, but the ways of the ancestors need to be continued in order to maintain our traditions.

The album has a list of our genealogy. I pass on this information to you with the request that

*you keep it safe and updated. Your mother would
want you to have it.*

*Julie, each day I have held you with love in
my thoughts. Pray for my soul. Bless you.*

Nana

Pray for her! Julie wondered what kind of sick game
had she been drawn into and what the magic words were to
end the game. She picked up the old tattered cardboard
photo album and a packet of photos fell out. Her
grandmother had scribbled a note and taped it to the top of
the packet.

*These photos were put away after your
mother died. Perhaps you could get a new album
for them. There aren't any pages left in this one.*

Reluctant to review the past but nonetheless curious,
Julie rummaged through the photographs. On the top of the
pile were her elementary school photos and ones of her
friends. There were photos of Anne's growing up years.
Julie glanced through them. She took out one of Anne and
Tom holding a baby. Entranced and confused, angry and
sorrowful, Julie took another sip of her drink. How could
her nana be so cruel as to leave her such reminders of the
life that she had missed sharing with Anne? Did she dare go
on to open the album? She remembered that album quite
well.

Right before her death, her mom had taken all of the

photos that had been stored in a desk drawer and spread them out on their large, cherry wood dining room table. She then asked Julie to help her label and date each one on the back before placing them in the album. When they were finished it was full of photos beginning with her parents' marriage and ending with her thirteenth birthday party. Her father had taken the birthday shot of Julie, her mother, her grandmother and her little sister, Anne, eating cake.

Julie poured herself another drink, took the album over to the bed, sat down, and using her towel, wiped thirty years of dust off the cover. After another drink, Julie had the courage to open it.

Inside the cover was a page recording dates of marriages, births, deaths and achievements of the Fitzsimmons' line dating back to 1860 when Thomas Fitzsimmons came to New England from Ireland. The oldest daughter in each generation of this large Irish clan had been custodian of the history, even if she had had no interest in doing so.

Julie slammed the album shut and glared at the painted portrait of her grandmother staring at her from the center of the dresser. She waved her fist at the woman in the frame and cursed at her.

"You old bitch, do you hear me? Do you? Wherever you are, I hope it's hell."

Julie tore up the sheet of information into tiny pieces. "I won't have anything to do with you!" She threw the album on the floor, "All of you! And that means Dad too!"

She went over to the portrait, ripped it off the wall and

smashed it against the dresser.

"Damn you, I don't give a damn about this crap! I told you it was over for me, I won't do this. Do you hear me? I won't!" Julie spewed the words out then screamed, "I C A N'T . . . !"

Her outburst opened the pit deep within her heart where she had caged the beast of rage. Her armor of protection cracked and the hot lava of her feelings burned through her body. Propelled by uncontrollable rage, Julie raced through the cottage smashing the vases, tearing prints from the walls, throwing knickknacks against the floor, and in the kitchen, breaking the china on the edge of the tile counter.

"Damn you, you fucking bitch, you God damn fucking bitch! You and your bastard son can go to hell! I hate both of you! Damn you. . . ."

Hysterical, Julie kicked the pieces of shattered history and stomped on them, screaming over and over at her grandmother. "Damn you . . . damn you to hell."

Her cursing, at first loud and shrill, became a whimper by the time all the reminders of her grandmother were destroyed. She went back into the bedroom, gulped another drink straight from the bottle, and pushed her overnight bag on the floor. Julie picked up a photo of herself with her mother that had been taken at the last horse show before her mother's death. It was just the two of them, smiling, happy, holding the trophy Julie had won.

"Mom, Mom." Julie clutched the photo to her heart, collapsed onto the bed and curled into a fetal position. She sobbed so hard that she convulsed and blacked out.

****

Dan was late leaving the hospital. By the time he could head down to Little Compton it was after ten. He knew the way well because his parents had had a cottage next to Julie's where he'd spent summers until his mid-teens. As he pulled into the Fitzsimmons' driveway, Dan struggled to contain his emotions.

He chastised himself for waiting so long to have this talk with Julie, for he knew that she deserved to hear the truth about why he didn't follow her to California. How will she take it? Will she understand? Will she forgive him?"

The welcoming glow from the cottage fooled Dan into feeling hopeful. He knocked and after not getting any response, looked through the window.

"Oh, my God, what happened?" He tried the door. It was unlocked.

"Julie. Julie!" he called out as he opened the door.

She didn't answer. Frantic, fearing that she had been hurt by an intruder, Dan raced through the cottage. He opened the bedroom door to find Julie passed out on the bed.

"Julie, dear Julie, what's happened?" He went to the bed fearing she had been raped, but as he stood by her, he saw a different truth.

Dan picked up the empty bottle of whiskey. His heart sank with fear. The doctor in him took over and he changed his focus from his own emotions to Julie's physical safety. He checked her pulse and the dilation of her pupils, and then patted her checks until he got a response. After unclenching her fists from the photo that she grasped over her heart, Dan turned it over to see that it was one of her mother and herself.

"Oh, sweetie, you're so hurt."

Her stoic reaction at her mother's funeral came to his mind. He encouraged her, "Cry, it's okay . . . it's okay. It's the crying you didn't do before."

Crying a little himself, Dan picked her up and carried her to the rocking chair in the living room.

Still somewhat in a drunken state, Julie surrendered to his protection. She felt him encase her. As if she were still the young teen at her mother's funeral, she sobbed and poured out the need for her mother, a need she had been pretending didn't exist anymore.

In the breaks from the crying, she whispered to him, "Dan, I can't stand it . . . I can't . . . I need her . . . I need her so much . . . I miss her so much."

Julie stopped to catch her breath, and then repeated again the mantra of pain, "I need her so much, Dan, I need her. I don't want her to die! Please, please Mom, don't die!" Julie cried over and over for her mother.

Dan rocked her until she fell asleep in his arms. He, too, cried.

9

SATURDAY MORNING

Julie was standing on the rocky edge of a deep canyon. Her father was on the other side. This time they were connected waist to waist by a rope stretching across the gorge. Rigid, unable to breathe, Julie started to slide out of the rope but it caught on her boots. The gorge was flooding with rushing water. She had a few seconds to get away from the edge before she would be swept away, tied to her father. She looked up to see that he was ready to jump into the water and was pulling on the rope so she would go with him. "NO! NO! NO! I won't go," she shouted at him and woke up in a sweat, gripping the blanket.

Julie reached for her dog for comfort but a felt cold empty space instead of Dixie. She panicked.

"Where am I?" She scanned her mind, hunting for a hint. Someone was in the house. She could hear noise and smell coffee. Then she remembered. "Dear God, I'm in Rhode Island."

"Good morning. I thought you could use some coffee after last night." Dan stood at the doorway of the room. He held out a cup to her.

"Dark, no sugar. Did I remember it right?" he asked.

He put the cup on the nightstand. "Just take your time, your head might feel heavy for a while."

She glanced around the room. "I don't remember your coming last night."

Dan sat down on the chair in the corner and smiled. "No, I don't imagine you do. You were pretty sloshed by the time I got here. Hope you don't mind my tucking you in. I slept on the couch."

"I'm so out of it," she said as she groped for the cup.

"You'll feel shaky for a good part of the day."

Julie rolled her head in bewilderment. She drank the rest of the coffee before moving.

"Thanks, that helps."

She sat up and wrapped her palms around her head, "Oh, the pain!" She rubbed her temples hard, leaned over the edge of the bed and picked up the empty bottle. "Guess I got drunk last night."

"You laid on a good one. I'll fix some food while you wash up. In about half an hour I have to get back to my place to dress for morning rounds. Why don't you follow me and stay at my place? It's just down the street from Providence General. You can sleep off your hangover there and go see your father whenever you're ready."

"But first, let's see what food Mr. Short put in the pantry for you." Dan went into the rustic bathroom and laid out towels and a toothbrush. He left her alone to get cleaned up.

Julie held her head as she got up. She recoiled at the smell of New England pine that lined the bathroom walls, bringing back memories of lost times, lost loves, and lost joy.

Even though the beach cottage had belonged to her grandmother, who grew up in Little Compton, Julie's mother had tended to it with love. Every spring she would rub lemon oil on the pine paneling until it shone clear and smooth. While working on the wood, her mother would tell her stories of how the pine panels were gifts chosen by forest elves to give to families so that humans would feel happy living inside. For a split second Julie felt again like an entranced young child, but the feeling left all too soon.

She picked up the toothbrush and looked into the mirror. She told herself, "Wake up and get out of here. What are you doing hanging around? Don't let yourself care about these people, especially him. Listen to me, get out of here!" She had chosen to stay at the cottage to get away from the old connections and here she was, immersed in her past. She regretted not having stayed at the hotel.

Just as she was about to subdue her emotional reawakening and reestablish her defenses, Dan's voice broke through. "Julie, breakfast's on." The familiar tenor of his voice helped dissolve her intent to shut off from others. Her mind not able to focus, she felt hurt, sad and very confused.

At the door of the living room, she froze at the sight of the remnants of her rage.

Dan turned from the stove. When he saw her standing there in shock, he went to her, speaking as he stepped over the debris littering the floor. "All these things are just old

crap that nobody wants. Don't let it bother you. So, you had a temper tantrum. You're allowed to be upset. I'll come down
later and clean up."

He put his arm around her and guided her into the kitchen. He had already cleaned off the table and swept the floor. "Sit here. Breakfast is almost ready. Want a fresh cup of coffee?"

"Yeah, another cup would be good," Julie whispered.

After eating, she smiled at her old friend. "That helped. I feel a little clearer. Thanks for being here and for not leaving me alone last night."

"This weekend, you're my top priority. Aside from working at the hospital, I'm not going anywhere else. It's just been too long since we've had time together."

"Dan, I'm not sure about anything right now. I feel like I stepped into a time warp. It's like I've been stolen away from my life and thrown into the past where everything is so familiar and yet, so different."

She shook her head, controlling her tears. "How am I going to deal with all this? I need my life back, I need myself back."

Conflicted and terrified, she was glad that Dan couldn't hear the words she wasn't saying. "I don't want to go back to missing you. I've put you away somewhere. Don't come out. I can't take one more emotional issue, least of all a decision about letting you back into my life. I just can't deal with any more feelings. I've got to stay in control."

Dan responded as if he had heard her thoughts. "Now

that I discovered that you, Julie Taylor, the famous scientist, are still the girl I loved in my youth, I don't plan to let you slip away from me before we have time to clear up our past."

He got up and kissed her on the forehead for he guessed that she was feeling more like being seventeen than forty-seven. He could wait, as he had waited before for her to heal her grief.

"Dan, I'm frightened, I'm falling apart. Please don't be offended if I can't reciprocate your attention. I'm so uncomfortable with what's happening to me here."

He sat back down in front of her and spoke with great gentleness, "It's scary to feel all those emotions that you buried so deep inside, but even though you feel like you're falling apart, maybe you're just falling into reality."

He took her hand and reached out to wipe a tear from her cheek. She didn't resist his comfort so he continued talking. With a voice full of compassion, he said, "When your mom died, you didn't cry, you didn't fall apart, you just went away. You built a good life and became a strong adult, but have you ever allowed yourself to grieve?"

"I'm not that young girl anymore. Don't be condescending to me," Julie responded and pulled her hand out of his.

"No, no, you're not that girl anymore, but you're a person who's losing one parent and remembering the unhealed loss of the other parent. I'm sorry if you feel that I'm condescending; I'm just concerned for you." He cocked his head down in a surrender pose and smiled at her.

"Damn you, Dan Hill, you're trying to manipulate me," she managed a smile. She tried to stay serious but found her resolve softening in response to his caring.

"You bet! I'll do what I can to manipulate the situation and get you to spend time with me. I don't like losing and I don't want to lose you again before we have some time together. So, sue me, I want you to stay open to me."

"You're still the charmer." She looked around and moaned, "I need to get out of here and be somewhere that doesn't remind me of all of this."

Dan held her eyes with a warm, loving gaze. He pleaded, "Come to my place and rest. We'll talk later. How about it?"

"Ump! Let me analyze the data." Her mood somewhat lighter, Julie gave Dan the assurance he wanted. "The man fills me with coffee and food, is willing to clean up my mess, and is going to give me a safe place to hide out. Seems like a good set up to me. I think I'll try your experiment."

"That's what I like to hear." Dan checked his watch then mapped out the day. "I'll show you my place in Providence and leave you a key. Later, I'll call and let you know a good time to come over to the hospital. That is, if you want to see your father. If not, just make yourself at home. I'll be free by five or six."

Julie got up and cleared the table. She thought about whether or not to see her father. "I'll see him this one more time; I've got some things to say to him," she said to herself as much as to Dan.

For the time being, Julie attempted to restore her sense

of equilibrium. How could she turn to her usual way to accomplish stability—working—in this mess?

"Do you have a secure internet connection for my laptop? I think it would help me be more at ease while I'm waiting for you. I want to check the latest data on my current project."

"Sure. I'll give you my ID and password."

Julie turned the hot water on and started to fill the plastic basin with hot sudsy water. Dan went over to the sink, turned off the water, and stopped her from washing the dishes. "These can wait until I come back to clean up."

"I think it would be better for me to come back here to fix the place up. I'm not comfortable having you clean up after me. Then, I'll be able to relax with you for the evening."

Dan came to her, kissed her cheek and asserted, "I'll help you if I want to. You can't refuse me, got it?"

"Oh, so now that I've agreed to stay at your place, I'm under your power?" Julie quipped, turned from him and started washing the dishes.

"You're under doctor's orders to allow me to care for you." Dan took the dishcloth out of her hand and dropped it in the sink. He took hold of her shoulders, turned her around to look right at him, and insisted, "Stop cleaning up and get your stuff."

She put her palms on his chest and pushed him away from her but did so with a feather-like touch. "Pushy, aren't you?"

"Some of my patients would agree with you. You're

just going to have to let me serve you."

"Okay, okay. I give in. You can clean my mess, but later you have to let me take you to dinner."

"That's a deal. Do you want help with your stuff?"

"That I will do," she answered with a smile and went back into the bedroom to get her bags.

He lived in an old colonial on Overhill Road. The dark red slats and gray shutters were weather worn, but the garden area lining the sidewalk was well maintained. The flowerbeds were full of perennials peeking through the soil. Julie imagined how in a month it would be beautiful with tulips and other spring flowers. Someone had already planted the window boxes with pansies. The old house wasn't so depressing to her with these touches of yellow and purple flowers.

Dan's apartment was another story. It was stark and modern.

"Take a look around while I check in with my service."

Julie walked down the hall and looked into the two rooms at the end. They were designed for children. She had almost forgotten that Dan had two children who visited him on weekends. Their rooms were full of life with colorful toys stored on shelves, posters on the walls, and stuffed animals lining the bright comforters on the beds.

She ventured through Dan's bedroom and adjoining sunroom before going back to the living room. There were no photos or other indications of a woman in his life. In fact, these rooms were devoid of any personal touches. It felt safe. There was nothing in the apartment to threaten

Julie. It could have been any number of hotel rooms that she stayed in during her lecture tours. Dan showed her where she could plug in her laptop, gave the access information, a key, and left her alone.

Still groggy from the hangover, she napped on the couch for several hours. When she woke up she felt clearer and ready to get to work. She set up her computer and opened her email account. After checking the statistics logged in from the day before, she made some notes for the team back at Stanford. As she worked, she once again had a sense of being inside herself. The emotional turbulence of the evening before faded. Dan called at noon to tell her that she could come anytime to visit her dad. Around two in the afternoon she decided that her energy was restored enough to walk to the hospital and face her father.

****

Julie made her way to the ICU of Providence General Hospital without running into Dan or anyone in her family. Mrs. Howe, her father's nurse, told her that she was today's first visitor.

"Can I have some time alone with him?"

"Sure. I can see the monitors from the nurse's station. Just ring if you need help." Mrs. Howe shut the door on her way out of the room.

Julie almost stopped breathing. Anxious, she stood at the foot of the bed and observed the reality of her father's condition. The day before, she had been in too much of a shock to take in his appearance. How could she identify with the fragile, old man lying there in the hospital bed, so still and silent? He looked more like her grandfather than the voracious, large and loud father she remembered.

She pulled a chair close to him so she could tell him in private what she had come to say. But, unable to contain years of built up rage, she stood up and walked around. Jack's being blank and unresponsive inflamed the intensity of her feelings. Her voice rose with the anger she had never expressed.

"Again, you're controlling me. I remember what it was like to live with you. How many times did you pass out? How many times did you leave others to pick up the pieces? Did you ever say you were sorry? Did you ever consider how mean you were to Mom and me? After all these years of banishment, you expect me to fix things for you?"

Julie went over by his head and whispered in his ear, "Why don't you just die? Do the decent thing, spare us all from any more involvement with your craziness. How dare you try to entangle me in your rotten life again? How could you?"

Mrs. Howe noticed through the room's window that Julie was getting agitated, so she called Dr. Hill to let him know that Jack Fitzsimmons' daughter, the one that was the legal surrogate, seemed to be having a hard time. Unable to get away from his office, Dan called Emma to see if she could come to the hospital to spend some time with Julie. And could she hurry? In the meantime, the nurse stepped into the room to check on her patient.

"Dr. Taylor, is there something I can do for you?"

"No, just leave me alone with my father. That is, if he's stable."

"He's in critical condition. Perhaps it would be best just to sit next to him."

"Okay. I don't intend to stay much longer, but I have some important things to say to him." Julie turned to look at her father. "Even if he can't hear me, I'm going back to California as soon as possible so I need this time with him. Don't worry, I won't cause any trouble."

Mrs. Howe checked the monitors and tubes then left her alone again. Not wanting to alarm the nurse, Julie sat down to talk with him.

"Remember, Dad, the time you came home so drunk that Mom and I had to drag you upstairs? Mom got really sick after that night. She wasn't strong enough to move you, so I had to undress you and clean up your puke, remember that? I can still hear you cursing and swearing long into the night when you didn't get what you wanted from Mom. Remember that? I sure do."

A wave of sorrow washed through her heart. She almost choked on the pain.

"Dad, you and Nana destroyed my life. How could you even think that I'd want to be near you? You stole my teen years and my mother and sister from me. You took everything." Julie couldn't hold back the tears.

She felt a gentle touch on her shoulder. She hadn't noticed Emma Quinn come into the room.

"Julie, why don't you come out into the hall with me?"

Emma guided the distraught woman away from Jack's bed. "Let's go sit in the intensive care lounge for bit."

Julie shrugged her shoulders and followed Emma. The lounge was decorated in soothing tones of green, blue and violet as if to create an oasis of comfort. The two women sat on a couch under a large window. A ray of sunlight streamed across the room.

"Julie, the nurses are concerned that you seem overcome with grief about your dad. They thought that maybe you needed someone to talk to."

"They couldn't be more wrong!" Julie snapped. The dazed state she had sunk into after confronting her father lifted from her mind. She looked up, puzzled. "Mrs. Quinn, why are you here?"

"Please call me Emma. Dan called me at home. He asked me to come over to spend some time with you. He's tied up for the afternoon and thought you could use some company. When I came to the ICU, Mrs. Howe told me how upset you've been."

Julie wasn't used to anyone being solicitous of her. She took out a tissue, wiped her face and ran her fingers through her hair.

"I haven't had a relationship with my father in many years; it shouldn't affect me this way. I'm a scientist, Emma. I like logic, order, and being in control of my life. Right now, I'm far from being in control. It infuriates me that my father put me in such a situation."

"He can be a stubborn man. Wish I knew his agenda but I don't have a clue about it. If you want to talk about your take on his decisions, I'm here. I've been told I have a good ear and a confidential one."

"Thank you, but it's between my father and me. But before I make a fool of myself, I need to get out of this hospital."

"That I can arrange. Come over to my house. My kids are away for the night and we can relax, go for a walk, or do whatever you like until Dan's free. When he called, he told me that he wants to spend the evening with you."

"If it wouldn't inconvenience you. Excuse me for a moment while I call Dan to let him know what I'm doing."

"It's settled then. You call Dan, and I'll let the nurses know that you can be reached through my service and then we can be on our way. I just have to drop off something at the office and pick up some food at Healthy Eats."

"Great, I'd like to pick up some carrot juice."

"Let's go."

On the way out of the ICU, Emma stopped at the nurse's station to talk to Mrs. Howe while Julie called Dan's service and left a message about going to Emma's. Then they left Providence General and headed across the East Side of Providence.

****

The bright, colorful atmosphere of the market helped to restore Julie's equilibrium. While Emma shopped, Julie browsed in the book section, rummaging through the latest books on running and nutrition.

Emma came by with a cart full of fresh fruits and vegetables and stopped for a moment. "Are you interested in running?" she asked.

"It's one of my passions. At home, I run at least two miles a day, often four or five. Did you get what you wanted?"

"Most of it. I thought we could pick out some dinner food together just in case Dan's held up at the hospital and can't come to get you until late. The counter at the back of the store has some prepared food, most of it natural. How about it?"

"I miss real food. I haven't eaten much today. Hospital cafeteria food isn't quite to my liking." Julie was starting to feel comfortable being with her new acquaintance. "Show me the way."

At the prepared food counter, Emma pointed to chicken wings marinated in tamari sauce and then broiled. "Those are my favorite. How about some of them with an order of oriental noodles and I'll make us a salad?"

"Sure you aren't from the West Coast?" Julie kidded Emma.

"Hey, Rhode Island's a modern place. We keep up with you California trendsetters."

"It's not the Rhode Island I remember."

"Well then, let's create some new memories for you to take back with you."

Even though they were strangers to each other, they found their way into an easy flow of conversation. While waiting in line for the cashier, a man waved to Emma.

"Do you need to speak with him?" asked Julie.

"No, I'll talk with him later. Patrick's the spiritual counselor who helped me when my husband, Bob, died. He teaches me meditation."

Julie thought of her Dr. Goldberg and how he wasn't anything like Patrick. He would never acknowledge her in public. "He's quite handsome."

"I agree--good gene pool. He gets a lot of his looks from his mother who's part of the Wampanoag tribe. His father's a mixture of Irish and Portuguese."

As they loaded the bags of food in the car, Emma said, "I'd love to stop for a latte before we go to my place and eat. I need a pick-me-up."

"Coffee sounds good," agreed Julie.

"There are several good coffee shops, but my favorite's The Coffee Bean. It's over on Wickenden Street," said Emma. She wondered if Julie remembered the street.

Over cups of hot latte, Emma broached the subject of Julie's obvious discomfort at being in Rhode Island. "It must be strange to be back here, especially under these circumstances."

"Everything seems turned upside down," Julie admitted.

"Hospitals always make me feel uncomfortable. My husband, Bob, battled cancer for four years and the hospital became part of my daily existence. I was an emotional wreck. I wanted to change everything. I had to learn that I had no control over his disease and what it was doing to our life." Emma took out a photo of her husband and sons to show Julie.

Julie took the photo and held it for a few minutes.

"It must have been devastating to lose him."

"It was. But probably no more devastating than a teenage girl being alone with her mother as she died, or an adult woman having to face the death of her other parent and be exposed to pain all over again."

"You know about my mom's death?" Julie sounded indignant.

"I'm so sorry to bring up such a personal issue. Dan told me. He wanted to fill me in so I would understand why this is so hard for you. I hope you don't mind. He's concerned for you."

"He shouldn't have told you. My mother's death is not something I want to think about." Julie stared at her coffee.

Emma waited for a moment until Julie looked up.

"Julie, I hope I haven't offended you."

"Dan and I were kids together so he thinks he needs to protect me," Julie said. She held back from adding that he didn't know her well enough to speak for her. She moved the discussion away from her family and asked Emma how Patrick Moore helped her with stress.

Emma nodded and went on to describe the healing center's room that's soundproof, padded and filled with lots of pillows and foam bats. Patrick had helped her face how during the final months of her husband's life, there were times when she needed to just let loose. She'd go into the emotive room with Patrick where he encouraged her to express all her frustrations and angers. She kicked, screamed, pounded, cried, but didn't hurt anyone.

"The healing that changed the way I handled the stress of loss came from the compassionate way Patrick accepted whatever feelings came up in me."

"I only let go in my dreams. They're not that positive an experience," said Julie.

"That's hard." Emma commiserated but felt it best not to share anymore of her own process. The healing process Patrick led her through did not feel positive; but it led to a more positive way of living with her husband's death.

Losing Bob was devastating. At first, rather than the emotional purging she did during his illness, she grieved in silence which led to silence within her soul.

"You know, Julie, I understand if you feel strange or lost with all of this. After Bob died, I couldn't hear my own inner voice and felt so lost."

"You seem to have come through it. I would never have guessed that you felt lost in some way," said Julie.

"Thanks to Patrick I didn't stay lost. After months of emotional purging, he taught me through meditation how to take hold of my life again and discover a new way to live. I had to find a way to appreciate my own existence and that of my children without my husband's help."

"Well, you seem to be calm now."

"At times. I'm sorry for talking so much about my own journey. I'm here to be a support for you," said Emma.

"I would rather hear more about you. How do you balance your professional life with your interest in meditation?"

Emma appreciated the smooth way Julie evaded sharing more about herself. She set out to have Julie relax and switched to chatting about raising active teenagers, studying yoga, riding her horse and taking on some of the biggest cases in Providence. Her tactic worked. There seemed to be a lighter mood between them. Guessing that a professional, bright woman like Julie was uncomfortable with surrendering control to Dan or to the legal system, Emma admitted how much she herself wanted to feel in control of her life.

"And even now, the lack of control causes me difficulty."

"What do you mean?" asked Julie.

"The part of me that couldn't stop Bob from dying and leaving me alone feels that I don't deserve to win and have a good time. Believe me, it was difficult to learn to forgive myself for not being all-powerful. It took time but I can, more often than not, allow good in my life and still feel sorrow or anger. But I don't ever want to go through that lesson again."

"That's how I experience being back here."

"It must be very difficult for you."

After sitting in silence for a few moments, Emma asked, "Ready to get out of Providence and go to my house?"

Julie smiled at Emma and said, "Okay."

****

As Emma drove down Wickenden Street and crossed the river, Julie remembered taking her little sister for a tour of the electric plant there. Feeling nostalgic, she inquired about Anne and her art. Emma filled her in on all the recent successes and on how her nephews and niece were doing. For Julie, it was like hearing about distant relatives instead of immediate family, for she had long ago made the separation from them. However, spending time with Anne's best friend had her wondering about her sister.

Julie let out a sigh when they pulled into driveway. "I love these old Victorians. What a beautiful spot overlooking the bay."

"I had that exact reaction the first time Bob and I saw the house. After looking all over Edgewood and the East Side, I was so happy to find this treasure."

Once settled into Emma's, the two women relaxed, collapsing into big, soft armchairs in the great room.

"One thing I do miss about Rhode Island is the big rooms," said Julie.

"This is my favorite room in the house. Would you like a glass of wine? I have some from Sakonnet Vineyards."

Emma took a bottle of local wine and some glasses from the bar area in the corner and poured them a drink.

"Since I'm in Rhode Island, I might as well taste the local fare."

Enjoying the wine, they continued their conversation.

"Emma, I'm grateful that you aren't trying to pry out of me the reason why I've kept away from my sister."

Julie held firm to her stance that whatever happened in her youth, needed to stay in the past. It had caused her enough pain. She guessed that it was hard for Emma to resist the temptation to ask more about her family history. After all, she was Anne's friend and Jack's partner. She opened the door for more conversation not directed toward her. She asked Emma, "Tell me more about you. Besides yoga, what interests you?"

Emma told her about her love of riding and how her son, Matt, shared her passion for horses.

"Does he also want to be a lawyer like you?"

"He has dreams of playing in the major leagues."

"Did you always want to be a lawyer?"

"I had to convince my father to support me in law school. My grandfather, father, and brother were lawyers, but there'd never been a woman in our brood who chose law."

Emma took a photo off the mantle of herself at her graduation ceremonies at Harvard Law School. Her grandfather, father, and brother had their arms around her. She put it back on the mantle and stood by the fireplace, lost in thought for a moment.

Julie just sipped her wine, waiting for her to continue.

Emma refilled their glasses and then brought up the subject of working with Julie's father. She told Julie about hearing stories from her father, who often entertained them at the dinner table with tales of Jack's fight against corruption in state government.

"When my father became Jack's partner, I knew that the day would come when I, too, would want to be a partner of the infamous Jack Fitzsimmons. When I grew up and realized what a challenge that fight was, I vowed to prove to your father that I was worthy of his trust and respect. It was quite a day for me when he accepted me into the firm."

"Is your father still in the firm?"

"No, he retired. It's great for me, however, since he has lots of time to spend with my sons. I've had to work hard to fill his shoes and become a partner that Jack values. I absorbed most of my father's caseload."

Emma turned her face to the water and waited to get a sense of Julie's feelings about her professional relationship with Jack. A silence cloaked them.

"Shall I continue?" Emma asked.

"It's all right for you to talk about my father. The man you admire is very different from the person who raised me. It's as if you're speaking about a stranger."

Emma explained that with her father gone from the firm, Jack asked her to step in and revise his will. She probably wouldn't have agreed to do it if she had known ahead of time it would stir things up so much for everyone.

"But he had a plan. In his typical manipulative way, he set you up." Julie's bitterness surfaced.

"Yes, indeed, he did have a plan." Emma agreed with Julie without betraying her mentor.

They sipped their wine and slipped back into another moment of silence.

What Julie couldn't hear was the rambling of Emma's mind that compared Anne and Julie to her sons. Julie reminded her of Matt while Anne seemed to be the more flamboyant one like Sean. She couldn't imagine what possibly could have happened to separate Julie from the others.

How could Jack not reach out to his child? Which one of them needed to make the amends, Jack or Julie? Did they bring out the worst in each other? What had happened? Why was Jack hardened toward his daughter? He had always seemed to seek the respect of everyone he met. Did he not care about Julie's opinion of him, or did he worry about it more than anyone knew? Jack had the money and the time to fly to California and set things straight. Emma assumed that Jack had been burdened with the truth of this relationship for many years. She believed that she could never maintain a separation from one of her sons for so long. The thought that Julie had done something evil flashed through her.

"Julie, I hope you don't mind my admitting that I just keep wondering about your separation from Jack and your sister. But of course, if you don't wish to talk about it, we can change the subject."

"My problems are with my father, not with you or for that matter, with Anne. She, I'm aware, might feel differently about it." Julie twirled her wineglass between her fingers.

She looked up at Emma and explained further, "To me, my father wasn't the lawyer fighting the good cause, but the drunk fighting my mother and letting his mother coddle him."

To Emma, this was quite a revelation since Jack never drank and even proselytized about not drinking. She had always assumed that he didn't drink as a lifestyle choice, not because of an addiction.

"I thought he just didn't drink. But thinking it over-- that was pretty naive, wasn't it?" said Emma.

"My father has an incredible ability to hide his true actions and motives." Julie picked up her glass, raising it to Emma's in a mock salute, "even from the best lawyers."

"That's for sure," Emma muttered. She walled off the emotional chaos Julie's confessions were creating in her. She wanted to set a tone of compassion to keep the sharing open.

Sensing none of the negative criticism that Julie assumed would come from a friend of her family, she let her guard down a little more and talked further about her father. She recalled the nights her mother was so weak with her diabetes that Julie had to take care of her baby sister, Anne.

"Some nights Dad would come home from the State House so drunk that he couldn't stand up. He would bang on the doors, cursing my mother for being sick. She always made excuses for him in the morning. He got angrier, more abusive and difficult to be around. Many times I'd have to clean up after him."

Julie paused, surprised she was being so honest about her negative memories. No one had ever evoked such openness before, even her therapist. Seeing the compassion in Emma's eyes, she went on, "I lived in fear most of the time. Towards the end when my mom was so sick, my grandmother was there a lot and, like Mom, she covered for

Dad. I knew she was there the night my mother died, but I can't remember it. She told me that I, not Dad, was with Mom when she died but, because of the shock, I don't remember it. After the funeral I left to live in Vermont with my mother's relatives, and I've never returned to Abbey's Run."

"Didn't you miss Anne?" asked Emma.

Julie pulled into herself and said almost in a whisper, "Very much, but I couldn't be there without my mother."

Emma took a moment to envision a healing light hugging and comforting Julie and said, "I'm so sorry you had to go through all that."

Julie explained to Emma how talking with Anne on the phone had been too upsetting. She didn't get along with her grandmother and resented her taking over, even though she had no choice.

"I hope that my disclosures aren't disturbing to you."

"I'm surprised about the information," was all that Emma managed to say. She had often wondered why Jack didn't remarry after his wife died. He seemed to be a man who needed intimacy and the love of those around him. In that old-fashioned way, he was a little standoffish to the outside world but very close and loving to his family and friends. It was somewhat shocking to her that there was another side to his nature that she was unaware of until meeting Julie.

They sat in suspended time. They finished their wine. When Julie made no attempt to deepen the conversation, Emma commented, "At times I'm a little too inquisitive. Forgive me for being too analytical about your family."

"In my experience, good lawyers are always trying to figure everything out. Again, no offense taken."

"Well, thanks for enlightening me about your experience as a Fitzsimmons. Anne's my dearest friend. I must admit, I like her big sister too." Emma smiled.

"Speaking of Anne, why aren't you spending more time with her this weekend?"

"Well, she's horseback riding and painting, neither of which leaves room for others to be with her."

"Tell me about her and her art."

Emma filled Julie in on her sister's paintings and successful exhibits, and the difficult moments with critics. She showed Julie photos of her niece and nephews at gallery openings of Anne's work. As Julie held the most recent one of Anne, tears came to her eyes.

"I can see how much you care for Anne. Do you want to see her while you're here?"

"I'm not inclined to open that door. It's best I leave my relationship with Anne in the past."

Emma didn't push any further.

Dan called to say that he would be later than expected. Emma suggested that she and Julie get some fresh air. "I can't run, but would you like to go for a walk with me? We can walk down to Pawtuxet Village, then down to the point and then back to the village for a cup of espresso at Bella's."

"That sounds terrific, but I don't have any walking shoes with me or any warm clothes."

"No problem. We're about the same size, so I'm sure we can find something for you."

They found clothes for Julie and headed out for a long, brisk walk along the bay. On the way down the hill to Seaview Avenue, Julie was quiet, digesting the fact that she had shared her frightening experiences with someone who knew her father. She was stunned that she was believed, not judged. It was clear why Emma Quinn was a successful lawyer. Her listening skills were finely tuned.

As they turned onto Seaview Avenue, Julie was reminded of how different Rhode Island was from California.

"I forgot how the very rich here gather in little hidden pockets like this one, just a few blocks from middle-class neighborhoods." She thought of how much she missed her home in Palo Alto. Has it really only been a day since she was tucked away safely in her hidden haven?"

"What's it like in Palo Alto? I've only been to Southern California."

Julie's spirit lifted as she described the town's year round temperate climate and beauty. She appreciated that there's always some vista to enjoy. When she first moved to the Bay area, it reminded her of the Mediterranean coastline in Italy. The trees had a similar feeling and the houses dotted the hillsides. Except for the earthquake threat that it could all crack open any minute, she found living there very much to her liking.

"It's so pretty all year. The city of Palo Alto is laid out in an orderly, pleasing way." Julie chuckled for the first time in days, "And besides, the weeds in my garden are much more controllable."

"There's a rose garden in front of the main house at Abbey's Run that your niece tends to. She told me your mother planted it."

"My mother and I worked on that rocky soil for a whole spring before she risked putting in her favorite tea roses. I'm glad it's still there. Would you tell my niece that for me?"

"Sure, but maybe you'll see her yourself at the hospital."

"Maybe."

They finished their jaunt in silence. As Julie walked, the frayed threads of her self-image wove themselves back together. She felt herself again. But by the end of the walk, she was a little worn out.

"Emma, if you don't mind, I'd like to skip the espresso and go back to your place. I need to rest a little before Dan comes."

"Sounds good to me. It's getting chilly. I'll light a fire and you can curl up on the couch if you want. It's nice and cozy. I have lots to do upstairs."

"Perfect." Julie craved to be alone.

10

SATURDAY AFTERNOON

Just past noon, Dan ended rounds. Exhausted, he left the hospital and headed down the hill to the medical building on North Main Street to clear up some unfinished business. He went around to the back door and slipped into his office so he wouldn't be seen by his patients in the lobby. He settled at his desk and buzzed the receptionist on the intercom.

"Sherry, please cancel my appointments today or have them referred to Dr. Long."

"Yes, Dr. Hill. I put some forms on your desk that need immediate attention. Otherwise, everything else can wait until Monday. Will you need anything more from me?"

Sherry Day had worked for Dan and his partners for the past six years and was the key person in the office.

"I don't think so. But if any of the Fitzsimmons family calls, beep me."

He had trouble concentrating on the mound of papers needing his signature and the emails needing a response. After an hour or so of plowing through the stack, he surrendered to his weariness and called it a day. He saved the files to his cloud server and put all his written notes in the top drawer of his desk, a modern oak version of an old steel medical one. When moving into his office he had insisted that it be efficient, but not sterile like the atmosphere of the hospital. "I can't handle anything else, this will have to do for today."

Dan went out into the empty waiting room. "Sherry, I'm going home to get some rest. Dr. Long's on call and will cover for me."

She picked up a mail packet and handed it to him, "Dr. Hill, before you go, here's an envelope that just arrived by messenger from the hospital administration office. Dr. Bell said to make sure you got it today."

He turned it over, looking for a hint of its contents but there were no markings on the envelope. "It's not stamped emergency so I'll take it with me and look at it later. First, there's some personal issues I have to attend to."

"Dr. Bell said that it's related to the Fitzsimmons case."

"Oh, all right, I'll review it at home and come back if I need to."

Feeling as if he would collapse unless he got a reprieve from the pressures of the hospital and his personal involvement in the Fitzsimmons family, he tucked the envelope under his right arm and left the office to go home.

Like a heavy dark cloud sitting over the earth on a hot summer day, a wave of depression pressed down on him. He walked up the hill, pushing himself to take long strides, swinging his arms back and forth. Since discussing Jack's case at yesterday's meeting, Dan felt as if all the liquids in him had turned to lead. Seeing Julie, still so beautiful, still so hurt, flooded his mind with painful memories. A part of his soul had died of heartache the day she moved to the West Coast and vowed she'd never return to Rhode Island.

He drove his new Chevy up to Bristol, Vermont, for her high school graduation. All the classmates and their families hung around in small groups, laughing and hugging. This was not the part of New England he belonged, but he didn't care for he belonged to Julie.

A group from her class partied that night at Julie's aunt's, then went for a nude dip in the local swimming hole of the New Haven River. After the other graduates had gone home, he and Julie had curled up together in his sleeping bag on a sandy spot along the river's edge.

After a night of lovemaking, Dan felt for sure that she would want to stay on the East Coast and accept the ring that he had bought with his graduation money. But when the morning came, Julie put up a wall of reserve around herself. Without talking to him about her move, she packed up her things and had him drive her to the train station. When she kissed him goodbye it was almost as if they had never touched. His heart broke that June and never really mended. Was his heart going to be broken again?

He struggled to ward off fear of being hurt again. Dan remembered how easy it was to talk with Julie's mother. Ma Fitzsimmons taught him to see life as an exciting challenge. A flood of melancholy washed through him. His heart spoke to her spirit, "I sure miss those nights when I wandered over to your beach cottage to share the secrets of my soul."

She had nurtured him; she had comforted him; she had taught him how to laugh at his own fears in ways his own mother couldn't. Julie's mother was able to reach beyond his adolescent rebelliousness to touch his genuine need to relate to others. It was because of her encouragement that he first started thinking about being a doctor.

Anger over her death surfaced over the sadness. He used to believe that being a good person guaranteed happiness. He learned otherwise. He walked faster and faster. It all seems so unfair. He didn't understand why God had let her die and he didn't think he ever would.

His mother had raised him to believe that being a gentleman and acting morally would be rewarded by God, the omnipotent being who doled out rewards for good living. But God forgot to care for him both that spring day when his second mother died and the week after when Julie left Rhode Island. With Julie's return, what was he to believe and how was he to behave?

As he passed the hospital, he thought how ironic it was that he, an expert in the medical field, a father of two children and an award-winning sailor, couldn't wade through his emotional confusion. He felt completely off balance.

What had been in his mind? Didn't he grasp that Julie's leaving would change his life? Why in God's name didn't he go after her? . . . Or go with her?

Once home, Dan unlocked his door and went into the kitchen to get a drink of cold spring water. His apartment's orderly atmosphere served as a welcome balm to his wounded soul.

He put the envelope on the table, deciding to ignore it for a while until he calmed down. Emotionally and physically spent, he fell fully dressed onto his bed and was asleep within minutes.

A voice called to him from the answering machine, "Doctor Hill, please call the hospital. Mr. Evans' test results are back and the resident wishes to check with you the dose of the new medicines. Dr. Long is handling an emergency and asked that you be called in to consult."

Dan jolted out of his nap. After a call to the resident in charge to assure her that the dose was correct, he went to the living room, sat at the table and leaned back against the wall.

He looked out of the window, immersing himself in the past, daydreaming of Julie and changing the way things had happened. What if the two of them had hitchhiked across country? They would have been part of the excitement at Berkeley; young lovers exploring new ideas, new ways to exist. That would have been great. Instead he let Julie go to California alone. What had he missed by not being with her? He wanted to have a second chance.

The hot spicy aroma of the food reminded him to eat. Drinking his coffee, he remembered that he had brought something home from the office. He picked it up from the center of the table and opened it. There were two letters, one for him and one for Anne and Julie Fitzsimmons.

Now what? Dan didn't want any more aggravations in

dealing with Jack's illness. He read Jack's letter. It stunned him. He read it again. Torn between relief that Jack found a way to clear his heart and distress for how his truth was going to affect Julie, Dan threw the letter down.

"Damn you, Jack! I knew you had a secret that was tearing you apart, but for Christ's sake, this? Oh, God, my poor Julie, that's why she left."

Even though the letter shocked him, he forced himself to put fantasies aside, stop his longing for dreams of the past and move into immediate action. He put the letters back into the envelope. Whatever Julie needed to help get through this mess, he would step up and provide it. This time he was not letting her run away! This time she'd face the truth with him by her side.

His mother had taught him an invocation to use in seeking Spirit's help whenever he felt overwhelmed by difficult choices. This was one of those moments of confusion.

"Set our minds ablaze with your light, Lord, so that we can see what we ought to do and have the strength to do it."

Dan repeated it several times, imprinting it deep within him. A golden light filled his heart, circled around his belly and surged upward into his mind. He saw what he needed to do.

First, he'd call Emma to see if Julie could hang out there until after his evening meeting. Then, he'd call Tom and have him get Anne to meet with Julie. He decided that it had to work and, with God's help, it would.

Dan went to his desk, found the number for Abbey's

Run and called it.

"Hi, Tom, it's Dan Hill."

"Has Jack's condition changed?" Tom asked assuming the call was from the hospital.

"No, I'm not calling about Jack's condition, but I need your help to resolve some problems."

"I'll do what I can. Just spit it out, whaddaya want?" Tom spoke like the heavy he was when he was on the police force.

"Can you come into town and drive down to the Fitzsimmons' beach cottage with me? I'll explain why on the way."

"What? Go to the beach cottage? What's the hell's wrong with you? We don't need to go there; we can talk right here on the phone. I'm in the office so no one can hear. I'm not going anywhere right now with Anne being so upset."

"Tom, this has nothing to do with Jack's present condition. I can't explain it over the phone, just trust me on this. I need to see you at the beach today."

"You gotta tell me more."

Dan explained that it concerned his wife, Anne, and her newly found sister, Julie. There was a delicate issue that they needed to find the best way to handle. He added that when the issue surfaces, it will affect the whole family.

Tom resisted leaving the kids, who were upset about their grandfather's illness. He reminded Dan about how Anne was struggling to keep things stable.

"Believe me, I understand Anne and the kids are

hurting, but what's come up is of the utmost urgency. You'll want to know about it, ahead of time, that is, to help Anne deal with it."

"Before what? Just what's so important?"

"It's not about Jack's physical condition but more about his personal state of affairs." Dan tried to appeal to Tom's protective attitude toward his wife.

Tom normally worked hard to maintain control over anything that affected Anne, not just because they were married, but also because it was part of his job as Anne's agent to keep her reputation scandal free.

"This is a sensitive issue. You'll want to help once I fill you in on it all. You'll want to see what's in the cottage. I promise you that!" insisted Dan.

Tom reluctantly gave in, "Okay, okay. For some God-forsaken reason, I'll come to the beach house with you. I'll need to figure out what to tell Anne."

"Since Anne doesn't want to come to the hospital, tell her that we're meeting to talk over treatment for her father which, in a way, is correct."

Dan didn't want to discuss the issue further until he had a chance to talk it over with Tom in person. "Please trust me on this, Tom. In the long run, what we'll talk over will help Anne."

"Since I'm going to trust you on this, you better be right. I'll meet you there as soon as I can. Are you at the hospital or at home?" asked Tom.

"Home. Just come over and please, whatever you do, don't mention this to your wife or anyone else."

"You got it. I just hope this isn't chasing shadows!"

Dan accepted Tom's vexing, for he knew that soon the circumstances themselves would justify the urgency. Reawakened and sharp again, Dan showered and put on casual clothes. Soaking under the spray of the hot water, he figured out how to handle what Jack wanted him to set up. Full of purpose, he noticed his depression lifting.

While shaving, Dan looked at himself in the mirror. He tried to see himself through Julie's eyes. Not bad. His hair was thinning a little but still had its red color. And his face was starting to look healthy again, but unfortunately, the damage from those years of boozing couldn't be totally erased.

He finished shaving, looked intently again into the mirror and imagined Julie staring back at him. She'd see that he wasn't an awkward teenager anymore. He was better at a lot of things and no longer worried that God was going to punish him for having sexual desires. He wanted her to forget how he had failed her in the past. "Hopefully, my love, we have a second chance."

He dressed in his favorite Levis and tan crew neck pullover. While waiting for Tom, he called Emma to ask her if Julie could hang out with her for a few hours. He told her about Jack's letter to Anne and Julie without filling her in on the details. He would need her assistance to bring about a meeting between the sisters.

"I'm going to help her, as best I can, to take care of this emergency. God help me, Emma, even though this is a horrible situation, I'm glad to have a chance to reunite with

Julie," said Dan. Inside his heart, he vowed that he would stick with her in a way that wasn't possible when they were just kids.

"I feel the same way, Dan. I'm happy to have met Julie, and I really like her, but I hate the circumstances that brought her back to Rhode Island. She's using the den phone to check in with her office. It'll be no problem for her to stay here. If she'd like to stay the night, we've got plenty of room."

Dan didn't think that would be necessary, but he would probably be late. He encouraged Emma to eat dinner if he didn't show up.

"No problem."

"I'm glad you're on the team, Emma. I have a feeling that both Anne and Julie will be looking to you for some help with all this."

"Well, Anne, as usual, is painting out her frustrations, but Julie, contrary to my first impression, is quite open and likable. Jack missed out!"

"Shall I give you a ring before I'm ready to head down to Edgewood?"

"Don't bother, just come. Good luck with Tom."

Dan put the letters on the table. He then opened the hall closet and got out of storage his box of mementos: photos of Julie and Anne, and the obituary of Margaret Fitzsimmons. He sat down and went over everything one more time. He put it all in a folder with the photos on the top of the pile. He thought that they might soften Tom's attitude toward Julie before reading the letters.

****

Tom's truck pulled into the driveway. Dan grabbed his jacket, tucked the folder under his arm and went outside before Tom had a chance to change his mind. He suggested that they take his car so Tom could read the letter on the way down to the beach.

"Dan, what's gotten into you? You seem to be driven, and it appears that you have gone way over the normal boundaries of being Jack's doctor. I know that you and Julie dated years ago but why are you so involved now? What the hell's going on?"

Dan attempted to smooth the way. He apologized to Tom for dragging him away from home but asked him to trust him, the meeting was important. He filled Tom in on the length and depth of his previous relationship with Julie. "We grew up together and I spent a lot of my childhood sitting in her kitchen talking with her mom."

He handed the file to Tom. "I'll drive to Little Compton. You read these on the way and then we'll talk."

Tom took the folder as he slid into the passenger seat of Dan's Mazda. "I don't like the feeling of any of this. I've never known you to be so mysterious and insistent."

"Believe me, Tom, this can't wait. It's worth being pushy about. Stop trying to investigate my motives and just read."

Dan could hardly contain himself as he drove away from the city. There was silence for about ten minutes. Then Tom exploded. He slammed the folder against the dashboard several times. Red-faced with flurry, he shouted, "Jesus, Mary, and Joseph! What the hell are we supposed to do with this?"

Understanding his friend's rage, Dan just listened as Tom ranted on about the effects of the news on his family, on Anne's sense of family and its reputation. But after a few minutes Dan could no longer hold back his concern about Julie.

"But Julie has already been destroyed by this. Her life has been sacrificed to keep this secret, which I don't think she even remembers."

Tom pounded his fists together then snarled a response, "This isn't your family. You can't understand the trauma this could cause. I don't want anyone else to know about this--no one! And I mean no one!"

Dan needed Tom as his ally to work through the situation so everyone could be helped, including Jack, so he tried to soften his reaction to Tom's rigid stance.

"True, I'm not family but I've loved Julie all my life and I knew all of them well when I was growing up. I'm Jack's doctor but...maybe I shouldn't tell you this, but what the heck, Jack's close enough to death to justify my telling you. I'm also his sobriety sponsor in the AA program. And we've been friends since you and Anne married. It can't end here! You'll see why I feel that way when you see the cabin."

"I didn't know that you and Julie had a past together until today and looks like a present, too, but I gotta protect my wife and kids. Julie's going back to California, Jack's probably going to die, and so what's the point in sharing these letters with the girls? Anne needs my protection from all of this. I don't care what's in the cottage."

Protection? Dan thought on how different they saw the situation. He knew that Julie shouldn't go back to the West Coast unless she healed this hurt or she'd be haunted by it for the rest of her life.

"Damn it, Tom, Julie deserves better than that."

"Julie's not my concern," Tom retorted.

"Well she should be! Anne wouldn't be so stable if it weren't for how Julie handled what happened."

Dan wondered if he should continue but chose not to push—not just yet. Besides, he assumed that Tom had to see that Anne, deep inside, must know the truth, and with Julie being back, things could never be the same unless this was cleared up.

They pulled into the cottage driveway. Dan hoped that Tom might change his mind once he witnessed how much hurt Julie had carried. He got out of the car and opened the front door with the key Julie had given him.

Tom followed him into the cottage but stopped short at the open doorway.

"What the hell! Did someone break into the place? Have the police been notified?" He kicked through the rubble and stood fixated on the mess.

"This is the manifestation of Julie's anger and pain. I found her here last night passed out, curled up into a ball and clutching a photo of her with her mother. It seems that her grandmother had left her some photographs that put Julie into a tailspin. A couple of Jack Daniels broke through her armor, sending her into a rampage before she passed out."

Dan walked around the room picking up pieces and putting them into a pile near the door.

"Can't you see that Julie's not a cold, unfeeling person? She's a hurting, confused woman with a tortured past. For God's sake, Tom, we can't just ignore the news in the letter and let her deal with this mess alone. Like it or not, we're stuck with what Jack did. We have to help him even if we hate him for causing this."

Tom sat down at the kitchen table and covered his face with his hands.

"Oh, God, Dan, I just don't know what the hell to do. This could destroy Anne. What if my kids find out and what about Jack's law partners . . . I just don't know."

Dan hoped that Tom would cooperate in gathering every one for a meeting. He placed a box of photos in front of him. "While I clean up, look through these. I think you're going to be surprised to see how close Julie and Anne once were."

Perhaps scenes set out before Tom would open his heart to Julie. Maybe, just maybe, he would then see that for Anne to accept her father's impending death, she would also have to make peace with her sister.

Dan got trash bags out of the pantry closet and went about cleaning up the mess. He put the bags of trash in his car and made the cottage look presentable for Mr. Short to close it up again. They certainly didn't need any local gossip to hit the papers.

Tom sat frozen, staring intensely at one image. Anne was about three when it was taken. She was sitting on the beach encased in her sister's arms. Their mother and father sat behind them in a loving embrace. They all looked so happy and content. He had never seen a photo of the whole family.

"We have a copy of their wedding picture in our hall but I don't recall ever seeing them all together. I just assumed that Anne's mother didn't like having any photographs around. I can't get over this big box of them. Where have they been?"

"Jack's mother had put them aside for Julie. As the oldest daughter in an Irish family, she would have the job of keeping them. I also think that she didn't want Anne, or Jack for that matter, to remember the family before Mrs. Fitzsimmons' death. She then created a different reality of the family, one with Julie not in it." Dan reached into the box and found a small album with photos of the summer cottage days. "Look at these."

He went over each photo with Tom, identifying the people he recognized. He put aside the ones with himself and Julie, remnants of his days of innocence.

"Hey, in this one you have a full head of hair." Tom smiled. "I can see how much you loved Julie but more than that, I can see how much my wife doesn't remember or doesn't want to remember."

He held up an image of Julie carrying Anne on her shoulders, both of them laughing and blowing kisses to the camera. Tom admitted to Dan, "Maybe Julie didn't reject them like Anne believes. Maybe there's more to it. Maybe the family rejected Julie."

"There's been a major trauma here that you and I have to handle for Jack," said Dan.

Tom's shoulders rose around his head. He looked like a bird of prey ready to pounce on its prey. "Right now I'm pissed as hell at Jack. He should've kept his goddamn guilt to himself and left our family intact!"

"But Tom, it's not intact--it's not. The togetherness is an illusion. It's not real as long as Julie's out of the circle."

Not in the mood to be accommodating, Dan aggressively countered his friend's resistance. "I'm not going to let this drop. In the way I see it, you're either going to help clear the way or . . . ."

"All right, all right, but drop the bully act. It's not your style. Anyway, I get it. You're not going to back away from this." Tom let his hand fall with full strength onto Dan's shoulder. "But from now on, I'm in charge. Got it, Doc?"

"Yeah, that's fine with me. I'd rather stick with the doctoring. I'm relieved that you're taking control."

Tom picked up the photo again, shaking his head. "It's just hard for me to believe that Anne and Julie were ever close. Once everyone starts talking, who knows what dirt will spill out?"

Tom paced around the room.

"How could he hide all this for so long and let his daughters deal with it? How could he have let his mother talk him into this? I just don't get it." Tom turned to Dan, "I knew that he had been a drunk in his youth, but I just never thought about it. He had stopped and that was that. Or so I thought."

He collapsed back onto the chair and shuffled through the box of photos until one struck him. Julie was holding a baby at a christening. The date on the back meant it was of Anne. Jack and his mother were standing next to Julie.

Tom sighed from a place deep within his soul. Will it ever be right again? As he looked at the picture, he saw his daughter staring back at him, but it wasn't her; it was Julie. He had to help get this straightened out--not for Jack, not for Dan and not even for Julie, but for his daughter, his wife, for their life. He looked up at Dan and said, "Let's get this fixed."

"You won't be sorry, Tom. Anne's trapped in this as much as Jack and Julie. It's clear that all you want is for her to be protected and safe."

The two men were silent as they placed the loose photos and albums back in the box.

Relief washed over Dan. Tom's demeanor had switched from the tense, warrior pose to a more reflective, cooperative one. He suggested that they close up the cottage and head back to Providence. They took the box, assuming that Anne and Julie might want them once the smoke cleared. Dan offered to store it at his house.

Tom looked around and grabbed his coat. "Let's get on with it."

Dan returned the key to the hiding place under the window. As he drove down the driveway he pointed to the cottage that his parents had owned until just few years ago.

"They came back to the beach for years, but after Julie left, I never could bring myself to be here. It was never the same again for me."

"The beach life just ends like that for some folks. After her grandmother went into the nursing home, Anne decided we wouldn't come to the beach cottage anymore. Whatever drew her back here year after year was over. It didn't matter whether the kids and I wanted to come or not, she refused."

"Maybe she had a similar reaction as I had. Julie's leaving left me wounded. Staying at the cottage where we had so much fun felt like walking back into a battle for another wound. It's a relief to know that the rejection I felt back then wasn't from what I did. Julie ran, but not from me."

Tom shook his head in agreement and added, "The race is over, now it's time to heal all the injured runners."

****

The conspirators sat outside Dan's apartment, finalizing their plan.

"I'll call you tomorrow morning with a plan for when and where Emma can meet us."

"Shit, I hate what we're about to do. It better be the right thing or we'll be buried with Jack." Tom blew out his breath and sat tensely like a soldier preparing to walk onto a battlefield.

Dan waited. He knew that Tom needed to concentrate and prepare to face Anne. Tom's head moved ever so slightly indicating he was ready.

"Talk to ya tomorrow." Tom got out of the car and headed for his truck. His shoulders slouched, heavy with the burden of truth.

Dan watched him leave. He prayed that God was with them in handling this. They sure were going to need all the help that the heavens could give them to pull it off.

He looked at his watch and determined that there was enough time to make the six o'clock meeting at St. Edward's Church. He locked the folder with the letters in his glove compartment and put the box in the trunk. By the time he drove across town, he was losing the strength he had marshaled to convince Tom to agree with him.

At dusk, the lights of the evening sky cast an aura of mystery around the church. Dan parked his car on the street in front of the church and noticed that there were just a few of the cars normally parked there before the meeting. Glad not to be rushed, he slumped against his car and quietly cried, "What have I done?"

"Hey, Dan, are ya gonna hang out here alone or are ya gonna come in?" Emilio, a street kid from the south side of town who regularly attended this meeting, jolted Dan out of his daze.

"Emilio, sure . . . sure, I was just getting myself together. Let's go in and help set up."

The two men entered the side door of the church and went down to the basement where the coordinator for the evening was setting up the chairs. Emilio chatted away with her. Dan, wanting to be alone, took one of the books to a chair in the far corner. Most of the people attending this AA recovery group had been together for more than a year. They had learned each other's signals indicating that they were in a deep personal process, such as the one Dan was in that evening.

The meeting was called to order and the business at hand discussed. Dan attempted to bring his thoughts and feelings into some sort of balance in order to share them with the others. One of the other attendees was talking about Step 4, making a fearless moral inventory of self.

The words engrossed Dan; his body filled with intense heat and he felt his heart burst open. He saw in his mind's eye exactly what he needed to admit.

Dan stood up and said, "I need to share."

Out poured the story of failing to protect the girl he loved when he was young. Dan then confessed that he didn't go to California with her, not because of fear or attachment to his family, but because he was drinking a lot. He couldn't face the truth that leaving Rhode Island with her would also mean that she would discover his addiction. If he had traveled with her, he couldn't hide and he didn't want to risk that. "You see, because her dad drank so much, she vowed not to drink anymore and didn't like it when I drank. The thought of being with her and not drinking, well . . . I . . . panicked."

Dan sobbed and sobbed. The others waited as if they knew there was more he needed to admit.

After a few minutes Dan was able to continue his confession. "I've lied to myself and to everyone else."

He had let Julie leave because he was a drunk, a hidden, sneaky drunk. He hid behind the pain of losing her and shut out his family. He became a master of illusion, hiding his drinking while becoming a doctor, marrying a loving woman and having great kids. Dan lifted his head and with tears still in his eyes, looked around, taking in the compassion and understanding coming from the others.

With more control he spoke, "I became a man with a smooth, slick surface and a cold, hard heart. I hurt my wife, robbed her of truth and love. I hurt my kids. I let them think I wasn't available to them because I was saving humanity. I was only saving my own ass and drinking to cover up the panic."

He shook his head in disbelief and admitted, "I even convinced myself that I, Daniel Hill, was the victim."

He described how his sick, alcoholic mind concocted a trauma story. Julie left him alone and in despair; his wife was rejecting and mean; his kids only needed him for money. He worked so hard only to lose his home and worldly goods; a sick tale woven to vindicate himself--poor Dan, abandoned and used; what a good guy.

The others were reverently silent. Dan sat back into his chair.

Emilio spoke up, "Yeah, I did that game. I play it in the streets with my bros in South Providence. I blamed everyone for my homelessness but myself." He turned and looked at Dan. No more words were needed.

At the end of the hour, the group members held hands, sealed their connection with a reminder to keep coming back to meeting. Dan made a decision. He would surrender to God his past with all the lies, the hurts and the poor decisions. And, he vowed right there in this circle of healing, not to pretend, not to close off but to be truthful with Julie and seek her forgiveness.

As the group was leaving, his sponsor came over to him and hugged him. "Tonight you moved into a deeper level of recovery. You don't have to fake it anymore. It's time to forgive yourself and get on with your life."

"Yeah, there's no time to waste anymore." As he left the church, he looked up at the stars and felt the angels were gathering to help him.

****

Tom knew he couldn't go home, at least not just yet. He left Dan's apartment complex parking lot and drove across town to the cemetery behind Our Lady of Peace Catholic Church. He walked down the path, around the grotto to the side area where his first wife, Mary, was buried.

He knelt near the head stone to pull the budding weeds from the grass and loosen the dirt around the young tulip blossoms. Even though she had been dead for over twenty years, Tom still came once a month to tend the grave. Today wasn't his usual day, but he needed this time to regroup. He longed to remember a simpler time in his life, a time when he felt more in command.

When he finished straightening the gravesite, he sat on the bench in front of the stone. Automatically, Tom reached into his pocket and took out an old blue beaded rosary that had been Mary's. He rubbed the worn, smooth glass beads through his finger and started saying the rosary, "Hail Mary, full of grace, blessed are thou among women."

It only took him about ten minutes to finish the rosary. He wondered if he would ever get over the death of his first true love.

"It's a nice spring day, a good day for grooming the site," said Father Ted Ryan. His best friend from high school was walking towards him.

"Hi, Ted. Out for a walk?"

"I was sitting in the grotto reading when I saw you walk by. I thought maybe you needed some private time away from that busy life of yours, but from the looks of you, I guess you need a friend. I've got some time right now. Want to talk?"

"Yeah, I got some things on my mind."

Tom and his friend walked back towards the grotto. "I'm really confused. I haven't been like this since Mary died. You remember how lost I was. My identity, my dreams, my reason for living—it all was connected to Mary. Then she died and a part of me died too. I got mad at others when they treated me as if I was still alive. Didn't they know that I died with Mary?"

"That was a long time ago, Tom. Why all the memories today? And why are you so upset?" Ted asked.

Tom bent down, picked up some of the loose stones on the path and absentmindedly tossed them ahead as they walked. He debated with himself how to answer Ted's question. Could he admit that although today he tried hard to stop thinking about Mary, he couldn't? Perhaps it was as simple as wanting a reprieve from the day's confusion. When Mary was his childhood sweetheart and young wife, things didn't seem so complicated. He understood Dan's feelings for his childhood sweetheart, Julie.

Tom remembered being ten years old and going into Mary's father's candy store on a Saturday morning to spend his allowance. He couldn't admit to his buddies that it was really the cute brunette he wanted to see instead of the penny candy. Her skin was rosy white and her eyes blue just like the clearest summer sky. He was captivated from that time on.

Their families went to the same church, but she went to a different school so that he could only talk alone with her at the store. As their love increased over the years they found other ways to meet, so that by the time Tom was fifteen he got in trouble for carving "Tom loves Mary forever" in a school desk.

All the love they shared washed over him. He thought of the innocent times of early adolescence when they daydreamed of a spending their lives together; of going steady in high school; of being engaged in college and of their wedding shortly after his graduation from the police academy. He also thought of their family life with their two boys in their North Providence home. It was a time of fulfillment, of laughter, of ease, but tragically, it all ended too soon when a drunk driver killed Mary.

"Tom, where are you?" Ted waited for his friend to

snap out of his daydream.

"Do you remember how Mary's sisters hovered over me after the funeral? That made me miss Mary even more. I sent Jamie and Paul to spend weekends with their aunts. That got Gail and Carolyn off my back." Tom tried to end his self-pitying. "At least God had the good sense to bring Anne into my life. Loving her has saved me from a very bleak existence."

Tom thought about the two years of feeling lost, of raising his sons alone before he found a new dream in loving the beautiful, exciting young artist. Being with Anne had given him new reasons to live. With her he felt strong again. He remembered feeling relieved that she didn't have a big family.

"Tom, you keep drifting off. You haven't been like this in a long time. What's going on--why don't you just tell me? Maybe I can help." Father Ryan grew more concerned and tried again to reach Tom. "Maybe I can't help but . . ."

"Why can't the dead just rise up and tell us poor weak souls what the hell to do?" Tom demanded.

"Unfortunately, they can't. But the presence of God in your heart can guide you."

"Ted, I go to mass every Sunday but to "feel" the presence, to "feel" the light, to "feel" the love or whatever, I just don't get it. It drives me nuts. Emma walks around talking about how Bob's spirit is with her. I try to feel Mary's. What do I get? Nothin' but empty space!"

"For most people it's simply a matter of faith." The priest spoke from his own view of spiritual awareness but it didn't touch his friend's confusion.

Tom's body swelled with anger and frustration. "Sometimes I think that God kidnapped Mary and hid her. I don't know what the ransom is. Why the hell can't I just reach out and have her with me?" He reached over and grabbed Father Ted's arm. "Don't get me wrong, I love Anne, but I wish I could feel Mary with me."

"It's fine, Tom, one woman doesn't replace the other. You can love them both."

They took the path into the grotto where they could be alone. Tom paced around picking up pebbles and throwing them into the small pond in front of the Virgin Mary's statue. Ted sat on the wooden bench and waited. As if taming a wild animal, he chose to sit very still, his arms open and his eyes looking down.

"Tom, maybe you feel that Mary's not here and God has forgotten you, but I'm here and I'm listening. Correct me if I'm wrong, but your depressed state isn't just from missing Mary. Something is upsetting you. Spill it out!"

"Swear that you won't tell anybody about this." Tom sat down, leaned forward, put his hands firmly on his knees and blew out hard, waiting for Ted's assurance before exposing the sordid truth.

"I'll act as your priest and as such, will be under the oath of confidentiality. Do you trust me?"

"Yeah, sure I do. Back when I was on duty, I investigated the break-in at Jack Fitzsimmons' office when he was a senator. After that and other times I helped him, we got close—or so I thought. He heard about Mary's murder by that drunken idiot and wanted to help me out. I moonlighted for him helping his daughter set up her shows. He acted like the most concerned, caring guy, another single father who knew what I was going through. Boy, was I fooled."

Tom looked down at his wedding ring and continued, "Anne was at the state house a lot. I got to know her better when I escorted her to some of the state functions when Jack was busy. Anne was so young and beautiful; it was easy to love her. I just fell for her." Tom collapsed against the back of the bench, sinking into silence.

An old woman walked into the grotto, stopping to put a flower at the foot of the Virgin Mother's statue. The men waited. After she was gone, Tom covered his face with his hands and cried. "Everything's changed and I don't think I can face it."

"Whatever it is, you are facing it. Why don't you tell me more?"

Tom reached into his pants pocket for a handkerchief and wiped his face. "Maybe you're right." He spent the next fifteen minutes or so talking about what he had learned in the letters and what he had seen at the beach house.

"I'm so mad. How can I tell Anne about this? I hate Jack . . . I . . . ." Tom shook his head, cried and coughed, sounding as if his heart was cracking open. "That son-of-a-bitch betrayed me. Now what do I do?"

Ted put his hand on Tom's back. "Forgive him."

"I can't."

"Forgiveness has never been easy for you."

"Yeah, I blame myself for Mary's death. She might not have been on the road that night if I'd been home. Then I abandoned my sons when they needed me the most."

"Tom, your sons love you and they remember their mother not just through their aunts, but more importantly, through your honoring her. It's time to let it all go. You didn't hide anything or lie, that's Jack's drama. It's not your job to judge him. You should concentrate on what needs to be done right now."

"I hope you're right. But what bugs me is that Jack got away with it for so long!"

"It seems to me, that Jack is about to face his actions with a higher judge than you," said Ted.

Tom bolted up and spun around to face Ted. "I know, I know but it gets me right here." He gripped his gut. "All these years he's hid this and, damn it, he knew that if I found out about this, I'd have to arrest him"

Ted stood up and took hold of his friend by the arms and shook him slightly to help him regain control of himself. "There could be another way to look at this. Denial can be a powerful tool of the mind. With Julie in California and his mother silent, Jack could have put all that happened in a compartment in his mind labeled "past," and then committed himself to giving his remaining child a good life. And, that, he did."

Tom wasn't calmed so easily. He broke away from Ted and threw up his hands in a gesture of exasperation. "But hell, look at what price, a life based on deception. What about Julie? She's the real victim here." Tom rubbed his temples searching for a clear thought. "Anne sees her as the villain and her father as the good guy. What the hell's going to happen tomorrow when it all blows apart?"

Playing the scene in his mind, Tom wondered out loud, "Who's it going to be harder on? Julie's been the victim all her life and now her sacrifice is going to be exposed. Maybe she doesn't want it to be. Anne's been living a fantasy all these years. How's she going to face the pain inflicted on her sister by the father and grandmother she always loved and trusted? Will she be able to trust anyone again?"

"Perhaps the truth will open more avenues for healing and love that you can't see while you're in the middle of figuring it out. Don't borrow trouble, as our mothers used to say. I sense that you need to stop obsessing about what Jack did and be with Anne. She needs your support. She's here and real, and for God's sake, she's in love with you."

Tom smiled for the first time in hours. "Yeah, you're right about that. Anne's gotta be my first priority. There's just one thing I have to do before going home."

Tom slapped Ted on the back. "Pray for us, would you?"

He left the grotto area and walked to his car.

****

The lights were dimmed. Tom sat next to his father-in-law, talking quietly so the nurses couldn't hear him. He wasn't aware that the nurses were already gossiping about how people who visited Jack Fitzsimmons sure had a lot to say to a dying man. At least he appeared more in control than Julie had when she had sat next to Jack.

Nonetheless, Tom poured out what was on his mind.

"You want us to see you as the good guy for confessing. Then you want us to forgive you. But you know what, Jack?" Tom leaned in and whispered in the old man's ears, "There's no way in hell I'm ever gonna do that. As far as I'm concerned you're the cause of any pain Anne, my kids, Julie, Dan and me are about to suffer. I can't and won't forgive you!"

In the subdued atmosphere of the room, surrounded by the blinking monitor lights and the steady sound of the respirator, Tom sunk into a melancholy reverie. He thought of times when he and Jack had bonded as father and son.

"I actually had you stand on the platform with me when the governor gave me that medal." Tom had received the medal for rescuing several children from a kidnapper. "I was so proud to have you there since my dad was gone."

He remembered how loving Jack had been when Tom held his first grandchild, Richard. Tom questioned what Richard would feel about that love now.

"When we moved into Abbey's Run I thought that living as a family would make up for the loss I felt after Mary died. I wondered why you accepted me, an older man with two kids, so readily into your young daughter's life. Right then and there I should have suspected something. You completely drew me in by the illusion of the loving father, protecting his family. What a sucker I've been."

Bile filled his mouth. Disgusted, he had to fight nausea.

Controlling the urge to reach up and rip the respirator off, Tom took his keys out of his pockets and rolled them around in his palms. The repetitive movement drained some of the energy built up in his chest. He had learned as a cop how to diffuse the heat of rage to the cooler feelings of detachment. Anne needed him, the kids needed him, and it might come down to Julie needing him.

"Just face the truth, the whole truth." How many times had he told criminals and their victims that the only path to setting things straight is to confess the truth?

Indignant at the deception, he accused Jack, "You used me, period, just used me. You've invalidated any love I ever felt from you. You knew that if you'd confessed this while I was still on the force, I'd have had to arrest you. Well, Jack, let me tell you that if you come out of this, I'll make sure you pay for it."

Tom thought of his own father. They had shared many good times that were part of the make-up of a middle class family—baseball games, fishing in one of the lakes in their Warwick neighborhood and camping in the summer.

"Jack, my dad was a good and honorable man. His kids were always more important to him than his own needs."

Sorrow swept over him. "Wherever you exist now, Dad, I want you to know that I realize that you had real power, a life without lies. I loved you, Dad. And I still do. Please forgive me, Dad. How could I've ever been so stupid to think that Jack was more powerful than you?"

Tom suddenly felt a lightness wrap around him. He could swear that he heard his father's voice saying to him,

"Son, I love you, too."

He pulled his father's love deep into him, trying to fill all the emptied spaces created by erasing the illusions of his life with Jack.

After a few moments, Tom refocused on the weak figure before him, a man unable to move, unable to recognize anyone or anything. A man lost within himself. He wondered how he could have ever respected this man: the silent, unmovable force wreaking havoc all around him.

Tom left the ICU renewed and determined to set things straight.

11

THE FAMILY

Almost in a trance, Anne slipped out of the house before the children were awake and headed to the barn. She tended each of the six horses, and then went directly to the studio. Leaning against the wall in the front area of the workspace was a large wooden frame fitted with a piece of untreated canvas. After running her fingers around the edges, she leaned into the middle so she could see if the art supply shop had tightened it to her liking.

"Good, nice and taut. Erica finally got it right on the first try," Anne sighed with relief. She didn't have the patience today to send the frame back to the shop to be stapled and glued again.

Standing in front of the frame, she concentrated on the large empty space in front of her and slipped into a deep thought. The painting's vision started to take form in her mind's eye. Swirls of color would be set off against dark shadowy forms dissected by shrieks of sharp lines; all these aspects merged together in the image she would strive to create. At this point in her creative process, Anne didn't dare stop to figure out what the images meant or resembled. She wanted the surging energy of the vision to take over her body. All thoughts or reality would need to cease to exist except for the forms dancing in her mind. Then, she would be ready to paint the vision.

After putting on her oversized shirt, she picked up a wide, sable brush and went over to the sink to fill a plastic jar with warm water. Everything was comforting, normal. She dipped the brush into the water, and then gently tapped the bristles against her hand to shake off the excess. She flipped through the hairs to make sure all the loose ones were out.

Anne rummaged through her supplies looking for the half-empty can of gesso base paint. All her concerns were about the frame, the paint and the image, not of the impending loss of her father or the exasperating presence of her sister. The familiar routines and the sensual experience of the paints reinforced her illusion that there was nothing as important as the work before her. Anne was feeling calmer. Her personal life was completely pushed away. The illusion of the image became the illusion of denial.

Using long, smooth strokes, first up and down covering the canvas, then over again side-to-side to even the tone, Anne covered every inch until she faced a large field of white space. While the gesso dried, she started to strip a sheet of aluminum into thin, long strips. Cutting the metal evenly took a lot of determination, so much so that she did not notice her daughter come into the studio.

"Mom, can I talk with you?" Rose called from the doorway, but Anne was so engrossed that she didn't hear her.

"Mom! Did you hear me? I need to talk to you."

Anne looked up from her hunched position but didn't put down the metal cutters.

"Rose, sweetie, I'm in the middle of something. Can we talk later?"

"It'll only take a few minutes. I can talk to you while you cut."

"Come closer but not too close so you don't get slivers in your eyes." Anne gestured to Rose to move to the side of the table.

"While I finish this cut, tell me what's so important," Anne said. She bent over and started to cut the metal again.

"But, Mom, I really need to see Grandpa! Richard said he would drive John and me there."

"I just can't take you there right now. Where's your father? Why can't he take you?"

"Dr. Hill called about an hour ago. Dad left to go see him. He told me to tell you when you came in for lunch."

Rose nervously twirled a string of hair hanging over her eyes. "Mom, why aren't you at the hospital?" She could barely speak, "Is he already dead?"

Anne put down the metal cutters and went over to Rose. She pushed her fingers through the strands of hair covering her daughter's eyes and tried to comfort her; after all Rose wasn't unaware of the strange turn of events.

"No, not physically, but his mind's dead."

"I can handle it, Mom. I just want to see him."

"I wasn't sure you'd want to go there without Daddy or me. I guess I had assumed that Daddy was taking you to see

Grandpa, but it's all right with me if you go with your brothers. Just be prepared because Grandpa will not be awake."

"I'll go tell Richard." Rose kissed her mother and left.

Worry about why Tom was meeting with Dan flashed through Anne's mind but she quickly pushed it aside. She was determined to stay focused on her work. Rose's visit had disrupted her concentration. Anne rubbed her hands, sore from cutting the metal, closed her eyes and brought the painting's image back to her mind.

"Okay, get back on track. Think. Where was I?"

She went back over to the art supply shelf. Sitting on the edge of the top shelf was a box with the smaller brushes. Part of her creating ritual was sifting through all the well-worn brushes and the new ones until just the right mix of textures came to her. Looking for the ones she needed, Anne stopped short when an old small brush came to the top of the pile. She picked it up and spun it around in her hands. It brought back memories.

As a seven-year old, Anne hated getting off the school bus and walking up the long driveway only to open the door to emptiness. Her home had been full of sound and activity when her mother was alive, but after her death, the house took on the quiet, slow pace of her Nana.

Memories woke up in Anne. She and her mother would bake cookies together and sing, sometimes loud, funny songs, and sometimes soft, dreamy songs. When her mother wasn't feeling sick she would sit at the old dark upright piano and play all the old songs passed down from her mother. Anne curled up on the chair next to the piano and dreamt of fairies and angels dancing to her mother's beautiful music. At night, she would lay in bed listening to the strange music that her sister liked, some group called the Beatles. But one morning she woke up to a silent house.

Anne twirled the brush between her thumbs, fighting off reliving the intense grief of her younger self. She had lost so much. After her mother died and her sister left home, Nana had moved into Julie's room and her father moved into the guestroom. Except for the times when her father would take her for riding lessons, she spent most of her time alone in her room.

Unlike her mother, Nana was a meticulous housekeeper. Anne didn't feel free to play in the house anymore. Before her mother's death, she and Julie would build forts in the living room and put on plays in the dining room. The memory of her mother's laughter echoed in her heart.

Anne's body contracted, reacting to the pain she had buried. "Oh my, oh my," she whispered as she soothed herself. "I haven't thought of those days in a long time. I almost forgot how awful it was before I started painting."

As a young child her play was limited to her room. She had managed to keep all of her sister's pens and pencils to draw doodles and pictures in her notebooks. Her father surprised her when he noticed one of them and smiled. The next evening he came home with a big box. He moved everything off the dining room table and spread a plastic sheet over it, opened the box and announced to her grandmother, "Anne can use this area whenever she likes except when we have guests."

She ripped the wrap off the box, tore open the top and squealed with delight when she saw the paint brushes, paints, watercolors, paper and painting shirt.

"Daddy, I love you!"

"You look so happy when you paint and I want to make you happy."

Her father had set up the watercolors, then sat down and playfully explored them with her. It was the only time anyone but her touched her paints.

Anne clutched the brush to her heart and cried, "Daddy, Daddy, what am I going to do, how am I going to handle things without you?"

Anne sank into a chair and wept. After a while, her grief spent, she picked up the brushes, mixed the paints and started to fill the empty white canvas.

****

A strong hand gripped his shoulder. "Dad, are you okay?"

Tom jumped in response. "Yes. Yes, I'm fine. Guess I just dozed off sitting here."

"I was on my way to pick up John from his game at East Side High and thought I'd stop in to see Grandpa. Mom said Rose could come, but I wanted to see what's up with you first."

Richard walked around the bed and touched his grandfather's hand. It was hard for Tom to witness his son's love and concern without bursting out with the truth.

"How's he doing? Is Grandpa gonna die?"

Tom nodded, "Yeah, he won't come out of the coma."

Richard rubbed the old man's hand and gently put it on the sheet, a purposeful act of surrender. Mrs. Howe came in, checked the IV and left. Tom and his son, alone with the dying family elder, were now being initiated into the rituals of death. They sat by the body like sentries guarding an old, collapsing castle. Soon all the mortar would crumble and their job would be finished.

After an unmeasured moment, father and son looked at each other with an acknowledgement that the old family order had changed. They were free now to speak of the present.

"Dad, Mom's acting weird. Why isn't she here with Grandpa? And why is she in her studio and not here with us?"

Richard, his oldest son with Anne, was so much him. They both found it hard to stand by and not know what to do.

"Remember that time, Dad, when her friend Barbara left town, and she stayed in the studio for several days from early morning to late night. It's like he's already gone. He hasn't died yet."

Tom stood up, put his arm around his son and walked him out into the corridor. "Pick up your brother and go home. I'll be there soon. When I get there, I want to talk to the three of you about what's happening."

They left the hospital together but before leaving the

city, Tom stopped at his favorite coffee shop on Weybosset Street, where he hung out when he was a young cop on foot patrol. The small shop drew a mixed crowd of students from the colleges, street people looking for a rest stop, blue-collar workers and local police. The business people tended to go to the upscale coffee shop near Kennedy Plaza. Like most Saturdays, the shop was empty. He took his coffee and donut over to the counter by the window.

Sitting there, staring out at the few people milling around the downtown area, Tom sipped his coffee and dunked his donut in the hot drink. He felt too weak to hold his shoulders back and his stomach in. Looking up at his reflection in the donut shop window, he almost didn't recognize himself. The lean, strong, young cop on the beat had completely faded away, leaving in its place a somewhat worn, graying, older man. It had been so much easier to be a rookie cop. Taking on the responsibility as head of the family was daunting. He wondered how the world would judge him—powerful, loving, arrogant, wise, foolish or distant.

In ruminating about his position in life, Tom almost forgot what was awaiting him at home. The events of the day rattled around inside his mind. He shook his head in disbelief that it was just this morning that he had faced the blunt truth of what really happened in the past.

It seemed like days ago that he and Dan were at the cottage. It also seemed like it would be years before they were out of this mess.

After taking the last gulp of coffee and swallowing the

remaining crumbs, he walked outside. Tom had hoped that being in his old hangout would help him feel in charge of his life again. He had hoped to be able to be clearer before talking with Anne and the children, but there was no escape from the dismal reality of the situation facing them.

On his way back to Abbey's Run, he stopped at the local deli to pick up some food. He was sure that no one at home had figured out what to have for lunch. By the time he got home, the three of them had set the table and were waiting in the den, arguing over what movie to watch and who could use the phone.

Tom opened the door and called to them, "I'm home. Help me with this food."

"Dad, I thought you were right behind me. What took you so long?" Richard took one of the bags out of his father's hands.

"I went downtown and had a cup of coffee. I needed some time to think after being in that hospital most of the morning. Hope you guys didn't fix any lunch, I got chicken and the works."

Rose took the other bag of food out of his hands, went over to the counter and rummaged through the containers.

"Great Dad, my favorite. Did you get the potatoes I like with the scallions roasted in them?"

"Sure, honey."

His arms free, Tom put his hands on Richard's shoulders. "You okay?"

"Yeah, but it's real hard, Dad. It hurts like hell to see Grandpa so sick. And what's with Mom? She's been in the studio all day."

"You know how she gets wrapped up in her work. I'll go talk to her after supper."

"Dad, I want to see Grandpa," Rose insisted.

"I know, honey. Soon, but first, let's eat."

As they filled their plates, John joined them, fresh from the shower.

"How was your game?" Tom asked his younger son.

"Nothing new, we lost," John shrugged.

After serving themselves, they sat down. Tom opened the conversation. "We're gonna need to help each other through the next couple of days. There's a lot going on. I don't know where to start. First of all, I appreciate how you're pulling together. Rose, you and John took care of the horses and did some housework. Thanks."

"Dad, just drop it on us; whatever it is, we can handle it." John turned to his brother and sister, "Right guys?"

"Yeah, Dad. I don't like the way you and Mom are keeping us out of whatever the hell's going on. Is Mom having a breakdown or something because of Grandpa? Just tell us, we can handle it," Richard demanded.

"It's nothin' like that, believe me. I'll tell you some of what is going on with your mother, but I can't tell you everything until after tomorrow."

"Why?" Rose asked.

"I have to talk with your mother first."

John had been quiet but couldn't contain himself anymore. "Mom's acting scary. I watched her this morning when she was grooming Spade; she didn't know I was in the barn. She was crying real hard, saying something about the bitch and about Grandpa being stupid." John swirled his fork around several times until the food on his plate was all mixed together. "I never heard her talk about Grandpa that way. And who's the bitch?"

"Your aunt."

"Who?" The three of them said in unison.

"Your mother's older sister, Julie."

"Wait a minute Dad, we have an aunt?" Richard blurted.

"Well, yeah, you do. But she and your mom haven't talked in years."

Tom faced them all and started to tell them about the situation. "For a reason that I'm not free to tell you right now, your grandfather arranged for your mother's older sister to come back." Tom stopped talking, put his head down and quietly ate his dinner for a few moments.

His children stared at him with shock all over their faces. The four of them sunk into a few moments of silence.

After what seemed like forever, Tom put down his fork and continued, "We learned yesterday that your Grandpa recently signed a living will naming your Aunt Julie as his guardian."

"But Grandpa's always lived here with us. Shouldn't Mom be his guardian?" Rose's body tightened up with confusion.

"That's what I thought, too, until I talked with Dan Hill today and got more information. It looks like your grandfather was trying to force Julie to come home to

Rhode Island. I don't think he realized how much this would hurt your mother."

"You're not telling us everything, are you Dad?" Rose leaned toward him and demanded, "Tell us. What is it?"

"I did discover something that even your mother doesn't know yet, but . . . ." Tom took in the confronting glares of each of his children. "I can't tell you what it is, at least not tonight. First thing in the morning, your mother and I have an important meeting with Emma and Dan Hill. Hopefully, after that, I'll be able to share all of it with you."

Richard crossed his arms over his heart, tucked his head in close to his chest and leaned back away from the table. As if he had sudden clarity about the situation, he snapped forward, looked up at Tom and asked, "So, this is why you were so angry when I saw you in Grandpa's room this afternoon?"

"Yes, son, I'm afraid so." Tom hesitated for a moment. "Normally I'd never ask you to keep a secret from your mother, but just for tonight don't say anything about all this. And, definitely don't mention her sister."

John pushed his father, "Why not?"

"Mom has a lot to deal with. Grandpa's in critical condition and she has no say in his care." Tom struggled not to show how concerned he was. The look in his children's eyes showed enough worry.

John continued pushing his father, "What did this sister of Mom's do?"

"I honestly don't think it was something that Julie did or didn't do. Anyway, the next couple of days probably won't be easy for Mom. She's going to have to face the fact that the sister she crossed off her list of family members is back. It's hard enough on her to deal with your grandfather's crisis."

Tom was talking to them all but aimed his request mostly at John, "Can I count on you to not mention Julie tonight? Can you give me a day to work this out with Mom?"

"When you put it that way, Dad, I can wait as long as you want if it will help Mom." John seemed relieved.

Tom pulled a photo out of his shirt pocket. It was an old black and white glossy one that he had taken from the old album. He passed it to Rose.

"That's your mother and your Aunt Julie at a horse show. Show it to your brothers when you're finished."

"Mom's so young here. We never saw a picture of her at that age," said a surprised Rose.

"I guess your mother is about four when that was taken. Your Aunt Julie is ten years older than Mom."

Richard grabbed the photo, glanced at it and then shoved it at his brother.

"How come nobody ever told us about this so-called Aunt Julie?" Richard demanded.

"I said I can't tell you now, but you'll know the whole story soon enough," Tom said impatiently.

Richard kept pushing his father. "Didn't anybody talk to her?"

"From what Dan tells me, Nana and Julie stayed in touch. After your grandma died, Julie went to live with cousins in Vermont until she graduated from high school. Then she went to college in California and stayed there."

"You mean she never saw Mom again? But they're sisters . . . ." Rose was dumbfounded.

"No, honey, they haven't talked since Aunt Julie left Rhode Island. Dan told me why she left, but you'll have to wait until I talk to your mom." Tom tried to comfort his daughter even though the questions in his own mind were multiplying. He began to ramble, "And, I just found out that we don't use the beach cottage anymore because Nana had willed it to Julie."

"What? I thought that Mom just got bored with the beach. I can't believe that she'd hold back so much from us." John looked dumbfounded.

"Son, your mom hasn't held back from you, she's just been operating under some false information that will be cleared up tomorrow. You'll understand more when I can tell you all about it. I know it's hard to wait."

Richard gruffly pushed his chair back from the table, picked up his plate and threw it into the sink. He swung around and faced his father. Tom held him in a steady, calming gaze until John agreed. "I don't like any of this. But all right, tomorrow."

Tom turned to the others and said, "I'm really sorry that things are such a mess. I have to go talk with your Mom. Clean up here, would you?" He didn't wait for an answer. He left the house and walked over to the studio.

****

Tom opened the studio door and leaned against it for a moment. Anne was at the far corner bent over her worktable holding a hot welding gun. The light from the gun stung Tom's eyes as he watched her.

After about ten minutes, Anne stepped back, lifted the safety hood, and eyed her work. She was welding long thin strips of steel to each other in random pattern. Tom had learned over the years not to interfere in her creative process. Even at times when it might look like she was just standing there, she was mentally organizing the image she was trying to achieve.

He couldn't wait any longer. He reached back and locked the door. The lock's click disturbed Anne. She looked up at him.

"Tom, I'm really onto something."

He walked over to her and took the tools out of her hands.

"What are you doing?" Irritated, Anne pulled at the tools.

"I want my wife." Tom put the tools on the table and took her in his arms, holding her tightly. "Anne, I need you."

"Not now Tom, I'm in the middle of something."

He let go of her, but stayed planted in front of her. "Yes, now."

"Tom, I only have a few moments."

Driven by his passionate need to connect with her, his desire fully awakened, he let out a deep-throated moan, "I'll take them."

He kissed her hard and full. The smell of the studio intoxicated him. He thrust his tongue deeper and deeper; again and again painting the colors of his arousal. She gave way to his aggressive urges and responded to his passion. He left her no room to pull back. They collapsed onto the floor, kissing and touching, melting into each other's arms. Their lovemaking was fast, staccato like. Together, they released.

Anne clung to her husband. Encased in the aura of their fulfilled passion, Anne cried.

When he felt her body drain of the built up tension, Tom opened the conversation. "Honey, we need to talk about what's going on with you and your Dad."

Furious, Anne sat up and punched him in the chest, "No, we don't! You bastard. How could you bring this up just after we made love?"

She punched him repeatedly but her blows were weak and childlike. Tom let her vent on him. As she slowed down and sunk back against him, he drew her into a full embrace.

"Honey, I need you. I love you. I was desperate to find a way to connect with you, to bring you out of that space where you've been hiding. I'm not sorry for pushing you or worrying about you. I love you."

His words softened her resistance. She leaned into him.

"I'm feeling so confused. I don't want to lose my father, but what he's done really hurts and the thought of facing him is too much for me. Sometimes I think I can handle this and then it all becomes overwhelming."

"You're not the only one who's overwhelmed. This is tough for me, too."

She reached up and gently touched his cheek. "Oh, this is so hard for all of us."

"Yeah, it is."

Anne sat up and straightened her clothes. "Why, Tom, would he ever want her back here? I just can't get over it!"

Tom controlled himself even though he was tempted to spill the beans and reveal what he had learned from the letters. He held firm to his belief that it would be best if the truth came from Jack. His job was to get Anne to that meeting.

"Jack had his own reasons for bringing Julie home, and those have nothing to do with the quality of your relationship with him. Who knows, maybe he had tried other ways and they didn't work, so to your father, this seemed the only way to get her back to Rhode Island."

"I don't give a damn about her, and I certainly never want to see her again!"

A fleeting thought crossed his mind. Tom wondered whether Julie had been the loving sister that Dan claimed she had been. Maybe Anne was right. Maybe Julie was evil.

He stood up, buckled his pants and then with a quick movement, reached out and pulled Anne back to him. He held her tightly. Tom longed to do the right thing, whatever the hell that was. She tried to break free but he wouldn't let go. He just kept talking.

"Honey, it's important for you, for us, and the kids to separate the issue of Julie's return from the fact that your father, who you love, is dying. We need you to grieve with us, to go through this with us; it's our loss too. You have three kids waiting in the house for their mother to share her sorrow with them, to let them love and comfort her, and to help them let go of the only grandparent they have. Don't pull away like this, we can't take it anymore." Saying his piece, he loosened his grip.

Anne twisted away from him. She rubbed her temples and repeated, "I'm so confused!"

"Just open your heart to us, let us comfort and help you."

Tears came to her eyes and Tom took advantage of them, "Come on, honey, come into the house and be with the kids. You can deal with Jack and your sister later. We're here for you, and we want you to come back to us. Rose thinks you're having a breakdown. Don't you want to reassure her? Do you really want them to feel so abandoned? Do you want them to lose their strong, nurturing mother and their grandfather, too?"

He gently took hold of her arm and guided her toward the door.

Anne resisted him a little, but then softened. "You're right. I've been forgetting that this is hard for them. The last thing I want is to have Rose thinking that I'm out of control. Tell you what, I'll finish the work on the table and then come in. It'll only take me about ten minutes."

Standing on her toes, she kissed him. "Thanks for not letting me be alone."

"I need you too much to lose you to a piece of metal.

Your work is good, but it's not you in the flesh." Tom continued the thought in silence, "And I don't want to lose you to your memories."

Like her normal self, Anne gently chided Tom, "You'd better not pick on my creative visions."

"I wouldn't dare do that. Don't be too long." He kissed her once more and left for the house.

All three kids were watching a movie in the den. Tom stopped at the doorway and said, "Mom will be in soon. She's almost done in the studio. I'll be upstairs or in the office."

Tom showered. He first stood under a strong stream of very hot water. When he felt faint, he switched to the coldest setting. This was his way of alerting his mind and senses. He needed to be sharp and focused. Rummaging through the pile of unfolded clothes on the bedroom bench, he found his favorite jeans and sweater.

Refreshed, he went downstairs to his office and put on his favorite Ella Fitzgerald CD. He worked his way through a stack of correspondence, including a letter from the Boston gallery concerning Anne's upcoming show. The music and the busy-work distracted him from the truth hovering like a tornado over his family.

****

Anne came in the side door that opened to the office. "I thought you'd be hiding out in here. Where's everyone else?"

"Waiting for you in the den," answered Tom.

As Anne started to leave, Tom took hold of her hand and asked, "How about all of us going to see your father? I think it's important that we do this as a family. Whaddaya say?"

"I don't feel ready for that."

"Just for a while." Tom let go of her hand, gently grasped her by her arms and looked directly into her soft, green eyes and said, "Honey, you're having a hard time with it all, but so are they, so am I."

"Oh, my darling, you're so good at the guilt. I bet you used it to wring many a confession out of the bad guys." She smiled for the first time in days.

"I'll go check in with the kids before I decide," Anne said to her husband and left the room.

Tom slumped back into his chair. He sat perfectly still, drumming his fingers on the desk—a warrior sending out the message to gather round for the ceremony about to begin.

Tom's approach to Anne was successful. She decided to stay out of the studio for the night and go with the family to visit her father. At the hospital, Anne was deeply moved as she watched Rose stroke her grandfather's hand and thank him for loving her. Richard stood silently behind his sister with a look of sadness in his eyes. John went to the other side of the bed and gently touched his grandfather's shoulder.

Witnessing the love that her children showed toward her father, Anne found herself opening to him. She felt her own love overtake the rage and disappointment that she had struggled with since hearing about Julie.

"Tom, take the kids to the waiting room. I want some private time with my father." Anne sat down and took hold of his crumpled hand.

At first she had no words, just memories. In her mind's eye her father was young, strong, loud and commanding. Moments of simple pleasures flooded her senses: the smell of his after-shave as he kissed her before leaving for the office, the movement of his hands as he talked, the swirl of energy around him as he told one of his tales and the softness of his voice as he comforted her when she was injured.

She looked at him, the shadow of the man she remembered, and quietly spoke, "Daddy, I'm not going to spend my last moments with you upset about Julie. For some reason I might never understand, you felt the need to bring her back here. It's fine, Dad, if you have to forgive her before you die, I understand. I'm all right. You can let go of suffering and go to Mom."

She bent over him, gently putting her face against his heart as she had done thousands of times.

"Thanks for doing your best to make my life as happy as possible after Mom died and Julie left home. I remember the time you dressed up as the clown for my seventh birthday and when you came to my play at school and got up to cheer when everyone else just clapped."

She sat back and looked up at him. Anne tried to envision how this small, caved-in man, struggling to hold onto life, could have been the powerful authority that at times scared her and infuriated her.

"You know, Dad, when I had that accident and you made me pay for it, I hated you for a long time, especially since you took my driver's license away for a year."

Anne, a mother of teenagers herself, found it easy to agree with the way her father had handled her drunk driving accident. She drove home drunk from a party and fell asleep at the wheel. Her car left the road, crossed their neighbors' lawn, plowed through a stone barbecue pit and hit a statue of Jesus, knocking off its head. No one was hurt but her father was livid. He made her spend her savings to buy a new statue and the materials to rebuild the barbecue pit. For four Sunday afternoons he supervised her in putting every stone in just the right place.

He was serious, yet funny; he was kind, yet stern. And, he was leaving her. How could he do that to her? She looked up into his eyes, seeking some sense of him, but there was no response. His spirit had already left.

Anne kissed her father on the forehead and bid him goodnight. Connecting with her father, even in his unresponsive state, comforted her. She decided to return the next day.

The nurse came in to check on the monitors. "Don't worry, Mrs. Riley. Your father's condition probably won't change tonight. You all look so tired. Go home and have a good night's rest. He's in good hands here."

Anne found her family in the waiting room watching the news.

"Let's go," she said in her strong mother voice.

They jumped up and rallied around her like a swarm of bees around their queen. In an unusual act of surrender, Anne accepted their attention and hugs.

"My sweet darlings, I'm so sorry for the way I've been behaving, keeping you at a distance and not sharing this with you."

She looked from one to the other and vowed to them, "As long as Grandpa is here, we'll deal with this as a family. I promise."

John kissed her and spoke for them all, "That's all we need Mom."

Tom herded them down the hall and out of the building. "How about getting a bite to eat at Dakota's over on Thayer Street."

Anne smiled at him and gave him their special "look" that meant, "I cherish you."

"I'm starved," said Richard.

Rose spoke up. "I don't think I could eat. Seeing him in that hospital all hooked up to machines really upset me. I'm losing Grandpa. It's awful that he's never coming home."

"Sweetie, one of the hardest things for any one is to live while someone you love is dying." Anne hugged her daughter as they walked to the car. "Allow yourself to reminisce about all the special things you did with Grandpa. You'll have those memories forever." Then, as much to console herself as her daughter, she said, "He's leaving to go on to another kind of life. We need to help him leave peacefully."

"I'll try, Mom," Rose whispered.

John put his arm around his sister and said, "Let's have some ribs for Grandpa. They're his favorite."

Rose smiled a little and walked with her brother to the car. Anne was relieved that Rose's mood lifted a little. Her emotional reserves were low. Since finding her father lying on the floor, her own moods were on a roller coaster of extremes. For reasons she didn't feel free to share with her children, she felt as though her life was crashing in around her.

For so many years she had played a silent game with her father, that of never mentioning her sister. Anne had always assumed that he didn't want to see her again; that he never wanted to face what she did the night her mother died. But now, while locked into silence, he broke the spell they wove together.

"Mom, Mom, what are you thinking about? You seem a million miles away?" John tried to draw her back.

"I'm just tired and hungry," Anne lied.

"You guys get out here and I'll park the car." Tom let them all off in front of Dakota's. Saturday evening on Thayer Street meant that all the Brown and Rhode Island School of Design students were milling around looking for some action. The buzz of the street felt good to Anne, helping to anesthetize her against the emotional pain she struggled to manage.

They got the last available table and were soon enjoying their meal. In between munching on ribs and fries, they spilled out stories of their life with Jack.

Rose said, "One of the best days of my life was when I turned thirteen and Grandpa took me on that trip to New York. We went everywhere: the Empire State building, the museums and a boat ride around Manhattan. We had dinner at Lindy's. He even took me for a carriage ride through Central Park. It was so much fun. And, I didn't have to share any of it with my brothers."

"Well, we had our own times with Grandpa. Remember, John, when he took us on a canoe trip to fish in Maine? We roughed it up, caught a few big ones and heard lots of fish tales." Richard matched Rose's intensity in the telling of his story.

Anne had her own special moment. "I'll always cherish my thirteenth birthday when Grandpa gave me the saddle that had belonged to my mother. It was as if he had given me the world."

On and on went the stories of the impact Jack had had on their lives.

Tom hid his negative feelings for the moment. "Jack never seemed to be at a loss for gifts and love for his family. When we got married, he helped Jamie and Paul feel welcomed as his new grandchildren. I wish they could be with us." Tom reached out, held Anne's hand and said, "And he was very helpful when I retired and became your agent. He didn't judge my leaving the force. His trust meant a lot to me, then."

Anne heard conflict in his voice but for the sake of the kids, she tried to shake off a foreboding feeling. She promised herself she would talk to him later.

"That reminds me, Dad, do Jamie and Paul know about Grandpa?" John asked.

"I called them this morning. Jamie will leave Albany tomorrow after his seminar and pick up his brother in Bennington," Tom answered.

"Good, then we'll all be here," said Richard.

Anne flinched at Richard's statement, for she thought he didn't know how prophetic that really was. She wasn't aware that Tom had already told them that they had an aunt.

In unison they stood up to leave the restaurant. No one needed to say anymore. They knew that the storytelling shared during the evening was part of the dying ritual. It was silently acknowledged among them that Jack Fitzsimmons would not recover and return to Abbey's Run. For time to come, they will organize their family around his absence instead of his presence.

On the way home, Anne was overwhelmed by the energy conjured up by them all coming together in such an intense way. She watched Tom as he drove. He was her warrior, her wise man, her lover, and now the elder of the family. Passion flushed through her. All thoughts of her father's condition moved aside. She knew what she needed that night.

Tom looked over at her as if he was touched by her thoughts. When he smiled in recognition, Anne relaxed. Tom had felt her desire.

When they got home, the boys went to check on the horses while Rose headed for the phone to call her friend.

Tom and Anne didn't have to say much, they went right upstairs to their bedroom.

****

No words, only the habit of their shared intimacy guided them into lovemaking. Tom locked eyes with Anne as they undressed each other. Anne exuded an urgent hot energy. Tom kissed her as if to drink in her heat. She opened to him and played him with her tongue. She guided his mouth to her breast and moved down onto the bed. He moved down her body, consuming it with kisses. Anne rolled Tom over. She kissed, licked and caressed him and he was quickly ignited. She mounted him and rode him as if speed, sensation and wild rhythm would save her from the demons biting at her heart.

When Tom could no longer hold back, he lifted himself up to embrace her. He kissed her fiercely, matching her rhythm. With their bodies merged face to face, heart to heart, she sank down hard, taking him higher inside of her. As they moved together, separation dissolved. They cried out as they reached total release.

He fell back against the pillows and pulled her close. They clung tightly to each other until their heartbeats slowed and they could feel the boundaries of their own bodies. Anne slid off of him, curling up into his arms.

After a few moments, she felt his shoulders and neck tighten. She recognized the signs that he was ready to bring up a difficult issue.

"Darling, we haven't made love like that in a long time so whatever you're scheming to discuss with me while I'm so nice and relaxed, just forget it."

"I can't. We've got to talk."

Anne flew out of bed and stormed into the bathroom. She tried to slam the door but Tom had followed her. He blocked the doorway and insisted she listen.

"We've got to talk about a meeting that's happening tomorrow."

She ducked under his arms and grabbed her hairbrush. Waving it around in front of his face, she screamed, "I don't have to talk about it!"

Tom didn't flinch. Experience taught him that it would be best to hear her out.

"I don't have to listen to anything! Don't dump something on me that I don't want to hear. It's probably about Julie anyway! I won't be forced into dealing with her." She pushed him back and slammed the door.

Tom didn't retreat. He opened the door, went over to the sink, and stood behind her as she brushed her teeth.

"Except for tonight with the kids, you've been storming around in your studio or tending the horses, anything but telling me what's going on with you."

Anne rinsed out her mouth but didn't turn to face him. She felt thick, heavy with rage and resentment.

"Leave me alone! I can't go from love making to fighting so quickly and usually you can't either, so back off and drop all this talk. Just go to bed, I'll be there when I'm ready."

But Tom didn't stop. Instead, he took hold of both her arms and swung her around.

"I hate ruining my time with you, time I get so little of lately, but this won't go away. Your sister is here, and personally, I don't give a fuck whether you and your sister ever work this out, but right now you have to listen to me. Jack's not my father and I refuse to handle this totally for you."

Anne pushed him away. "What's gotten into you? You have the gall to come after me like that!"

Tom backed up and sat down on the edge of the tub.

"Don't put it all on me. I didn't mean to grab you, but I'm so damn frustrated at not being able to get through to you. I've wanted to talk with you for the last two days but you've managed to never be available. I can't wait anymore for you to be ready!"

Sparks of anger flew from her.

He changed his tone. "Please won't you just listen for a minute so we can get past this? We both need to get some rest."

Anne softened as she watched Tom, naked and tense, sink into himself. The anger cleared from her eyes, she saw how disturbed he felt.

"All right, all right, let's go to bed. You're acting so Strange. You might as well tell me what you want," she said in a gentler tone.

She offered him her hand and hugged him as he stood up. "I promise I won't fall asleep before you talk."

Tom got into the bed and wrapped himself around her.

He spoke softly as he presented the plan, "Tomorrow morning at ten we're going to meet Emma, Dan Hill, and Julie in your father's office."

Rolling over to face him, Anne couldn't hold back her displeasure. "Why there and why do I have to see her? Why can't you and Emma handle the legal aspects of this mess?"

"Because there's more than the will that has to be dealt with. Your father wrote a letter which he requested to be read to both you and your sister if he became incapacitated or died."

"I never heard of such a letter."

"It was in an envelope that your father had given to Dr. Bell. He delivered it to Dan today. After talking it over with Dan and Emma, we decided that it would be best if she read it to both of you. She doesn't want to read it at the hospital or her office, so she suggested your father's office."

There was a long pause.

"Are you asleep?"

"No, I'm just trying to figure out how I can get out of it without upsetting you or Emma. Dad had no right to involve me in his scheme, or to draw you, Emma, and Dan into it. I don't want to hear what he has to say in that letter. I'll find a way not to go. There must be some compromise that won't disappoint you."

"There isn't," Tom confirmed.

Anne turned away from him and muttered, "Maybe by morning I'll think of something."

"I hope not. Would you not fight this so much? Do this for me." He kissed the back of her head barely uttering a goodnight before falling asleep.

Anne lay awake for a long time trying to recall memories of her childhood family--her mother, father, sister and herself. But she could only get glimpses and feelings of dread. Frustrated that she couldn't call forth the last memory of being with her mother, she recalled the last time she saw Julie, packing her suitcases. Her sister was sullen and dismissive of her. Julie went to live with relatives out of state and then, after high school, disappeared altogether from their lives.

Shortly after Julie left, Anne heard her grandmother and father arguing about Julie.

"We can't keep her here. She'll destroy everything. You have to think about Anne; she needs you. I'll take care of Julie," said Nana.

Although she never quite understood her father and grandmother's decision, Anne obeyed their orders to stop writing or calling her sister. She had cried and missed Julie, but her father had been so adamant about the separation that, as a young girl, she had no choice but to accept the situation. Over the years, she came to accept that because Julie had done something awful, she had been banished from the family. But for some reason, her father had given her power of his affairs. The prattle of confusion in her mind wouldn't quiet.

Anne cried silently. Her thoughts reached out to her father.

"Dad, you betrayed me! How could you change the rules without telling me why? I could kill her for what she did to us and you expect to meet with her, to share you with her. What the hell's going on? Dad . . . why . . . why?"

Tom had no trouble sleeping and from the sound of his snoring, he was unreachable for further talk.

Anne couldn't fall asleep. She tried to stop obsessing over the situation. She rolled around in the bed to make herself more comfortable, put a nightstand light on to read a novel, wrote in her journal, all to no avail. She gave up and went downstairs for a cup of chamomile tea.

With a down vest over her nightgown, she took a cup of tea and went out to the front porch. The clear night's cool, crisp air had just a hint of wind. She looked at the tall spruce trees lining the front yard and marveled at how, spring after spring, they grew and expanded, undaunted by the harsh New England weather. They had stood there all her life, asserting their right to exist.

She sipped her tea, then gazed upward. The night sky absorbed her. It was clear, making it easy to imagine the stars as points of interest along the paths of soul journeyers. The vastness of the universe expanding out beyond the stars soothed her. The stress of her grief subsided and gave way to a sense of inner peace.

Her mind slowed down and the tension in her shoulders eased. Whispers from her soul comforted her. Her father would die. Her sister might be in control of his last days, but her family and art would continue to be the core sources of love in her life.

After she finished her tea, Anne went over to the hammock stretched between two large maple trees in front of the porch. She curled up in a blanket Rose had left in the hammock and swung herself to sleep.

12

THE REUNITING

When Dan arrived at Emma's house, he had a few moments alone with her to discuss the meeting the next morning.

"Are we gathering in your office tomorrow?"

"I'd prefer using Jack's office. It's his business; it's his letter. His office feels best to me."

"What about Julie and Anne? They might not be comfortable being surrounded by his things." Dan pleaded with Emma, "Come on, how about your office? Julie might feel safer there."

"I'm not willing to do that. Remember, I'm not just a surrogate for Jack in this matter. This whole thing is upsetting for me too. I need to have some boundaries here"

"You're a lawyer. Everything you deal with is upsetting."

"I deal with contracts. I stay away from this personal stuff as much as possible. I only took on Jack's will because he manipulated me into it. There are limits to what I'm willing to do." Emma insisted, surprising herself with how stubborn she was being.

"Dan, I'm too close to all of this. I need to keep some part of my life away from what Jack has set in motion. You can understand that, can't you?"

"Sorry, Emma, for being so insensitive. I've been so involved with Jack's life and my reactions to Julie's return, that I've forgotten how this is affecting everyone else. It's all so damn crazy!"

Emma stepped back and eyed him from head to toe. "Well, you do look a little crazed."

They both laughed, breaking the tension.

"You're probably anxious to see Julie. She's napping on the couch. Let's go wake her."

Dan followed Emma to the great room and watched as she nudged Julie awake.

"Not yet, Dixie, in a little while," Julie muttered in her sleep.

"Julie, Julie, it's Emma. You're in Rhode Island, not home in California. Dan's here."

He sat down on the couch and said in the most comforting tone he could conjure up, "Julie, it's all right, take your time. If you need more sleep, I'll wait."

She opened her eyes and smiled at him. "What a nice surprise to have you here when I wake up. Just give me a minute to get myself together."

Julie sat up, looked around and nodded at Emma who was sitting in the high back chair by the fireplace.

"This couch is so comfortable. It's been a while since I've slept that soundly. Have I been out long?"

"Just about forty minutes. I like to crash on that couch,

too, sometimes. It envelops you like being held in big loving arms. Your nap gave Dan and me a chance to finish talking about some business that he'll fill you in on later." Emma turned to Dan, "You must be starving. Can I fix you something to eat?"

Dan realized that he hadn't eaten in hours. "If it wouldn't be too much of a bother, I'd love something."

"No trouble at all. Can I get each of you something to drink?"

"I'd love a cup of coffee; maybe it will help me get going again."

"Make that two. Can I help you with anything, Emma?" Dan offered.

"No, you stay with Julie." Emma left them alone.

"Julie, if you're up to it after we eat, I'd like to take you out to Regina's for a nightcap. It's good place to relax and talk." How about it?"

Julie gave him a guarded look and asked, "What do you want to talk about?"

"Some business around your father's situation, but mostly I want to catch up on what's been happening in both our lives." He couldn't admit that what he had to say might upset her.

After eating, they rode in silence back to Providence. Dan wrestled with himself as to whether he should just tell her what was in her father's letter or wait until the meeting in the morning; that is, if he was able to persuade Julie to be there. He turned it over and over in his mind, but longing to have her stay open to him, stopped Dan from bringing it up.

"I don't remember if Regina's was open or not when we were young. But of course, we weren't of the legal age back then," said Julie.

Dan laughed and said, "No, but we sure found ways to have fun."

"Don't worry; I'm not going to forget that we had fun together and some wild times. Remember when you visited me in Vermont and we snuck over the border into New York with our fake ID's. We sure partied that night!" Julie smiled for the first time in days.

"If I recall correctly, your aunt grounded you for a month."

"It was worth it. What's the atmosphere like at Regina's and do I need to go back to your place and change into something more appropriate?" asked Julie.

"What you're wearing is just fine. It's a casual place with comfortable sofas and small tables, ideal for conversation."

They found a parking space on South Main right in front of the bar. The place was full of Brown University visiting parents who were in town to retrieve their children for spring break.

As they entered, Julie commented, "This could be a scene in Palo Alto when the town is invaded by Stanford parents."

Dan checked with the hostess who assured them there would be a table for two in about ten minutes. They decided to wait outside. Dan enumerated all the changes in downtown Providence while Julie countered with rapid development in her California community. Each word distanced them from the emotional impact of the recent crisis. After the first flush of conversation, Dan grew quiet, uncertain of how to continue.

"Am I imagining it or has a wall come between us?" Julie called him on his retreat.

"Caught me, I'm wondering just how safe it is for us to get close."

Dan was willing to admit that much to her but silently wondered whether or not he should try being more intimate with her before she knew the whole truth. He knew she might need time alone to resolve the conflicts the truth would no doubt create.

He found himself in a quandary. Where should the boundaries be laid out? Should he tell her tonight what Jack confessed in the letter? What of the experience did she remember? What was she purposely ignoring and what was she unconsciously forgetting? What should he bring up for discussion?

Nothing in that moment felt right.

"Dan, it's good to be with you again. Let's just enjoy the moment."

The hostess came outside to tell them that a table had been cleared for them. They made their way through the close, intimate space to the back room dimly lit by gaslight.

"I'll have a glass of non-alcoholic champagne and for the lady . . . ?" Dan looked at Julie, waiting for her answer.

"A white wine, please," Julie ordered, and then turned around to see the surrounding decor. "Sure is different from

Pete's Dive."

"Oh, that old place, I'm surprised you remember it. You know, Pete still runs it and all the kids in Smithfield hang out there. We sure left our mark there. Remember the table you could write poems on? Well, ours is still there. I go in for a slice of pizza sometimes when I visit my sister."

"Your sister, Judy, how is she?" Julie slipped easily into the light banter she and Dan seemed to have chosen for the evening.

"She's great, married to a professor at Rhode Island College, and has three kids ranging from ages five to twelve."

"And your parents, what about them?"

"They moved to South Carolina last year to be near my brother, who has an accounting firm outside Charleston. They love it there."

"And you, do you love it here?"

He sipped the champagne trying to buy more time to center, to pull back, to hold back, but could he? He faced Julie, silently waiting for his response. Unlike the night before, she looked so together, so integrated. Was it an illusion or was she really that practiced in stepping away from traumatizing feelings? He wanted to burst forth with his dream of leaving everything in Rhode Island and camping out on her doorstep, convincing her to be his love. Instead, he spoke to her as if he were talking to a colleague.

"I enjoy working at Providence General and living on the East Side. It's convenient to cultural activities, sports, downtown, and the neighborhoods are well maintained.

And, of course, the most important reason is that my two children live a few blocks from me. Rita and I share custody. This weekend I asked her to keep them so I could devote my time to you and Jack. We'll catch up next week."

"It's strange to think of you as a father. We were just kids together ourselves. Tell me about them."

He told her about the creative bent of his son, Chris. "He's ten and goes to after-school art classes at Rhode Island School of Design."

His eyes lit up when he spoke of his daughter. "Cathy's twelve, head of her class, a whiz at computers, and loves science. She's interested in my work which, as you can imagine, pleases me no end."

Dan took a sip from his drink, looked up and saw a soft look in Julie's eyes. He decided it was the moment to take the conversation to a deeper, more personal level.

"When we went for coffee yesterday I told you about my alcoholism and recovery, and I want to confess something else. I need to talk about our separation when you moved to California?"

"Oh Dan, it was so long ago. Why go back there?"

"As part of my recovery, I've had to face what I did to others and make amends when possible. I was hoping there would be a chance to ask you in person for forgiveness."

Julie looked down and tapped the edge of her glass. After what seemed like forever to Dan, she lifted her eyes and responded, "I'm listening."

Tears filled his eyes as he confessed, "I let the world think that you broke my heart by leaving me when, in

Mariah Martin

reality, I caused the hurt to myself, and probably to you, by being a drunk. Through the years I played the drama over and over again. My girl, the girl I wanted to marry, deserted me. I used that drama to excuse myself from the sin of holding back love from my wife and kids, the love and respect they deserved."

Julie sat frozen. Dan was looking off to the side, wrapped up in guilt.

He continued, "Rita called me on it. After she moved out on me, I hit bottom. My sister and my doctor intervened. Thanks to a month at Beach Road Recovery Center, I'm alive and sober."

He turned back to Julie seeking her forgiveness. He saw that she had retreated inside herself and wasn't listening anymore. He touched her arm, "Julie, are you with me? I'm sorry, it was insensitive of me to talk about drinking after what Jack's alcoholism did to you."

Shocked, she snapped back and demanded, "How do you know about that?"

Dan remembered that Julie didn't know her father had been in AA with him or that Jack had confessed in the letter.

"Your father already gave me permission to let you know that he shared with me what he did under the influence of alcohol. We attend the same AA meetings. He told me how he ruined your childhood with his drinking. When we were younger, in and out of each other's homes, just about all the adults drank as a social sharing. Nothing seemed that different about your father's drinking. I didn't fathom what you were going through."

"No one did."

"I thought when you left for Vermont you were just getting away from the pain of losing your mother. Every time I went to visit you in Vermont it felt awkward between us. God, I was stupid and insensitive."

"What do you mean?'

"You were so serious about your plans to get into a good school, to move West—I just assumed you felt finished with all of us in Rhode Island. Sure we had some fun times but Julie, you had goals and what did I have, impulses. I just wanted to go out and get drunk or get you in the backseat of my corvette. When you asked me to go to college with you in California, I felt too scared to go. I didn't want you to see me as a fool. Also, on weekends when we weren't together, I was drinking a lot with my buddies. It's hard to admit that I didn't want to choose between you and my fun times. Besides, I doubted that you really meant it when you asked me to leave New England with you."

"You were my world then. My mother was dead, I wasn't close to my family anymore and you were the only person who I believed loved me. It devastated me when you chose Brown instead of Berkeley. But that was a long time ago and we're both grown-ups now. Let's just forget it and enjoy our visit."

"It doesn't matter how many years ago I flaked out on you, it still matters. I'm sorry, Julie. I want to be strong for you." Dan reached over and touched Julie's hand and added, "Perhaps to start new with you, at least as a friend."

"Let's talk about that later." Julie tightly clutched her wineglass.

"That's fine." Dan answered in his neutral doctor mode. He wondered if he exposed too much; if he blew his chance for reconnection. He pulled back a little and asked, "All right, I'll drop talking about us but can we talk a little more about your father?"

"Dan, he's not in my life anymore except in my nightmares. I want them to end. I don't want to think about him anymore, but my therapist has assured me that if I remember more about my childhood, the nightmares will stop."

"I wasn't aware that your memories were blocked."

"The time between my mother dying and Nana taking me to Vermont is very hazy--even memories of Anne. You're the only one that's clear in my mind."

It was Dan's turn to freeze up in reaction. He sat quietly, trying to figure out if he should just read her the letter from her father, tell her the contents, or wait until the morning meeting. He wanted to handle the situation in a clear, responsible way. He didn't want to hurt her all over again.

"Dan, you look worried. What's going on?"

He filled her in on the letter; how it was delivered to him this morning and how he was directed to have it read to her and her sister in the presence of Tom, Emma and himself.

Before he lost his nerve, he explained further his reluctance to give the letter to her, "Since Jack had confided in me, I feel the need to act according to his wishes. Emma has agreed to meet with all of us tomorrow morning in your father's office to read the letter out loud."

"You bastard! You have the gall to sit there and know everything but you're not going to tell me? What kind of power trip are you on!" She glared at him.

Dan wanted to run, to hide, and at the same time, he wanted to spill out all he knew, but for some reason he also felt compelled to honor Jack's dictates.

"You've every right to be furious. Maybe I'm being pig-headed about this, but I want to give Jack the respect that he would hopefully give me if I had confessed to him."

Dan picked up his drink and continued, "For too long I let booze and impulse rule my judgment. This time I'm going to risk losing your friendship, not because of the booze, but because of what my higher power tells me to do. Julie, tomorrow morning your father will bear his soul to you and Anne. I, in good conscience, can't short-circuit the process. I only hope that you can understand my choice!"

Julie sat stunned. She appeared to be fighting rage but Dan could only wait for her reaction. Would she accept his position? If she couldn't, he assumed that any hope of rekindling their love was over.

For what seemed like a complete spin of the earth around the sun, they sat in their own realities. Dan was too confused to be able to sense what Julie was feeling.

Finally, Julie broke down. She bowed her head, crying quietly as if she could pull the tears back into her heart as they fell from her eyes. "Dan, I feel like you have abandoned me again."

He reached across the table and took her hand. "I know. I wish you could feel how much I'm really here for you, but I can't break a vow to another member of AA to save you from pain. Believe me. I've done everything in my power to get this resolved for you so you can be free. I hate to see you haunted by Jack's deeds."

He moved his chair closer and hugged her. "Please, know that it's my intention that this situation is handled with sensitivity. If I were to tell you what was told to me in confidence, how would I have any integrity and honor?"

Did his words reach into her heart as he intended? He couldn't tell.

Julie closed her eyes and whispered, "Maybe you're right. I guess I do need to be able to trust you." She opened her eyes and looked at Dan. "That is, if we're going to get to know each other as adults."

"Yes, as far as I'm concerned, Julie Fitzsimmons Taylor is never leaving my life again. And I want you to feel sure that I'll never break my word to you. Never."

For an unmeasured moment they sat in the space of trust that they just created. He reached over and ran a finger along the side of her face. "You look tired. Do you want to turn in for the evening?"

She sighed, "Yes, let's go to your place."

With a quiet sense of reverence for what they had just shared, Dan drove Julie back to his apartment. While Julie checked for any information that her office might have emailed her, Dan listened to his phone messages. Both Tom and Emma had called to confirm the meeting.

Julie looked so worn out, so vulnerable that Dan wasn't even tempted to push any boundary of sharing or desire. When she finished looking over the statistics that were sent to her and sent back her opinions, she sat on the couch. She glanced around the apartment with a blank look. Dan sensed that she needed some time alone to regroup.

"You look like you're ready to crash. I have to go to the hospital to check on some patients. Why don't you take my bed and I'll sleep in my son's room. Use anything you need. There are clean towels on the top shelf in the bathroom."

She surprised him, suggesting, "When you come back, why don't you join me in the bed? I could use the company. I'm not sure if I'm ready for more, but I could use a strong man to fend off the nightmares."

"Sure. If just lying next to me will slay the dragons of the night, I surrender my presence to your service, my lady. It'll be like our old camping days when we shared a sleeping bag to guard each other from the spooks in the woods. I also need a good night's sleep and having you next to me will soothe my soul."

He smiled to reassure her that he wouldn't push for more just yet.

Dan walked back to the hospital, checked on some of his patients, saving his most important one for last.

The nurses and interns assured him that Jack's condition hadn't changed; the respirator was keeping him alive.

"Mrs. Howe, take a break. I can stay for ten minutes or

so."

"Thanks, Dr. Hill. I could use a cup of coffee."

He sat for a moment feeling his rage. In a one-way dialogue with his patient and friend, Dan poured out his emotions.

"How could you sacrifice your daughter that way? How could you pretend to have a happy home while Julie lived in exile? I know, damn it, I know much of it was the dry drunk behavior. Oh, Jack, you were sober but just as sneaky as when you were drinking."

Dan got up and walked around the still body in the bed. When the nurses looked in, they assumed that Dan was doing his doctor duties. But all the while, under his breath, he admonished the silent patient prone before him.

"All those years of being a dry drunk. Why the hell couldn't you just get yourself to AA before last year! Is this letter a fake, a way to stay important after you die? I know I'm not supposed to judge you, but, in God's name, why the hell did you wait so long?"

Dan had to hold back the tears that burned his eyes. His body ached with the pain caused by years of lost love, by years of his running away, by sacrifices he imposed on his own children, and the pain of lies compounded upon lies.

"Dr. Hill, is there anything you want to change in his orders?" Mrs. Howe came back into the room and reach up to hook-up a new IV solution.

"No, I was just in the hospital and thought I'd see how he was doing. Call Dr. Long if there's any problem."

He went to the doctor's lounge to pull himself together

so that when he went home, he could stay focused on what was good for both of them. Tomorrow would be stressful enough.

The lounge was too busy, so he went to the chapel. There was a big book from AA sitting on one of the benches. He opened it and read the part about turning confusion over to the higher power rather than trying to control it. Forgotten promises, buried in the tombs of his memory, arose and flooded his mind. Dan sloughed over with the weight of regret pressing down on him. One time in particular burned in his brain, the last day his daughter depended on him--the day he killed her trust.

His daughter had gotten all dressed up for a father/daughter dance in the sixth grade. She had shopped for weeks searching for the perfect outfit. Her mother had let her get a pair of high heels. Everything was set. He left the hospital in plenty of time to get home, eat, dress and escort his only daughter to the last dance she would want to attend with her father.

Thinking about what he did made him feel sick. He fought his shame. Distraught, his only connection with sobriety was surrender.

He admonished himself for not going straight home from work. No, not him, he had to stop at O'Leary's for reinforcements. Booze was his precious love that night, not his daughter. Before his eyes flashed images of her sitting by the door waiting for him, all dressed up.

How could he have done that, sacrificed his daughter's love and trust to the altar of alcohol? Who was he to judge

Jack?

Immobile with grief, Dan felt a light expose the core of his being and wash it clear with God's forgiveness. He thought of Jack and asked to be forgiven for judging him.

By the time he left the hospital, the sky had sunk into the deep dark of late night. Dan opened his apartment door very quietly, put his jacket on the back of a chair and went into the kitchen to have a glass of juice. Opening the refrigerator, he drank from the carton as he usually did when alone. He jumped in surprise when Julie's arms wrapped around him from the back.

"Welcome home. I've been waiting for you." Julie moved around to come into his arms. "I need you tonight. Come to bed with me."

Without hesitating, he picked her up and kicked the refrigerator door closed. On the way to the bedroom, they kissed with passion, with desperation. Not wanting to let go of each other, they fell onto the already warmed bed. The urgency of their need drew them into a quick, explosive release. As Dan withdrew from her, Julie clung to him. No words were necessary.

They slipped into dreaming together.

13

SUNDAY

Anne stood at the entrance of the Waterman Office Building, one she had been through a thousand times to visit her father. This time she approached the door and started to shake.

"I can't do it. I just can't go in there. I'm furious at Dad. I can't believe that he brought Julie back after all this time." Anne collapsed into her husband's arm and pleaded, "It's just too hard to be here in this empty office. Take me home."

Tom steadied her, ignored her pleas and guided her into the building. "You'll know soon enough why you have to stay for this meeting. I'll be right next to you all the way. You don't have to talk or deal with the others if you don't want to."

"Fuck you! What the hell's going on! I hate it when you talk "cop"! She pulled away and turned her back to him.

"Sorry. But for God's sake, can't we just do this meeting and get it over with?"

"Let's go home." Anne headed towards the door, but before she went in, Emma arrived and hugged her.

"Thanks for coming. I've been so worried about you. I

thought it best not to come out to Abbey's Run because Tom told me that you were painting and needed to be alone," said Emma.

Anne didn't respond.

Emma stepped back in reaction to Anne's coldness. "Look, Anne, I don't like what your father has done or the way he manipulated this situation with Julie, but I hope my handling it for him won't come between us. Jack engineered this meeting, but believe me, getting this cleared up will be best for all of us," she said.

Anne looked at Emma and after a few long tense moments, responded, "My father seems to be creating one mess after another, but I realize that he orchestrated this whole turn of events without any of us having a say in it. So, let's just get on with it." They walked upstairs and opened Jack's office.

Emma shivered. "I'm going downstairs to turn up the heat and make some coffee. Do either of you want a cup?"

Anne turned away and with a shrug of her shoulders and said, "I don't need more stimulation. Just being in my father's office is enough." She walked by her father's desk without looking at it, crossed to the far side of the room and curled up on the couch.

Tom sat next to his wife without a word. She had no idea how frantic he felt inside as he wondered how his wife would react to the news she was about to receive. Anne was used to him retreating when she was angry with him, but she didn't care what he was doing. A current of anxiety crept down her back sending erratic pulses of hot energy through her nerves. Wanting to jump out of her skin, she got up and paced back and forth, shaking her hands in the air to throw off her nerves' excess energy. She turned and looked at her father's chair and as if he was sitting there, screamed, "Damn you. Why did you have to bring Julie back?"

"I'm just as upset as you are about being here," Julie said as she and Dan entered the room.

The sisters looked at each other, molecules of fear filling the air between them. Anne was shocked at what she saw--a vision of her grandmother reflected in her older sister. It took everything she had not to burst into tears and bolt from the room.

Anne abruptly turned away from her sister and looked at Dan. "I didn't know you'd be here."

Dan responded to her anger. "Anne, I understand how difficult this must be for you. If you feel my presence is intrusive, I'll wait outside while Emma reads the letter from your father."

Anne brushed him aside and said, "I don't care if you stay. You're not the one I have a problem with."

Emma went over to Jack's large walnut desk and sat in the thick leather chair. Dan handed her the letter to read and pulled two armchairs close together for him and Julie.

Emma looked at Julie, then at Anne and said, "Let's get started. I, for one, am eager to get this over with. Before I read this letter that your father wrote to both of you, I want it known that I wasn't aware of this situation until yesterday. And if I had known, I would have advised your father to approach his concerns differently."

She gazed down at the letter and sighed, "Nonetheless, he acted in his usual determined way when he set this up. After the letter is read, you'll probably want to take time to digest the contents. Enough said." Emma began reading.

To My Dearest Daughters,

If these words are being read to you, I'm either dead or near so. It also means that I wasn't brave enough to face you with the truth and live with the consequences.

Julie, I imagine it took courage to return to Rhode Island. I can only hope that my telling the truth will spare you any more pain.

Anne, I've tried to be the best father you could have, but it didn't make up for what I robbed from you, even if you're not aware of the immensity of that theft. It is time to set the record straight. Don't blame your sister for leaving you, blame me.

What I'm about to reveal is the actual reason why your sister left us. Forgive me, my dearest Anne, for all the lies of omission that were left to rot in your heart. Let the truth unravel the web of deception that Nana and I created.

Anne, dearest, you might not remember how your mother's health was fragile with diabetes for the last years of her life. What we never told you, for obvious reasons, was that after your birth,

*your mother's disease progressed to the point
where it prevented her from participating fully in
life. She withdrew from me and turned her
attention to her children.*

*Julie, as the older daughter, you took on
many of your mother's responsibilities. That
freed her up to share the best of life with both of
you: the horses, the singing, the cooking, and her
favorite stories. It was as if she knew her time was
short and she wanted to leave her love imprinted
in each of you.*

Anne couldn't believe it—he praised Julie as if she
helped her mother. What was going on? She had trouble
listening to Emma read, and it was almost impossible to
hear what was being said.

*Rather than being appreciative of your
mother's love, I turned to alcohol. After work I'd
go for a couple of drinks, then I'd go home and
drink some more. Sober, I'd never raised my
voice to your mother; drunk, I'd spewed my rage
at her. But nothing could excuse what I did the
last night of your mother's life. It is excruciating
to admit to you and to myself that I could be the
cause of so much pain.*

Emma paused, looked up from the letter and took in
silent stares of the sisters.

"Anne . . . Julie, I could stop here and leave things as they are. . . ."

Neither responded. Tom encouraged her to continue, "Go on with it, Emma. They need to hear this. Just read it and get it over with."

"Very well," Emma sighed and began reading.

I spent the evening at a fundraiser for my upcoming re-election. The wives of the other candidates accompanied them to the event. Disappointed that Elizabeth was too weak to join me, I went from table to table drinking with each group trying to cover up the social disadvantage of having an absent spouse.

In those days not having your wife with you was political suicide. By the end of the evening, I was an out-of-control drunk. The last conscious memory I have, is of leaving the Grange hall and being driven home toward Abbey's Run.

Jack went on to report how what happened that night changed all their lives but, to his horror, he didn't remember any of it. He remembered waking up in a detox unit at Beach Road Recovery Center. His mother was standing over him holding a document for him to sign. It was an agreement that he'd never drink again. She made him promise to get sober and stay sober or she would take both of his daughters away from him. If he drank, she would go to the police with the truth.

Anne sat frozen. She looked at her sister who stared down at the floor. There was no way to see what Julie was feeling but her body seemed to be shrinking. Anne shut her eyes as if to close off from the words, but Emma kept reading Jack's letter.

According to his mother, he created chaos in his drunken state. Julie had come downstairs after doing her homework. She noticed that look in her mother's eyes signaling that her blood sugar was dropping. From taking care of her mother so much in the last year, Julie knew that her mom needed some orange juice to avoid losing consciousness. Julie was walking into the kitchen to get the juice when Jack stormed into the house.

Furious, I yelled at your mother for abandoning me and not acting like my wife. Julie, you tried to calm me down, but I grabbed you and started saying that maybe you could fill in for your mother. Elizabeth got up to protect you from me. I pushed you away and went after your mother to force her to kiss me, but she backed away. This action fueled my rage and I hit her.

She screamed. This enraged me even more. I pushed her hard and she fell down against the fireplace, hitting her head against the stone edge of the hearth. I didn't even bend down to see if she was all right. I turned to you, Julie, and told you that I felt avenged that she was suffering as much as I was and the score was even. I then went upstairs.

Anne's eyes flashed open and fixed on her sister. Julie was still staring at the floor but now her fingers were pressed together as to take on a pale, bloodless look. Her lips pressed together in a crunched tightness. Anne recognized that look, it was one that Nana had—tight lips, tight jaw and fixated eyes—right before blowing up over some mishap or crying for no apparent reason that Anne could tell as a child. It was easier for Anne in that moment to obsess over what Julie was doing or looking like than hear the toxic words her father wrote.

Your grandmother came to the house right after I left the room. She found you, Julie, bent over your mother, crying. You told her what I had done. Somehow Nana convinced you not to let the paramedics know the full story when they came to the house. She had you lie and tell them that your mother passed out from lack of sugar and fell.

The paramedics believed your story. Then, somehow, you and Nana got me into the car and she drove me to the treatment center. That was the last time we were together.

It was hard for me to accept that I killed my wife and almost molested my daughter, tearing our family apart. Until her death, Nana shamed me into staying sober. After she died, I fell off the wagon. I had several car accidents. Because I was an ex-senator and my son-in-law was a retired cop, the police looked the other way.

"Stop! Stop!" Anne wanted to scream but sat silent, horrified by what was being said. She couldn't believe what she was hearing. Her father went on to confess that he was found out as an alcoholic by Dan during a physical examination. He accepted Dan's invitation to an Alcoholics Anonymous meeting not out of caring for his family, but out of fear of being exposed. This couldn't be her Dad.

She never saw her father drunk or have even one drink, for that matter. She had always assumed that he choose not to drink out of respect for his profession and responsibilities as a single father. What was really happening here—a confession or a story to cover for his lost daughter, Julie, the true culprit and cause of her mother's death? Anne could barely sit to hear the rest of the letter.

Julie, how can you ever forgive me for letting you live so isolated, so burdened with the truth of what really happened? Anne, how can you ever forgive me for letting you think that Julie didn't love you enough to come home? My only hope for salvation is that you can rediscover your love for each other. So often I longed to see the two of you together again, my beautiful daughters, but my cowardice was stronger than my dream. I never had the courage to do what it took to bring the two of you together.

Please don't let my weakness of character stand between you anymore. What more can I say except that my heart cries out to you. I can't even begin to hope for your forgiveness; all I can hope for is that you will be able to forgive each other and rediscover the love for each other that your mother always had for you.

Dad

Emma closed the letter and waited. The air in the room ceased moving. Everyone sat still.

Rising up out of the calm, Anne stood and shouted at her sister, "You lying bitch! I knew it, you made up that story. You didn't give Mom her juice in time. You had Nana and Dad believe that he killed her, but I don't believe you. I hate you." She grabbed her purse and ran out of the room. Tom rushed out of the room to attend to Anne.

****

Dan and Emma turned to Julie. She was mumbling to herself. Dan knelt down in front of her, held her hands and coaxed her to tell them what she was saying to herself. She looked at him and said, "I always thought that I had killed my mother by choosing to take care of Daddy instead of getting her juice in time. I thought they sent me away because they were ashamed of me. Mom depended on me and I let her down. I let her die. That's what I thought happened."

"You don't remember what happened, do you?" Emma asked in a tone of disbelief.

"No," Julie mumbled.

Emma leaned closer and said, "It's hard for me to think of Jack as a murderer, but I don't believe that you let your mom die without doing your best to her help her."

Dan touched Julie's hand and looked squarely into her eyes, "Even though he doesn't remember what happened that night, your father believes that in his drunken state, he killed your mother. Anne's upset but she was too young to understand."

"My father was drunk and out of his mind. He might have made up that story to justify to himself why he let Nana send me away. It would be like him to claim the power to kill rather than admit that he raised such a weak daughter. Or, Nana told him that story to cover up what I did. She would never talk about what happened, always saying some things are best buried with the dead."

"No. No. I remember the kind of woman your grandmother was, proud and stubborn. She couldn't stand the thought of having her family business become public. She sent you away so she didn't have to face having such a weak child, your father. It was her shame that hurt you, not yours," Dan insisted.

Julie covered her eyes and pulled herself into a ball. After a seemly endless minute, she uncurled, sat up straight and said coolly, "I just want to get away from this. I don't care what Anne believes. It doesn't matter anymore." She stood up and turned to Dan. "I want some time alone. Do you mind if I go to your apartment and rest."

Dan was taken aback by her coldness and sudden withdrawal. "Sure, I'll drive you." He answered calmly, but his heart raced with fear that he would lose her again.

"I'd rather walk. Don't worry about me. I'm relieved to have seen Anne again, even if she'll never forgive me. Dad's dying so we'll have to live with the confusion, but at least it's all out in the open." Julie faced Emma and said, "Thank you for your help. I'm sorry we all put you through this."

"You're not doing this. Jack's the one who created this situation. Believe me, Julie, I don't want to accept what your father confessed to have done, but freedom from this nightmare is what I wish for you."

"Having us all face the night my mother died is about as much freedom that's possible here. We need to get on with our lives. I'm in the middle of an important research project and I miss my dog. I'll go to court with you tomorrow and then leave for home. We'll talk later."

Julie reached out, shook Emma's hand and smiled at her. "I'm glad that my sister has a friend like you. It makes it easier for me to leave. See you in the morning."

Dan looked downhearted as Julie turned and walked out of the office.

"Give her some time," said Emma.

"You've been great. Hope you don't mind if I leave. I have to get to a meeting," said Dan.

"You do what you have to do. I need some time, too. Call me on my cell after the meeting so we can make plans for tomorrow."

Emma walked out of the office with Dan, neither of them saying anything.

14

THE CLEARING

Dan called his sponsor, Susan. "I want a drink. Oh, God, help me."

"There's a meeting over at The Rhodes Center in twenty minutes. I'll meet you there."

"Thanks Susan."

It had been a long time since his sobriety was so threatened. He could lose it all—Julie, his work, his kids, his health.

He took the stairs to the second floor of the science library and saw Susan waiting for him by the conference room door. He wanted to turn around, dash down the stairs and go to O'Leary's Pub. Nobody there cared what he did. It was his right to get drunk. He could turn around before she noticed him. He could tell her to get lost, that he would do what he wanted to do. He wanted to give in to the devil, to the gnawing in his belly, to his fear. But instead of running away, he forced himself to stay put.

Someone came up the stairs behind him and tugged on his elbow. "Hey man, you coming to the meeting?"

"Hi, Rick. I was just catching my breath. The stairs

remind me of my age," he lied as he walked down the hall with his friend.

Susan reached out and hugged him. "Glad you decided to come down the hall instead of running back down the stairs."

"You saw me?"

"Dan, you were deciding to stay sober or run. You had to make the choice. You've made it, at least for this moment. We'll talk after the meeting."

Feeling hollow, empty of all substance and strength, Dan sat and tried to focus on the other members as they shared their stories. How did he come back to this addictive feeling? Truths that he had learned over the years at AA flooded his consciousness. Let go of control. Turn to the high power. Live through the drama and detach from the outcome. Choose to live sober one moment at a time. Sobriety comes first. He repeated them over and over, to no avail. He still wanted to drink.

Everything and everyone drifted to the background except the desire to drink. Silently, he called out to God. "Lord, I'm lost. Take me over and fill me with your love and strength."

A wave of energy flowed from the top of his head to the bottom of his feet. He heard the voice of his higher power say, "My peace be with you."

The meeting's moderator asked, "Is there anyone else who wants to share?"

Dan stood up, walked to the podium and faced the group. He poured out his story of how he had reconnected with his old love and how the fear of losing her again had triggered his addictive feelings. Although it had been years since his last drink, in the last days he had felt like a drunk. He closed by sharing how he had reached out to his sponsor, prayed to his higher power and finally felt the healing power of surrender.

After the meeting he and Susan talked awhile, which helped anchor his renewed sobriety. No matter what happened between him and Julie, he would stay focused on his AA program and loving her.

****

Sean and Matt were waiting for her at home, but Emma couldn't bring herself to go there. She called Patrick on the car phone. "Glad I caught you. Do you have an hour or so for me?"

"You've been on my mind all day. Come down to the center and we'll talk," Patrick answered.

Emma found him in his office. He greeted her with a hug.

"Have a seat. I made you some kava tea."

"Aaah, that sounds good," she said.

Emma sighed slowly, letting her shoulders drop down and relax her ribs. How many times had Patrick encouraged her to notice that whatever crisis was happening in her life, if she stayed focused on her breath, she would be okay. Well, this day counted as one of those crises.

She let the warm steam swirl around her face, inhaling

the tea's aroma before sipping it. Feeling a little more settled, she looked at Patrick, who sat next to her and waited for her to speak. "I don't know if there's anything else I can do for Anne and Julie. I just needed some time with you to talk about all this. What we say will not leave this room, agreed?"

"Of course," Patrick answered.

Emma filled him in on what happened at the letter reading.

"I'm so mixed up about all of this—it's hard for me to accept that Jack killed his wife and rejected Julie. I just don't know what to do or for that matter, how to feel about it all."

"I understand, Emma, why you're so upset. Do you want to meditate together?"

They sat in silence for about half an hour. Emma pictured an angel shining light around her, her boys and the whole Fitzsimmons/Riley family. The meditation calmed her and helped her let go of the tension from the morning meeting. She opened her eyes and looked at Patrick, who was looking at her with a well of kindness.

Patrick spoke first. "Emma, I want to help."

"What do you mean?"

"Before Julie leaves Rhode Island, I could do a hypnotic regression and take her back to the moment of her mother's death. Do you think she would be open to that?"

"I don't know. It's hard to tell. But that's a generous offer, you're so busy."

"It would have to be today. Why don't you call her and

ask her. When we were meditating, I sensed her mother's presence and got the impression that she wants Julie to be free of this burden."

"Should she come here?'

"Ideally, with such short notice, regressing at the scene would speed things up, but don't worry about that right now. Find out if she is willing."

Emma called Julie at Dan's and explained Patrick's offer to her.

"Is that the man we met at Healthy Eats yesterday?" Julie asked.

"Why, yes. I'm glad you remember him. We've been meditating together and he was inspired to suggest this to you. I trust him."

Emma waited while Julie took time to consider the regression.

"It sounds similar to the work I do with Dr. Goldberg, my therapist. I do want to get to the truth, Emma, not the truth according to my father, but one I lived. If it doesn't work, I'm going to California and putting the whole thing out of my mind."

"I'll make the arrangements and call you when things are set. I have a good feeling about this. We all want it cleared up. I'll call you soon." Emma hung up and turned to Patrick, "I'm going home and will call Tom from there. He and Anne can decide if it's all right to use Abbey's Run for the regression. Should I call you here or at your house when we're ready?"

"I'll be here." Patrick reached over and gave Emma a

hug. "The Great Spirit is in charge here, not us."

"I feel that too. Talk to you soon," said Emma. She rushed out of the center and went home.

At her house she found her sons rummaging through the refrigerator for lunch food. "There's pastrami in the meat drawer. Make me a sandwich too--only leave off the mayo."

"Where you been, Ma?" they asked in unison.

"I'll tell you in a minute. First, I have to call Tom and Dan." Emma kissed them each on the cheek before going to the den for privacy. She was deeply relieved when Tom let go of his initial reluctance and agreed to set it up so they could use the living room at Abbey's Run. Maybe Julie felt she could let it all go after returning to Palo Alto, but how could she, Emma, stand to work at the firm, see her friend Anne and live with the confusion? Since this regression was as much for her peace of mind as it was for the sisters', she did her best to connect with Tom. "Thanks Tom for setting this up."

"I want this cleared up once and for all! I'll take Anne to town while you're here," Tom said and then asked, "Are you going to include Dan in this?"

"If he's not at the hospital, I'm sure he'll want to be there for Julie. Expect us around three."

"Remember, just use the living room," insisted Tom. "We'll be careful. Let's hope this works. See you later."

Over lunch, Emma told Matt and Sean that Jack's older daughter, who'd been estranged from the family, was in town and was in need of her help. She felt it best not to tell them anymore.

"What? Mr. Fitzsimmons has another daughter? God, that's weird," said Sean.

"How's Auntie Anne doing?" asked Matt.

"She's having a hard time. It looks like Jack's going to die and that's hard enough for her. And now she has to face a sister she hasn't seen in almost thirty years. Don't the two of you ever allow that to happen--understand?"

"Don't worry, Mom, we're stuck with each other," Matt assured her.

"I have to go out to Abbey's Run for a while. What are your plans for today?"

"We'll be here. I don't know about Matt, but I have tons of homework to do."

"Me, too. Don't worry about us, Mom." Matt touched her hand to reassure her.

Emma hugged them each and retreated to her third floor suite to ready herself for the challenge to come.

****

Dan drove through the gates of Abbey's Run and stopped the car for a moment. It had all happened so fast: the confession, the AA meeting, and the talk with Julie to convince her to stay and try one more thing to heal her memories. He turned to Julie, who sat frozen with fear and asked, "Do you want to leave?"

"No, I'll never be free until I face what happened here, but I'm surprised that Anne's allowing us to come into her home to do this. Will she be there while Patrick works with me?"

"She'll be around. But at this point, she doesn't want to see or talk with you. Tom will let us in, but only Emma, Patrick and I will stay with you. I really question the wisdom of this, but if you want to give it a try, I'm with you all the way," Dan said.

"Thanks, but even if you left, I'd still need to do this."

"Why put yourself through the trauma again?"

"If I go back to California without knowing the truth, I might never be able to be free of the nightmares that have interrupted my life." She reached down to cover his right hand that still gripped the gear stick. "Let's go. I'm ready."

As he drove toward the house, Dan wondered if Emma, who was already there, had been successful in explaining Patrick's plan to Anne and Tom. His concern was well founded, for Emma was at that moment working hard to overcome Anne's resistance. Despite Tom's efforts, Anne had refused to leave her home.

"Honey, you think your father is lying to protect Julie, but what if he isn't? Do you want to always wonder what the truth is? That doesn't sound like the Anne I know, the one who always tackles things head on. Patrick believes that doing the regression in the room where your mother died might unlock Julie's memory."

"Yeah, but she could lie about what she remembers. I hate the idea of letting her back into this house!" Anne said. But underneath her resistance, she was opening to the idea of Julie coming to Abbey's Run.

Tom responded quickly to the slight easing of his wife's rigid stance against Julie coming to their home. "Honey, you're accusing Julie of the worst of crimes without giving her a chance to clear herself. This is not just for Julie; this is for our family. You're angry, you're sad, you're confused, but don't be unfair and cold hearted."

"That bitch! You dare defend her! She's the one who let my mother die and then took off without even caring what happened to me. How could you ask me to allow her in my home? My home! It's not hers anymore."

Wise in the ways of dealing with his headstrong wife, Tom changed his approach. "You're right. You're absolutely right, she's asking a lot of you but please, honey, do this for me."

"Why?"

Tom pointed out to his wife that he was in a bind because if her father confessed that he murdered his wife, he, as a retired policeman, was still obligated to defend the law. "Have you forgotten that I have to have someone arrested if I know they committed a murder? Don't you see, Jack knew that? Was he hiding from me all these years, or was he just protecting Julie? I've got to do whatever I can to find the answer."

"So what are you saying to me—you're going to be a cop again? If Julie remembers not giving my mother her juice, you'll arrest her? Or do you plan to arrest my father before he dies?"

Tom grabbed the sides of his head and pulled his hair as if he could open his skull and pull out the right answer.

"If Julie remembers that she's guilty of neglect, of course I won't turn her in. Your father and grandmother were responsible for your mother's care, not your sister. But, honey, if it comes out that Jack is guilty, I'll have to arrange for him to be arrested when and if he comes out of the coma."

"Well, well, aren't you the good citizen?" Anne snarled.

"Either way, we have to do what it takes to clear this up. If we don't, I'll always feel that I was part of a conspiracy and I don't want that. I can't stop being a cop just because it's family."

Tom didn't share with his wife the suspicion that Jack had made it easy for him to leave the force and run Anne's business by giving them Abbey's Run. Was he bribed? Tom wanted to know.

Anne took food out of the refrigerator, slamming bags of potatoes and carrots onto the cutting board. Both Tom and Emma knew enough not to speak or try to reason with her until she calmed herself. The potatoes were scrubbed raw and the carrots were chopped into little pieces before Anne let down her guard.

"Fine! Fine, let them do it but they can only use the living room. Got it?" Anne pronounced.

"Yes, honey, I'll take care of it. Are you going to wait in the studio?"

"I don't know. What about the kids?" asked Anne.

Tom had it all worked out. He wanted them out of way and not exposed to the story of death and loss. Rose was at Tracy's and John was at Kyle's. Richard dropped them off

250

on his way to the library.

Anne turned to Emma. "I hear a car in the driveway; take care of my home. You hear me?"

"Believe me, Anne, I won't let anything happen that will harm anything here or disturb your family. I promise you," Emma stated with strength but she was not so sure of herself.

"Bring them in through the front door right into the living room. I don't want to see them," Anne said and left the room.

Tom went out to greet Dan and Julie, and Emma joined Patrick in the living room.

****

"I'm going to check with Tom to make sure it's all clear," said Dan. He left Julie in the car while he walked up the stone walkway past the rose garden to the door.

Tom stood in the doorway with his arms folded tightly over his chest.

Dan approached but stood back a bit. "Hi Tom, thanks for arranging this with Anne."

"Look, Dan, like I told you yesterday, I'm doing this to protect my family." Tom didn't wait for Dan to respond. He walked by him and went to the car. "Hi, Julie. Patrick and Emma are waiting for you in the house. Your sister wants Emma to stay in the room with you and Patrick. Anne's not comfortable with all of this. She and I will stay out of sight. You can use the living room but that's it."

Julie stepped out of the car and swayed a little. Tom automatically reached out to steady her. "Are you all right?"

She leaned back against the car. "Just give me a moment to gather myself. Being back at Abbey's Run is a shock."

Dan came over to her and took her hand. "You're not alone anymore, hold my hand."

She gently squeezed his hand in return and whispered, "I'm ready."

They walked up the path to the front door. Tom opened it and stood aside. She stopped in the foyer and came home.

"I don't recognize anything. This won't work. I don't know what I'm doing here. It's all strange to me. It's not the house I lived in."

"Julie, we renovated most of the house to modernize it. We had to make it our own. This hall, the stairs and the rooms to the left are all new. Come this way, you might remember more." Tom led her into the living room.

She froze. "My God, nothing's changed." Her words were barely audible.

"Yeah, when your father gave us the house he stipulated that this room remain the same until after his death. We changed the wallpaper and slip covers several times but always kept the same patterns. You looked shocked."

"I . . . I just can't believe it."

Patrick walked up to her and said, "We won't begin until you feel comfortable being back in this space. We'll wait for you to let us know. Walk around, get used to being here. Take your time."

Julie looked at Emma and said, "I'm so glad you're here."

"Just let me know if you need anything of me. I hope it clears up the confusion for you and for us all."

"If you have everything you need, I'll go be with my wife. I hope this works. Good luck," Tom said.

"We're all set," Patrick assured him.

Before joining Anne in the kitchen, Tom put his hand firmly on Julie's shoulder and in a calm tone told her, "Take your time."

Tom turned and hugged Emma and said, "Be careful. I'm depending on you." He then nodded head to Patrick and Dan as if they were speaking the silent language of the male protector tribe as Julie has seen him in her dreams.

Julie slowly made her way around the room. She stroked the thick, floral patterned chintz couch slipcovers. She picked up one of the two of pillows that had hand-woven roses on them. Holding it to her heart she closed her eyes and sighed, "Mom!"

After several moments she put the pillow back down in the corner of the couch, patting it gently a few times before turning to Emma. "My mother had these made to match her favorite flowers in the garden. Sometimes when my father was out drinking, Mom would sit here in front of the fire, clutching a pillow. She would call out to me for help. Now, I need her help."

"I know that she can hear you and is probably with you

right now." Emma stepped a little closer to Julie, picked up the pillow and offered it to her. "Maybe it would help if you held this."

"Maybe." Julie brought it once again to her heart as she continued to move around the room.

She walked over to the shelves that lined each side of the fireplace, pausing to run her fingers along the edges of the collection of old books. "My grandmother was so proud of this first edition collection of Dickens. Mom loved to read to me after Anne had been put to bed and we were alone. So many nights we were alone while Dad was out drinking."

Julie leaned forward, resting her head on the edge of a shelf and whispered words by Dickens, "It was the best of times, it was the worst of times.'" If you really knew, Mom, how bad it's become."

She stopped, drew into herself and gathered her resolve. She looked up and nodded to Patrick and said, "I'm ready."

"Before every healing session, I dedicate my work to the Great Spirit by using the rituals my grandmother taught me. She's a Cherokee elder. Every time we gathered she would start our time together by doing a medicine circle blessing. I always felt so much love and peace when she lit the sage."

"I lived in South America where I witnessed healers in their trances, so I'm somewhat aware of what you're about to do. I'm comfortable with whatever you need to do," said Julie.

Patrick opened his backpack and took out a white

candle, a peace pipe, an eagle feather and some loose herbs that he placed in a small ceramic bowl. He laid them out ceremoniously in a circle on the coffee table.

Julie stood in front of them between Dan and Emma.

Patrick explained, "First, I will smudge the room."

Dan asked, "What's smudging?"

"Blessing the room with sacred smoke," Patrick answered.

He lit the herbs, blew out the flame, and moved through the room, waving the smoke with the feather while chanting an ancient healing prayer. Without waiting for approval, he waived the feather in front of Dan, surrounding his body with the smoke coming from the smoldering sage and cedar. Continuing, he then did the same to Emma and Julie. Next, Patrick handed the bowl to Emma, who respectfully reciprocated the ritual around him. Sacredness filled the room, making it easier for all of them to relax.

Patrick sat in front of the coffee table lighting the white candle of protection before proceeding to the peace pipe. He turned to Julie and said, "I'll first offer the pipe to the guardians of the four directions, then to Father Sky, Mother Earth and to each of you. It speaks of our unity with the Great Spirit."

At that moment, Julie wasn't a rational scientist or a disturbed daughter but a seeker receiving the blessings of a shaman. The shadows of the underworld were ready to be faced.

The spiritual ritual completed, Patrick turned to Julie

and said, "Come sit here on the couch. Julie, there are two ways we could continue. I want you to choose the one you are most comfortable doing with me. First, we could do a soul retrieval, during which I will visit your soul reality to experience the truth as you know it on the spiritual level of existence. Or, I could use a procedure of memory recall."

"How would you do that? Dr. Goldberg, my therapist in California has tried to help me remember, but it hasn't worked."

"Has he hypnotized you?"

"No, not that I am aware of."

"Well, we could try a light hypnotic trance and see if that helps open your subconscious. I am a trained hypnosis counselor."

"Yoga, readings, and hypnosis—you sure are different than Dr. Goldberg. I trust him and sitting here with you, I trust you. What do you think is the best way?'

"Because of your familiarity with memory recall work, let's do the hypnosis today."

"That sounds good to me."

"You stay right here on the couch and I'll sit in this armchair. Emma and Dan, make yourselves comfortable on the window seat."

"Dan, Julie might express some intense feelings as she recalls the event. If you'd have difficulty holding back from reaching out to her, perhaps you should wait in another room. Any disturbance while she's in a depth state of concentration could upset her."

"No, no, I'm staying," Dan insisted.

"I'll sit with Dan," said Emma.

"Very well then, but please don't speak or move about during the session."

Patrick proceeded to lead Julie into a hypnotic trance, giving her the suggestion that she could come out of it any time she wasn't feeling safe. "You're in charge of this experience; I'm only here to guide you and help you move along in your memory recall. Lift your right pinky if you're ready to go deeper into the trance."

Julie raised her finger and slipped into a state of deep relaxation—her eyes almost closed and her head bent. She heard in muffled tones the directions being given to her. Somehow, Julie found herself in the past, on the night her mother died. She looked around and found herself in the upstairs hall. It was dark. She heard her mother downstairs, crying. She went down and sat next to her mother on the couch, trying to comfort her.

"Jules, sweetie, I'm going to be fine. I just had a hard time sleeping and I feel a little faint. My blood sugar must be low. Would you get some orange juice for me and then you better get to bed. You have a big day tomorrow with the show at the Barrington Stables."

"Don't worry about the show, Mom. I want to stay down here with you until you feel better."

"Just get my juice and I'll be all set." She patted Julie on the cheek.

Julie leaned over to kiss her mother before getting the juice, but stopped short on her way to the kitchen. There was a cab pulling up to the house.

"Oh, Mom, it's Dad coming home in a cab. He must be drunk again. Here, let me get you upstairs before he comes in; then I'll help him to bed."

"No, No! You hurry off to bed." Her mother sounded frightened.

Her father had been getting more and more out of control and no way did Julie plan to leave her mother alone with him.

"I'm staying right here with . . . ." Before she could finish, her father stumbled through the front door.

"Go to bed, Julie, right now. Please."

Jack looked at his daughter hovering over his wife and exploded, "Ah, my precious wife, sitting home, being catered to, being loved but me . . . me!" He got louder and louder.

As Julie remembered that night, she started to shake and hyperventilate.

Patrick touched her arm and whispered, "It's all right to step back away from the memory. You're in a safe place, just observe the memory. Breathe and let yourself find the way."

She calmed down but continued reliving the scene in her mind. Her father grabbed her and pulled her away from her mother.

"Go upstairs. Leave me alone with your mother. Go on, get out of here!" he screamed at Julie.

"No, Dad, Mom needs my help," Julie insisted.

He turned from Julie and went to pick her mother up off the couch but stumbled backwards falling against the fireplace mantle, cursing.

Julie, frightened that his temper was heating up, tried to calm him down before he became uncontrollable. "Come on Dad, I'll help you upstairs." But it was too late.

"The hell with both of you! I'll get what I want. Go to bed like I told you to. I gotta have some time alone with my wife."

He lunged at her mother but Julie stopped him. Furious, he pushed her aside.

"Get out of my way! It's time that I get some loving and attention."

Elizabeth pleaded with Jack to stop ranting. "Honey, come sit on the couch so you can tell me about the dinner at the Biltmore. Julie will get my juice while you fill me in on what happened and who was there."

"Oh no you don't, you're not fooling me. You want me to pass out on the couch. Well, I'm not that drunk! You get up! Give me a kiss, now." Jack spun around on his heels pointing to his mouth and insisting with slurred speech, "Give it to me now!"

"Honey, I'm dizzy and feeling weak. I'll kiss you after I have some juice. Julie, go get it, I'll be fine with your father. Go ahead, leave us."

"Get up and come over to me. Light my fire." Jack leaned back against the mantle.

"I can't Jack, I'm just too tired."

"Well then, I'll take myself into the kitchen to get a kiss from Julie, she's old enough to enjoy a good kiss." He snatched Julie as she came back through the door. She dropped the glass, the juice splattered all over the Oriental rug. She struggled to free herself from him.

Her mother screamed out. "Get your hands off of her, she's your daughter. Get away from her, get away . . ."
Elizabeth stood and reached out to pull her husband away from Julie, which further enraged Jack. He turned and pushed her down with a strong sweep of his arm. Julie screamed as she watched her mother fall backwards, hitting her head on the stone border of the fireplace. Her father muttered something about stupid, cold-hearted women, stepped over his wife and stumbled upstairs to his bedroom.

Julie knelt next to her mother. She touched her face. It was turning gray. She picked up her mother's wrist but felt no signs of life.

"Oh my God, oh my God," she cried. "You're dead, you're dead, oh my God, you're dead! I'm sorry, Mommy, I'm sorry!"

Julie was totally unaware of how long she sat holding her mother's hand before her grandmother showed up and took control.

The living room was still as Julie relived the moment of her mother's death. Patrick suggested that she envision herself stepping away from the scene in her mind and look back at the memory, to see if there was anything more she needed to remember or discover.

After a few seconds Julie whispered, "Yes, yes. There it is."

"What?"

"The Chinese fireplace screen that is right behind my

mother's head. It . . . it has a scene of a cliff and a canyon. That's why, that's why," Julie repeated it over and over, but Patrick knew not to push for the reason at that moment.

Julie let out a scream.

"It's stained with her blood, it's all bloody. NO!" Julie broke down and let out deep wrenching sobs.

After a while she quieted down, opened her eyes and looked at Patrick. She felt a little dizzy and had trouble focusing. Feeling drained she reached over for Patrick's hand.

"Give yourself time to come back into the present," he said reassuringly.

Finally, the color came back into her cheeks. Julie squeezed his hand. "Thank you. It was hard to see that, but at least now I know what happened."

"Julie, what did you see in the screen that released so much emotion?" Patrick asked.

"For years I've been dreaming of falling into a canyon. The scene on the screen was the setting of that canyon. Why for all these years could I remember such a superficial thing, but not remember what Dad did? Why, Patrick?"

"Your father's rage, your mother's death and your own fear of being harmed were too great to allow yourself to remember. You automatically chose sanity by transposing the unbearable emotions into the image on the screen. The part of your psyche having the nightmares protected you from being deeply split inside. Your mother's murder was too horrible for you to remember. Your dreams stored the memory for you until you could face it. You're strong, Julie;

you've held yourself together even if it was through repression and nightmares."

Patrick squeezed her hand and released it as he leaned away from her.

"I'm grateful it's over." Julie closed her eyes for a few minutes then looked up at Dan, her rediscovered love, and Emma, her new friend. No words were necessary.

"Emma, would you accompany me to my mother's grave in the high meadow? I need to be with her. Dan, I hope you don't mind my asking Emma to go with me. I feel the need to be alone with Mom, but I don't think I could find my way to the grave. Emma, do you know the way?"

"Yes. I'll be happy to take you there."

Dan walked over to Julie, kissed her on the forehead and said softly, "Whatever you need to do is fine with me."

Emma handed Julie her jacket. "It might be hard to walk on the paths because of the spring mud. Are you feeling up to riding up on the horses? I have some boots in the barn you can use."

"That would be fine." Tears rolled down Julie's face as she accepted the offer.

"Good," Emma said and turned to Dan. Can you help her find everything she needs while I get the horses ready?"

"That's why I'm here—to help in whatever way she needs."

Dan, Emma and Julie went to the barn while Patrick stayed behind to straighten up the living room.

****

As Dan watched, Julie and Emma rode out of the barn towards the high meadow, his beeper went off.

"This is Dr. Hill. I left a message not to be disturbed. I hope this is a real emergency."

"Dr. Hill, the hospital called. Mr. Fitzsimmons is failing and they thought you might want to notify his family to come to the hospital."

"Thank you, I'll be there soon."

Dan went back to the house to tell them about Jack and find out what they wanted to do. As he entered the house he saw Patrick sitting with Anne on the floor in the far corner of the dining room. Anne seemed very upset.

Tom met him at the door.

"What's happening here?" asked Dan.

"Anne got too nervous waiting in the kitchen. She went to the dining room so she could hear what was happening in the living room. She was listening to Julie and all of a sudden, she collapsed and huddled in the corner, looking like a frightened child. I tried to help her but she didn't respond to me. After Julie left the house, I got Patrick."

"Maybe I can help."

"Thanks, but she's responding to Patrick. Wait here for Julie and Emma."

"I can't. Jack's condition is worsening. Do you want to come to the hospital with me?"

"Hold on a minute, I'll check on my wife first." Tom looked into the dining room and saw that Anne was upset and talking intensely with Patrick. "I'm staying here. You go, but call me when you know more."

"Tom, his organs are failing. It's time to turn off the respirator. Julie has signed the forms. Do you think Anne wants to be there?"

"From what's happened here today, I'd say no. We all said goodbye already. Let Jack just die, then we won't have to deal with this mess anymore."

"I think that's best. Emma has her car so she can take Patrick and Julie home," Dan said. He looked down, fingered his keys, and said, "Tom, I promised Julie that I'd be here when she comes back from visiting the gravesite. I don't want her to feel abandoned."

Tom slapped his arm around Dan's shoulders and eased him towards the front door. "I'll make sure she doesn't, but right now I've got to get back to Anne. Talk to you later."

Still feeling uneasy about leaving Julie at Abbey's Run, Dan raced back to Providence General Hospital, sure that except for the life support, Jack was already dead. When he got to the ICU, the attending nurse filled him in on his patient's weakening condition. She asked if Jack's family was coming.

"Doctor Hill, do his daughters want to take him off the respirator?"

"Let me see the file to see if the permission slip is signed."

The form was filled out and authorized the hospital to remove the respirator at the doctor's discretion. Still in shock himself from witnessing Julie's regression, he would have to make a serious decision without her. Before going further, he made a call.

"Look, Tom, I'm ready but I wanted to check once more to see if everyone has had a chance to have a last moment with Jack."

"Well, the whole family did that last night except for my two older kids, but I'll explain the situation to them. What does Julie want?"

"Well, Julie signed the papers."

"Dan, are you all right doing this alone?"

"Yes. Thanks for asking. I'm doing this for all of us."

"Hopefully, he won't hold on too long and we'll all be saved from any more traumas."

****

Washed and wrapped in a clean blanket Jack almost looked at peace. Dan removed the respirator and had the nurse disconnect the other monitors. After the room was cleared of all the equipment, Dan sat on Jack's bed and waited.

Jack lay in a coma, his chest heaving and his breath rattling. The nurses reluctantly followed orders to leave Dan alone with him.

Sitting close to his friend, his sobriety partner, Dan struggled not to slip into judgment and resentment. He thought of some of the pain he had caused his own family during his drinking days and reminded himself that Jack had attempted to heal the wounds he had caused.

"Well, Jack, the secrets are all out now and your daughters will hopefully reconnect. Tom will take care of both of them. You might want to know that I'm still very much in love with Julie and if she lets me, will share my life with her."

Dan sat back and took a moment to reach into his soul for compassion.

"Jack, you've done all you can, so I beseech you not to linger in this weakened state. You can let go now, free yourself. Don't cause more difficulty for yourself and your family. Come on old friend, release the control; allow yourself to move from this body to a better place."

Dan placed his hand over his friend's heart and reverently recited the AA prayer they had often shared. "God, grant me the serenity to accept the things I cannot change, the courage to change the things I can, and the wisdom to know the difference."

He leaned close to Jack for a few final words, "Let go Jack. I'll stay here with you as you go over to the other side. May God embrace you and liberate you of your soul's turmoil."

Dan closed his eyes to pray. Little did he know that at that very moment, Jack was experiencing a healing of his spirit.

Jack felt himself lift up, as if he were still in his body but expanded in light right above it. He could hear the death rattle of his breathing, but he could no longer feel where the boundary of his body was. All of his attention was on the light spiraling upward from his heart. A vision appeared before him.

He was amazed to see his own eight-year-old self in a

translucent body moving upward out of his heart, smiling at him and waving a paintbrush. As the young boy disappeared into the beam of light, another vision floated up out of his body. It was of himself at fourteen reaching out to him, "Our friends are waiting for us, don't take too long."

He started to lift higher away from the body, glancing back briefly to see Dan sitting on the bed. He felt the bond of love between them, but the magnetic power of the light moved him farther and farther away. He had an overwhelming sense that God was all around him. Peace flowed through him; he completely surrendered.

Elizabeth came before him. Radiant, smiling, she beckoned to him, "Come with me. Now we can rest."

John Michael Fitzsimmons died at 4:33 p.m.

****

At Abbey's Run, Patrick sat close to Anne and asked her what was happening. She could only respond in spurts. "I'm scared. Mommy . . . Mommy."

Anne looked up at him from her crouched position and pleaded with him to help her. "I'm so scared."

Tom tried to move close so he could pull her out of the emotional state she was lost in, but Patrick intervened. "Tom, she's in the middle of a flashback. It could hurt her to stop it too abruptly. I'll talk her through it. It's all right, really. She needs to remember something about that night. Let it come through."

Patrick sat next to her. "Anne, tell me what's happening? I know you're frightened. I'll stay right here with you. How old are you, Anne?"

That question got her attention and she answered quickly, "I'm seven."

"Where are you, Anne?"

"I'm in bed, hiding under my covers. Julie's downstairs with Mommy and Daddy. Something really bad is happening. I don't know what to do."

"Do you stay in bed?"

Anne shook her head. "No. I sneak into Mom and Dad's room and call Nana." She bent her head down and tucked it into her arms.

Patrick waited a minute and then asked, "What are you doing now?"

"I'm hiding under the covers of my bed. Nana told me to go back to bed. She said she would be right over, but she's not here yet. Where is she?"

"It must be very scary waiting for her."

Anne looked up at Patrick with terror in her eyes. She could barely talk but did manage to get the words out. "He's coming upstairs. He's . . . ."

He encouraged her to keep talking. "Is he near you?"

"No, no. He . . . ," she let out a little breath and went on, "he passed my room and went into his. Daddy's falling on his bed." She became very quiet.

"What are you doing now?"

"I'm listening to hear if he's asleep."

Anne sat very still for a few seconds then continued

reporting what she was experiencing. "He's snoring. He always does that when he's asleep. I think I can get by his room to the top of the stairs." She stopped talking.

Patrick whispered, "Where are you, Anne?"

"I'm on the top step. I can peek downstairs from here."

"What are you trying to see?"

"I want to know what's happening to my Mommy."

She rocked back and forth and cried before continuing. "Julie's crying. She's leaning over Mommy . . . she's crying that Mommy's dead."

Anne's emotions broke open and she screamed, "Don't kill Mommy!"

"Anne, listen to me. There was an accident but it's not Julie's fault. Your mommy got hurt when your Daddy and Mommy were fighting."

"Mommy, Mommy!" Anne called out for her mother.

Tom sat down next to his wife, picked her up into his lap, and held her tightly to his heart.

"Anne, my sweet love, I'm here with you. It was so scary for you to see your mother hurt."

After several minutes Anne emerged from her memory and refocused. She touched her arms as if to affirm she was back in the present moment. Her body relaxed. "Wow, I was really there! Oh, my God, what a horrible, scary night." She hugged her husband and stood up. She hugged Patrick and said, "Thank you so much for helping me." She then turned to Tom and asked, "Where's Julie? I've blamed her long enough."

"Emma went with her to your mother's grave. They

rode up on the horses."

"Tom, I've got to talk with her! I'm going to ride up there too."

"Take it easy, honey. Why don't you wait until she comes back? There'll be plenty of time to work things out with her. Take some time to get yourself back together." Tom was reluctant to have his wife ride after going through such an emotional shock.

Anne looked around. "Where's Dan?"

"He was called back to the hospital to be with your father." Anne stiffened.

"My father, humph. How could he have lied all those years and kept Julie away from home? I'm not sure how to feel about him."

"I've been just as confused." Tom hugged her.

"Tom, you're so concerned for Anne's state of being and Anne, you're still shaky from what you just remembered. Both of you take a moment and get centered," suggested Patrick.

"I don't have time for that. I've got to get to Julie," Anne insisted.

"Well, it seems to me that you and your sister, your whole family for that matter, need to let the truth settle so that a healing can come about in its own time," said Patrick.

"But she's here now. If Julie goes back to California, I might never get a chance to make it up to her. We've got to do it before it's too late."

"The emergency was over the night your mother died, but you all have been reacting to it ever since then. Perhaps approaching this more calmly will help." Patrick tried to reign in Anne's panic.

She took in what Patrick said then, took a deep breath and became more stable and collected.

"Be kind to yourselves. Give yourselves enough time and space to reflect. Allow the spiritual strength to come forth from your hearts and souls so that each of you can face whatever you need to in order to heal," said Patrick.

Anne grasped his hands in hers, held them tightly and said, "Thank you for your advice and willingness to be the mediator of our family's mess." She released him.

Patrick raised his hands to cross over his chest, smiled and responded, "It touches my heart to witness the healing that is taking place here."

Tom excused himself and went into the kitchen to call the hospital. A few minutes later he found Anne with Patrick in the living room.

"You look better, honey."

"I am. While Patrick thanked his spirit guardians for their help today, peace filled my heart."

She turned to Patrick, "Now I know why Emma likes being with you."

Patrick bowed slightly, then, with a deliberate respectfulness, gathered his things together.

Anne looked to Tom. "What's wrong?"

"I'm sorry. Your father just died. Dan was alone with him at the end. He's going to make the arrangements with the funeral parlor." Tom didn't reveal any of his own confusing feelings so as not to upset his wife. "Do you want me to go get Julie and Emma to tell them or should we just wait for them to come back from your mother's gravesite?"

Anne found herself devoid of emotion for her father. She stood up and kissed Tom. "I can't feel anything for Dad right now, but for the first time that I can remember, I miss my sister." Tears came to her eyes. "I can't believe how much I really miss my mom and sister. What a fool I've been!"

Tom swept her up into a bear hug. "Don't, please honey, don't be so hard on yourself. Jack played everyone for a fool." He put her down and held her face in his hands, "Your father's gone, but you have a sister who probably has missed you just as much as you missed her."

Anne took in his words. "You're right. You stay here and call the kids. I'm going to saddle up and ride up to the grave."

"They've been gone for a while. It's getting cold and it will be dark soon. Why don't you wait here for them?"

"I have to go to her. I'm going to put some riding clothes on and will be right down. Why don't you fix Patrick a cup a tea and give him some of my ginger bread."

"I guess there's no talking you out of going, so go on, get ready and I'll take good care of Patrick."

"Tea sounds just perfect right now." Patrick smiled and walked into the kitchen with Tom.

Tom and Patrick came into the front hall as Anne was leaving to go to the barn.

"Tom, don't look so worried. For the first time in many years, I need to be with my sister. I want to tell her that I remember the truth about our father. This is an important time for us. I want to be free to talk about our mother. Then maybe, together, we can face burying our father."

"Anne, do you think that you should be riding alone? First you had the flashback and then you found out Jack died. Come on, honey, think about it," Tom insisted.

"I'm fine! I'm too mad at Dad to be upset about his death. Recalling my mother's death didn't harm me or make me weak, just furious. Besides, Julie's leaving soon and this might be the only time I can have with her. I'm going."

Tom waved his arms in surrender. "All right, you win. But, if you have to do this, don't stay too long. If you're not back in an hour, I'm gonna to go up and get you."

Patrick had been watching them. "Anne, if you don't mind, I'd like to ride up with you just in case Julie needs a little more help. If everything's okay, I'll ride back down with Emma and leave so you and your sister to have some private time."

"God, you guys are too much! I'm not a fragile woman, I don't need help. Thank you, Patrick, but no thank you. I'll go alone."

Patrick bent his head as if to agree but continued to pressure her. "Forgive me if I implied that you're too vulnerable, but I'm concerned about Julie. Please, I won't even talk on the way and will leave the moment I see that she's okay."

"You're quiet but I've got to hand it to you, your stubbornness works. Tom, can you lend Patrick a pair of riding boots and saddle up Midnight?"

As the two men headed out to the barn, Tom patted Patrick on the back, thanking him for finding a compromise.

"At times like these, it helps to be an outsider. I could hear how frightened you were to think of her riding off alone. It's my honor to escort her to the grave. If you don't mind, I'd like to suggest that you take time while we're gone to review your own feelings about your father-in-law. It will help your wife if you don't hide anything," Patrick said and then asked, "where are those boots?"

"Emma sure picked the right person. Thanks again. The boots are lined up in the tack room according to size; just pick the ones you think are best for you. I'll saddle the horse. You take care of Anne!"

Tom joined his wife in the stalls to help get the horses ready. The gray late afternoon air wrapped around the barn, seeping in through the walls and enveloping the riders bearing the news of death.

****

Instead of taking the long winding path through the meadows, Anne took a shortcut through woods near the property's boundary. Somber, the two riders barely spoke. It gave Anne a chance to sort through the day's revelations.

She had woven a security blanket around her life using the colorful personalities of her father, her grandmother, her husband and her children, but the pattern was unraveling. Lines and forms and spaces all floated through her mind.

At one point, Anne stared at the sky, broken by the empty tree limbs, and knew for the first time why chaotic metal lines had increasingly shattered her canvases. "Of course, my art all along has been showing me that the design was flawed. So, deep inside I've known, I've known."

With that acknowledgement, deep sorrow welled up in her heart. She wondered how her sister could ever forgive her for not remembering their shared love, the safe place of sisterhood.

As the horse set the rhythm with a gentle trot, Patrick moved into a light trance. He merged with the energy of the woods, the air, and the small rays of sun that broke through the clouds. Using a method learned from his grandmother, he directed the healing energy to Anne and to her horse, who Patrick knew was feeling his mistress's emotions.

Not feeling limited by the boundaries of the physical body, Patrick mentally projected himself ahead to the gravesite. He visualized a protective energy field of spiritual light around Julie. He performed this inner ritual to help set the stage for the sisters to open their hearts to each other.

"Patrick, in a minute, we'll make a sharp left turn." Anne guided him across a small creek and up through a pine grove where they saw Emma with the horses.

She had taken her jacket, laid it on a pile of pine needles so she could sit and meditate. It didn't appear that she heard them approaching. She was sitting cross-legged, her hands resting on her knees and her head bowed slightly.

Patrick dismounted, left the reins of his horse for Anne

to hold, and walked very quietly up to Emma. He sat next to her waiting for her response to his presence. After a few seconds, she opened her eyes and smiled at him.

"I thought that energy felt familiar. Are you alone?"

"Anne's over there waiting with the horses. We didn't want to go any farther until we checked with you about Julie's state of mind. How's she doing?"

"She cried on the way up here. Since reaching her mother's grave, she's been quiet," said Emma.

They stood up, stretched and walked over to Anne who handed Patrick the reins to his horse. She then tied hers to a tree and turned to face Emma.

Emma embraced her and said, "I've been worried about you. How are you doing?"

"Better. Forgive me for hiding out in the studio and leaving you to take care of my family. You're quite a friend!"

"Boy, am I glad you're back with us." Emma stepped back and looked at Anne. "But you still seem distraught. It's a lot to handle, isn't it?"

"A death, a murder, a mystery cleared, a sister I forgot--all of it." Tears came to Anne's eyes. She turned to look through the trees and saw her sister, Julie, sitting on the bench next to their mother's grave.

"Emma, my father died a little while ago. Dan was with him. It's too much to sort right now, but I need to be with my sister. Would you wait here with Patrick? We'll be down in a little while."

Patrick looked over at Julie. She appeared composed, so he agreed to stay with Emma.

Emma warned Anne about the delicate fabric of Julie's emotional state. "Your sister might seem strong to you, but from being with her these last two days, I know that she's very vulnerable. Be careful, Anne, there's been enough hurt already."

Hugging her friend, "Thanks for the clue. I need her back in our family; I'm not going to punish her anymore. I promise. Thanks for being with her."

Anne walked into the clearing, going very respectfully to the bench where Julie was sitting. She approached her sister, gently saying her name.

"Julie? Would you mind if I joined you?"

"What?" Julie looked up, surprised to see that it was Anne instead of Emma. "I thought you were too angry to speak with me."

Sitting down with her head bent, just like she did as a young child each time she wanted to ask something of her big sister, Anne sighed and then confessed, "I've made a terrible mistake. I know that you didn't kill Mom and that you didn't forget about me when you left home. I'm so, so sorry. Please forgive me."

Stunned, Julie looked at her forlorn sister. "Did they tell you what I recalled during my regression?"

"No, they didn't need to tell me. I was sitting in the dining room, right across from where you were, and heard it myself. But, more important, I know the truth because while you were remembering the events of Mom's death, I was also thrown back in time. After you left the house, Patrick helped me process the flood of the scenes that came to me in a flashback. Oh, Julie, I was so wrong to blame you."

Julie touched Anne's hand and spoke with great kindness, "We both have been hurt enough. I tried to protect you but I've made a mess of it."

"No, you didn't. Instead of questioning Dad, I always believed him. Now I remember what really split us apart. It wasn't you; it was Dad's guilt and Nana's conspiracy."

"It seems strange to me that you'd go from completely blaming me to putting the blame on Dad and Nana. Are you saying that you realize that Dad confessed the truth in the letter?"

"You have every right to question my motives for being here with you and for accepting the truth. But you see, that night, that horrible night when Mom was killed," Anne swallowed hard, barely able to admit that it was murder, "I wasn't asleep. The flashback brought it all back with terrifying clarity. I was awake the whole time. I was the one who called Nana for help after I heard Mom scream."

"You? You called her? I never knew why she came over that night." Julie shivered against the assault of the memories.

Anne moved closer to comfort her distraught sister.

"When I saw you crying over her, moaning about her being dead, I assumed, in my young mind, that you killed Mom. I never found the courage to ask anybody about it. Nana probably guessed my confusion but never spoke up to defend you to me. When she came into the house that night, she saw me sitting on the stairs staring at you. I'm so angry at her."

"Nana's first priority was always to protect her son. Mom was never good enough for Dad in her eyes." Julie's voice cracked with anger.

"I can't even face my disappointment and anger at Nana right now. Jules, I feel robbed of you and wonder if you can ever find it in your heart to be my big sister again."

Anne sat back, surprised by the intensity of her outpouring to Julie.

Shaking, Julie uttered under her breath, "You used to call me that all the time."

Anne forgot her own confusing emotions and reached out to embrace her hurt sister. "Jules, I still love you; I've never faced how much you mean to me, but that's over now. I need you in my life. Don't go away again, please!"

Julie held her tight, tighter than she ever held anyone. Shaking, she said from the depths of her heart, "Anne, sweet Anne, I've missed you, too."

They sat quietly, holding each other, stunned by the passion of their reunion. After the intensity ebbed, they sunk back against the bench, still connected, with their hands interlocked.

Anne found herself wondering something very disturbing.

"Do think that my birth is what really ruined Mom's health . . . and Mom's and Dad's life together?" Anne asked her older sister.

"Absolutely not! Don't you see that even in his letter, Dad couldn't face up to his problem? He had the audacity to imply that your birth caused their intimacy problems. Mom didn't conceive alone. Even though she was sick, he pushed her for years to have another child and then couldn't live with the consequences. How dare he set you up to feel guilty!" Julie was enraged.

She struggled with the force of her anger, an emotion she had spent years denying. She tried to speak with more reason, "Mom had diabetes, a disease that gets progressively worse, especially for some people, and Mom was one of those. Sure, having another baby was stressful but she was already quite sick. She gave into him and paid a heavy price."

Bitter and indignant, she continued, "Besides, it was Dad's drinking that destroyed all of our lives, not your needs as a young child! You get that idea out of your head."

"But I can't help but wonder if his drinking started after I was born. Maybe it was guilt instead of love that he's been sharing with me all these years. Maybe, just maybe, taking care of me had been his penance rather than his choice."

Anne couldn't hold back the tears. Her firm resolve to stay strong so she could support her sister crumbled under the weight of her doubts. Her sobbing welled up from the hidden places of her being.

Her younger sister's pain helped Julie regain her control and strength. She lovingly admonished Anne. "You listen to me, little sister. Dad might have destroyed Mom's life and my life with his boozing, but one thing is very clear: he worshipped you. You were part of his salvation and thus, his love, his joy, his sobriety. If parenting you was solely driven from guilt, he wouldn't have been able to maintain his sobriety all these years. He gave you what you needed to become the happy, full adult you are!"

Julie touched her sister's face, wiping away the tears. She held Anne in her gaze until she was sure that her sister was hearing all she was saying.

"It helps me to know that you made it. You've had the best of him, you've had the children Mom would have loved to grandparent and you've been able to find a great, true love. Don't you see that your life, your loves, your art, your care of the home and of the earth are part of all of our transcendence over the devastation of his addictions and of Mom's illness?"

Anne took in the loving acknowledgement of her successes, smiled at Julie and reciprocated her sister's compassionate support.

"I haven't been the only one to succeed. Don't you think that Mom's looking down from the heavens smiling at her daughter, the great and famous scientist? The gentle and good woman who was," she choked a little on the truth of what she was going to say, "the person who gave up so much of her life so that her sister could have happiness and family, a life rich and full of loving people."

"It was worth it. You've had the life I had always hoped you were having."

"Julie, all that I have is part of you, too. You're a part of me, got it?"

"Thanks." Julie kissed her sister on the forehead as she

had every night during the years she mothered Anne.

Anne smiled, sat back and looked serious again. "Julie, there's one more thing I need to know, but I'm not sure whether or not it's all right to intrude further into your memories."

"Let's get it all out in the open. What is it?" Julie asked.

"Mom fought Dad off because he went to grab you. Did he ever do that before that night?"

"Not that I remember. I think that's why Mom moved off the couch to stop Dad. She had put up with a lot over the years, but never that kind of behavior. I never saw her confront him when he was drunk. But that night, before she fell down, she was full of rage and didn't hesitate to stand up to him." Julie spoke without emotion; her words lingered in the air.

A sleeping volcano suddenly erupting, her rage exploded. "Damn him! I hope to God that he doesn't get away with this, that somewhere he has to face what he did to Mom, to me, to all of us!"

Anne shook her head in agreement. "I wish I could take your hurt away."

There was a pregnant silence. Finally Julie asked, "Did he ever touch you? Did I leave you to be hurt by him?"

"No, in fact, he rarely touched me in any way. I just thought it was because of his sadness over losing Mom. Now I see that it was his guilt. Now I see so much. I feel so betrayed. It scares me that I have so many memories of a man who tore our life apart and so few of the mother I lost."

"That I can help solve." Julie took Anne hands and started talking. They sat until the light dimmed, sharing their memories of their mother and of the good times they had all spent together.

As they walked away from the grave, Anne touched Julie's arm and said hesitantly, "Before we leave I need to let you know what I came up here to tell you."

"I think I've already figured it out. Dad's dead, isn't he? I saw the sorrow in your eyes. Don't hide your pain over losing him on my account."

"I'm not. I'm confused by my own reaction to his death.

Anne reached over to her dearest friend, "Emma, how can I help you. Dad has put you through so much. I wasn't here for you."

"Not your fault. For days before the stroke, I sensed that there was something wrong. He didn't want to talk about it. I understand now why he reluctant to let anyone know what he planning. I guess he set-up his redemption in the only way familiar to him, controlling the situation and Julie, your return," Emma mused.

"My father knew the only person I'd come back to Rhode Island to help is Anne, not him." Julie gently touched her younger sister's face and said, "It's hard to admit, he was right."

Anne clung to her sister.

Emma told them, "It'll take time for me to forgive him for what he's put us all through. I don't know if I told either of you but your mother had come to me in one of my visions right before all this blew up. I understand now that her soul was reaching out to help us all. She's here with you. I'm sure of it."

The three women hugged.

"It's getting late. We need to return to the barn and get away from the dark," said Emma.

She helped the Fitzsimmons sisters mount their horses and head home to their family.

The End

ABOUT THE AUTHOR

Mariah Martin had two stories, *Danny* and *Freedom*, published in **More Hot Chocolate for the Mystical Soul,** by Arielle Ford, by Plum, Penguin Group. She also has published book of spiritual messages, WE SPEAK, Lulu Press. She and her family now live in Rhode Island.

♥

Book 2

Emma Quinn Mystery

THE LIGHT

Emma's has new, repeated visions. Only by following the Light from the spiritual realm can she discover the meaning of her dreams and save her family.

Mariah Martin

The Return

64659447R00163

Made in the USA
Charleston, SC
02 December 2016